Walter,

He's My Dog

By Roger K. Droz

Walter, He's My Dog
by Roger K. Droz

Paperback ISBN: 979-8-9911560-3-5
eBook ISBN: 979-8-9911560-4-2
Library of Congress Control Number: 2024915460

Published by Personal Chapters LLC
Wakarusa, KS and Independence, MO
www.personalchapterspublishing.com

Dedication
and Acknowledgements

For Margo, and dog owners everywhere.

Thanks to my wife, Margo, for proofreading, suggestions, and support. To Mary Phelan for proofreading and suggestions. To Aimee and Tom Gross for their ideas about both content and cover. And thanks to Anne Spry for publishing this book.

Contents

Chapter 1
The Bearded Man

Me and Walter (he's my dog) have been going on walks since I first got him from a friend who found him abandoned. Sometimes our walks are long ones. Walter's spoiled and it's my fault he thinks he needs to walk every day. On the days I don't feel like walking he insists we go anyway. On bad days at work or when the weather is rotten, I just want to kick off my shoes, lay back and relax in my Barcalounger, close my eyes, and visualize some tropical island. You know the one; the one where a scantily clad young woman brings you a drink, adjusts your beach chair, removes your shoes, and asks in a cooing voice, "Is there anything else?" Walter won't have any of it though, he meets me at the door with his leash in his teeth, ready. He won't leave me alone; he bothers me until I give in. Lately, Walter has begun to dictate the length of our walks. They are almost always longer than I want, and his walks are always increasing in length, to the point where I am exhausted when we finally get home.

It's not so bad though. Since the separation, it's just me and Walter against the world, and frankly, a guy could go batty sitting in his recliner, alone in his apartment with nothing but four walls and a television.

Walter, he's all I kept in the separation agreement, and it's only because Theresa didn't want him. "You and that damned dog…," she'd say. She didn't like dogs much and I never understood why. Walter's been a better friend to me than she ever was so when I think about it, I got the better end of the deal.

It would be fair to say Theresa and I didn't part on friendly terms. In fact, it would be an understatement. I do miss her cooking though.

I've lost almost twenty pounds since the separation. The first and most obvious reason is now I have to do my own cooking. The second, and just as significant: Walter's walks keep getting longer. He has taken me to neighborhoods I have never seen before. Just two days ago, we found a new park (well, new to us). It certainly wasn't new. It was about four square blocks of ancient Chinese Elms, the ones that stand fifty feet tall and cover the ground with dead sticks and limbs with every storm. Clean-ups can take days.

This new-to-us park lies between two hills, and before man built a fence around it, was a beautifully wooded meadow. Still, with a stream meandering through it, a smattering of children's antique swings, slides, and even an old merry-go-round, it is a park.

The merry-go-round has little steel triangle-shaped sections painted red, yellow, orange, and blue. The handrails between each section were white once, but now are dull and rusty from lack of use. Also, there is one of those old curly Q slides. It has several earlier colors showing through the final coat of orange paint. Just like the handrails on the merry-go-round, the metal was rusted where once it was smoothed by the bottoms of small children who screamed gleefully as they descended.

The park is mostly deserted now. Only an occasional jogger or elderly couple out for an afternoon of fresh air frequent it.

I unhooked Walter's leash and watched as he sprang to life, running, sniffing, and of course, peeing on every tree. I smiled as I watched. I wished I could live in the moment like Walter. Sure, he would recognize our new apartment when we got back. Sure, he would recognize my ex when he saw her. He would even wag his tail as he futilely begged her to pet him. Right now, though, Walter was completely engrossed in the exploration of this new-found wonder.

I followed slowly, watching with envy as he explored. Walter occasionally would look back to make sure I was following, then mark a new tree, splash into the stream, or sniff a slide or swing set.

Today Walter found something interesting in the water and was splashing and frolicking around like black Labs do, so I walked on ahead. I abandoned the pathway to follow the edge of the stream, knowing this would be Walter's chosen route when he came bounding back to me.

Soon I heard his panting and his paws pounding the ground, then felt the rush of air as he flew past me, brushing my leg as he went. In seconds he was ten yards ahead, when suddenly, he lowered his hind end, dug all four feet into the ground, and locked up. Before the leaves and dust could settle around him, Walter froze.

Ahead of us, sitting on a bench facing the water, was a white-bearded old man. He looked like one of those poor people from an old black-and-white movie, sitting there in a tattered gray jacket and black pants. He heard Walter's approach and turned to face us. Tired eyes peered from between the bill of his tweed cap and his wrinkled cheeks. He didn't try to smile.

Walter's ears twitched like they always do when he wants to break and charge, so I reattached his leash.

The old man didn't seem to be a menace, only tired, worn from a hard life. I moved to Walter's side, patted him on the shoulder, his signal to relax, and said, "It's okay, boy."

Then we began our approach. The old man made no motion, either to acknowledge us or leave. I quietly sat on the opposite end of the bench and unfastened Walter's leash. Walter's signal to begin.

First, he approached the old man from the side and sniffed the ground around him. He inched closer, sniffing all the while, until he was next to the old man's leg. Surprisingly, Walter laid down next to the end of the bench, close to the old man.

The three of us sat quietly.

The bearded man was the first to break the silence, "Nice dog," he said.

"His name is Walter," I answered. "He's friendly."

"I can see that," the bearded man answered as he reached to place his wrinkled hand on Walter's back.

We sat silently for a few more moments, him with his hand gently rubbing Walter's back, both of us staring straight ahead.

"Walter and I are out for our evening walk. We just discovered this park a few days ago. Walter likes it here. This is his new favorite place, because of the water, I guess."

"Yes, Labs like water," the old man answered.

Again, we sat in silence.

"Well, Walter and I should be getting on," I said, breaking the quiet.

"It was a pleasure to meet you, Walter," he said and patted my dog on his head.

Walter looked up as if to say to me, "Do we have to go already?"

The old man didn't try to either extend the conversation or his hand.

I turned toward home. Walter reluctantly followed.

It was a nice evening, the sky was clear and only a slight breeze rustled tree leaves; a big change from the last two days. Yesterday and the day before were miserable outside. Two days ago, it rained all day and yesterday the wind blew unceasingly. Walter and I were cooped up for two straight evenings. We needed a walk.

"Come on boy, let's go," I said.

I paused at the end of the sidewalk. Should we go in a new direction today, find some new street or neighborhood or park or should we walk to the Dairy Queen?

Without hesitation, Walter decided for both of us. Straining on the leash, he practically dragged me off my feet. Walter wanted to go to the park to see if the old man was there.

Walter is friendly, he likes people, begs to be petted, licks hands in thanks, and makes friends easily. He enjoys each new encounter but is always ready to move on. But the old man, clearly, he instantly liked the old man and wanted to go find him.

I tried to keep him on his leash. It was quite a distance from the edge of the park to the old man's bench, but I finally caved to Walter's demand. So, to satisfy his urge and relieve the strain on my shoulder, I unclasped the hook on his leash. I don't run anymore, youth has betrayed me, but I did the best I could to keep up.

When the bench finally came into my view, Walter was already there, silently lying on the ground at the end of the bench next to the bearded man.

Today he raised his head, turned and with a slight smile said, "Nice dog."

I took his smile as my opportunity to talk. "Yes, he's a great friend. I don't know how I could get along without him," I said and scooched a little closer on the bench.

"Do you live close?" I asked.

"I have an apartment two blocks away," he answered.

"So, you are not a native to the city?" I inquired.

"No, I have a farm about seven hundred miles south," he said.

Again, we sat quietly for a bit. I didn't know whether I should continue to pry or just shut up.

After a few moments, he broke the silence. "I need to get back," he said and rose to leave.

Walter looked at me with eyes that begged, "Can we go with him?" or more correctly, "Can *I* go with him?"

The old man limped away with the aid of a cane. He crossed the bridge over the creek, climbed the steps, and disappeared through a growth of forsythia.

I sat quietly wondering for several minutes, then decided to begin our walk home.

As luck would have it, it rained all afternoon and when I got home from work, the weather was so bad, Walter wouldn't go out. The weather must be bad for a black Lab to pause at the door and then go back to his bed. I made up for it by ordering a pizza. Walter likes the pizza delivery boy. He recognizes the sound of his car and sprints to the door in anticipation when he hears it. Pepperoni is Walter's favorite.

Saturday we walked to the park. Walter sped to the bearded man's bench but to his disappointment, and mine, it was occupied by a young couple who were obviously consumed by their new love. I thought they must have arrived at the old man's bench before he got there. So, Walter and I looked around, thinking he might have found another place to sit. Walter couldn't find him anywhere, so with drooping heads, we resumed our walk until it was time to trudge home.

Sunday we went back again, this time only to find the bench empty.

I was worried now. *Have we seen the last of the old man? Did something happen to him? Was he in an accident?* I wondered.

On Monday we went to the park to look as soon as I got home from work. The old man was back, sitting on the same spot on the same bench. We hurried over and sat, me on the bench and Walter on the ground next to him. "We missed you Saturday and Sunday," I said.

"I'm busy weekends," he responded without clarification.

We talked a little about his farm. "I inherited it from my father. Our farm has been in the family for four generations. My wife, Emma, always wanted to remodel the house. She wanted to make it her own, but we never did. It just didn't seem right to change anything. I thought if it was good enough for my parents, grandparents, and great-grandparents, it should be good enough for us too."

"Do you have any children to leave it to?" I pried.

"We had just one, a girl. She didn't like the farm. She was always taking music and dance classes in school. She didn't want anything to do with the local boys. She was always saying, 'I'm moving to the city when I grow up.' We used to argue about it a lot. The day after she graduated high school, she ran off in the middle of the night without even leaving a note. We never heard from her again, not even a birthday or Christmas card. It broke Emma's heart." he said.

"Well, at least you still have your wife and the farm," I answered, trying to turn the uncomfortable conversation.

"Yes, I still have the farm, but Emma died a year ago. Now there's nothing left for me there but a few head of cattle and a lot of memories," he said.

His words were coming hard now. I regretted turning our conversation in this direction. I couldn't think of a way to change it, so we sat in an uncomfortable silence for a time. I wondered if I asked too much. *Have I stepped over some line? Is he so upset that I have driven him away?* I wondered.

"Would you like to walk with Walter?" I asked, trying desperately to ease the situation.

"No thanks, I best be getting back," he answered.

Again, Walter and I watched as he limped to the bridge, up the hill, and out of sight. Again, without turning back to wave or even tip his cap.

On the way back to the apartment, even Walter seemed to sense we might never see the bearded man again.

The next evening we found him sitting on the bench. Walter was ecstatic.

"I guess I shouldn't have bored you with my story yesterday," he said.

"No, not at all," I answered, "I was afraid I pried too deeply. I was glad you took me into your confidence. The way things have been going for me lately, I needed someone to talk to."

"Tell me about yourself, son," he said.

"Well, there's not much to tell really. I just got divorced about two months ago. After three years of marriage, my wife and I drifted apart. We didn't have much in common and our jobs kept us from having enough time together. I have a classic nine-to-five office job, and now with Covid, I do a lot of my work at home alone. Her work kept her busy most nights and weekends, so we didn't get to do the things normal couples do. She was bitter that her career hadn't panned out as well as she hoped, and I became the target of her frustration. Without a word of warning, she served me with divorce papers. She took everything except for Walter here," I told him.

It felt good to hear those words. I hadn't talked to anyone about any of this since Theresa and I parted. I sent a letter to my folks and exchanged texts with my brother, but I didn't have a real conversation with anyone.

With a sense of ease, I asked, "So, what brings you to the city?"

"My daughter," he answered. "I thought I might be able to find her here. I thought Saturdays and Sundays would be the best days to try to find her. It's the reason I don't come to the park on weekends. I've been searching all over, going to stores and restaurants, showing people her picture. But I'm lost in all this new technology. I don't understand anything about mobile phones and all the texting and messaging that goes with them, so it's hard for me. The phone companies don't put out phone books anymore, so I am lost. I went to the police, but they weren't of any help. They told me I needed to file a missing person's report. I didn't think it was the right thing to do, having the police investigate, I mean. Besides, she might not have the same last name or even the same first name for that matter. I planned to search for a month, and my time is about up. My neighbor is taking care of the home place, but he goes to Florida for the winter every year, so I need to get back. Friday, if I haven't found her yet, I'm giving up and going home," he said.

Our conversation ended there. Neither of us knew what to say next and the finality of Friday caught me off guard.

The silence was extremely uncomfortable. Even Walter sensed something was wrong.

After a few minutes, the old man broke the quiet, "Well, I guess it's time for me to be getting back."

It was hard to put one foot in front of the other on the way home, and Walter couldn't or wouldn't keep up.

I opened a beer and collapsed into my Barca. Tonight, I didn't even turn on the TV. Instead of climbing up and crowding against me in the chair, Walter shuffled to his bed and lay with empty eyes, whimpering.

I left a half can of warm beer on the nightstand. Walter didn't move when I got up. We each slept alone, fretfully.

Wednesday afternoon is the time Theresa and I talk if we have anything to say to each other. Either I call her, or she calls me. The conversations are short, to the point, and strained. "Meet me at the Twenty-Seventh Street entrance of Fillmore Park," I told her.

"Why?" she growled.

"I need to talk to you about something," I answered.

"You are talking to me now, why can't you just tell me over the phone?" she said, still growling.

"No, we need to be face to face for this. Six-fifteen, Twenty-Seventh Street, at the park, just be there," I insisted.

I planned to meet her at six-thirty, but I knew she would be fifteen minutes late.

"Alright, but this better be good and it better be short!" she said, still with the same tone. He was already sitting on the bench when Walter and I walked up. More correctly when I walked up, Walter took off at full gallop the instant I unhooked his leash. By the time I came in sight of the old man on the bench, Walter was eagerly licking and jumping at his feet. "I'm glad you came this evening," I said.

"I thought I should," he answered. "I'll look for her one last time tomorrow, then Thursday evening I will have to pack for the trip back to the farm."

When I saw Theresa's blue Prius come into sight, I excused myself. "I'll be back in a minute," I told him and walked toward the Twenty-Seventh Street parking lot.

She jumped out of her car, already in one of her moods. She was wearing her big city outfit, leather jacket, scarf up to her chin, big dark sunglasses, and stupid purple hair. Without any sort of cordial greeting, she barked, "This better be good."

"Please, can't you at least be civil? Come with me to the park bench, I have something to show you," I said.

"Why the park bench? There's some bearded old man already sitting there, and that damned dog of yours is there too."

"I know, Walter and I like that bench, and sometimes the old man is sitting there when we arrive. He doesn't bother us though. You and I can sit at the other end," I said.

"This better be good!" Theresa growled again.

We sat, her on one end, me in the middle, the old man on the other, and Walter on the ground next to him.

My phone rang right on cue.

"Excuse me, I need to take this call," I said, rose, and walked away.

I walked to the far side of the park, thanking my buddy Will for calling me on time.

From behind a bush, I watched. Walter jumped to my spot on the bench between Theresa and the old man. He pestered her until she relented and petted him. The old man instinctively reached to pet him too. They sat silently for a few moments, each with their hands on Walter's quiet body. Then I saw her lips move.

A few seconds later, I saw his lips move in response.

I could see they were both crying now.

Weeks later, I lay comfortably, fully reclined on my side of the couch, watching *Casablanca* for the umpteenth time. The old man with the beard, Theresa's dad, Henry, lay sleeping in my Barca.

Walter jumped up and snuggled in between Theresa and me.

"That damned dog of yours," she smiled.

"Yeah, if it weren't for that damned dog, your dad wouldn't be asleep in my Barca, and you wouldn't be here beside me on the couch."

Chapter 2

Our Friend Mike

Henry needed to get back to the farm so his neighbor could leave for his Florida home.

I talked Theresa into going back with him. "Just try again," I told her. "Help him get used to living without your mom. Maybe you can patch up your lives, or at least make peace with each other. Then you can come back here and resume your career, fresh, with a clear mind and conscience."

Theresa held Walter's leash while I hugged Henry goodbye, with promises by each of us to "come visit." Then she passed Walter back, shook my hand, gave me a peck on the cheek, and boarded the train for their trip back to the farm. I stood, waving at them as the train left. Walter pressed against my leg as the train vanished from sight. The walk back to my car was excruciating. Walter and I both sensed our lives just changed and were never to be the same again.

During the time she was back on the farm, Theresa and I exchanged texts and video chats. Our first visits were hopeful and friendly, but after a while, they degenerated into strained and uneasy. Theresa would no longer phone me, and her texts were short and vague. It was clear it wasn't working between them. Her distaste for the farm was ingrained; she couldn't or wouldn't change.

A disappointed Henry choked on his words when I called him to find out.

"It isn't working," he said. "She doesn't want to be here, and I no longer want to try to change her mind."

Henry, not Theresa, called to tell me she was coming back. The spark which we rekindled before she left, died. The instant she arrived I sensed the old coolness between us return, at least on her part. The remoteness of her career had softened her memory of its disappointments. She didn't want to live on the farm, and she wasn't enthused about living with me and Walter again. She was ready to start over again - alone.

When Henry entered our lives, I had reason to hope he might change Theresa's outlook. But he couldn't and now I knew she wouldn't. I could see there was no longer any point.

Theresa moved into a new apartment.

I opened an official-looking envelope to see the papers and a short, typewritten note with no signature.

The farm is just the same and I don't like it there. I have a new job with a cruise line, working as an entertainer. I have decided to give up my New York career, for now at least.

I didn't mind. I was willing to try again, but it was clear now there wouldn't be a third try. Walter and I adapted and managed just fine without her before, so being without her again wasn't difficult.

Walter and I went back to our daily walks, now with no need to honor her schedule.

Walter was chasing a squirrel when he stepped on broken glass. By the time I rushed to him, his leg was already bleeding profusely. I wrapped his leg with my shirt, picked up my wounded dog, scrambled back to my car, and rushed to the vet. Ernie, the custodian at the veterinarian's office, helped me as I struggled to get my bleeding dog out of the back seat of my car, through the front door, and into the lobby of the vet's office. Once inside, I stood in the center of the lobby, shirtless, holding my bleeding dog, calling for help.

A startled Mary looked up to greet me. "What on earth happened?" she asked, as she scurried from behind her receptionist's desk to help.

Mary is just who you'd picture as a receptionist at a veterinary clinic. If you saw her on the street or in a grocery store not wearing her smock, you'd think, *I'll bet that lady works at a veterinarian's office.* She has slightly curly black hair with a little gray. She keeps it too long for a woman her age, but she wears it proudly. I suspect she has worn the same hairdo since she was in high school. She is short, a little overweight and always wears a sincere smile between a pair of dangly earrings. She reminds me of the actor Kathy Bates, but not the character she played in the movie *Misery,* where she kept James Caan prisoner in his own house.

I suspect deep down Mary is a cat person. But she can go either way–cats or dogs. Her favorite pet is the one in front of her.

"He cut his leg on some broken glass," I answered.

"I can see that," she said, then turned toward the back and yelled, "I need some help out here, right now!"

Before I could begin to explain further, Ingrid appeared. The instant I saw her, I lost focus on the wounded dog I cradled in my arms. Her blond hair flowed in the air as she floated toward us. Her long legs carried her with an ease that was natural, not learned, as she hurried to inspect Walter's wound. Her sparkling eyes fixated on my dog, and her expression changed to sincere concern.

I often wondered what caused Ingrid to become a veterinarian instead of pursuing what would have certainly been a successful career as a model, a movie star, or a debutante. Those Emma Stone sparkling eyes. Those Keira Knightley sensuous cheekbones. Those Taylor Swift luscious legs. That Margot Robbie flowing hair. The woman was a goddess. *She must have a multitude of admirers,* I thought.

But none more sincere than me.

Back when Theresa and I were first separated, Ingrid began her career here at the Fillmore Neighborhood Veterinary Clinic. In my "B I" days (Before Ingrid) I never found time to bring Walter in for his scheduled appointments. When I did finally show up, a visibly perturbed Mary would lecture me on the necessity of Walter receiving his exams and shots *on time, every time*. But once Ingrid and I met over Walter's sleek, muscled body, I was never late for an appointment again.

When my phone rang, I would check the caller ID, and if it was the clinic, I would answer, "Yes, Mary?"

"Doctor Johansson asked me to remind you of Walter's next visit," her happy, knowing voice would say.

For some reason, those calls made me envision a mailbox in front of a small cottage in the country with the names, "Dr. Ingrid and Mr. James Williams," printed in bold letters.

Today, Walter had seen Mike before I could snap his leash. He bolted out of the car door, and they began their game of pursuit. Mike, a feisty red squirrel, is Walter's friend and tormentor. Each day, Mike waits near his tree at the edge of the park for Walter to arrive. Each day he sits a little further from his tree, daring Walter to catch him. And each day Walter fails, but just by inches.

As soon as they see each other, Mike bounds across the grass, leaps for the tree just as Walter grasps for his tail, then sits on his branch and taunts poor Walter until he gives up and trots to the creek. If it weren't for Walter, I think I could get Mike to eat out of my hand.

But today, the chase didn't go well. I saw the broken glass. Walter didn't. A shard pierced his left front leg as he bounded toward Mike's tree. He yelped, collapsed, and frantically rolled to a stop in the dust. When I got to him, he was howling, and blood was gushing from his leg and foot. I hurriedly swept him up and ran toward my car. I ripped off my shirt, tore the sleeve from it, and tied a makeshift tourniquet over his wound.

In the time it took to drive the four blocks to the veterinary, my blue shirtsleeve was completely blood-soaked, and a large red splotch had formed on my leather car seat. Walter lost a lot of blood.

"Have you been a bad boy again, Walter?" Ingrid cooed, as her long slender fingers pulled the matted cloth away from his wound. "Bring him to the examination room, Mr. Williams," she said, without even looking up.

Even during this emergency, I wished she would raise her head so our eyes could meet.

"This is a deep laceration. Walter will need sutures," she said. Then she looked at me and asked, "What was he doing?"

Before I could find the words to explain, she said, "Mary, can you find a smock for Mr. Williams?"

Embarrassed, I turned away to hide my nakedness and wished I was more diligent with my gym membership. No amount of chest puffing could compensate for the gentle roll of fat surrounding my body, almost covering my belt.

I detected a hint of a smile on Ingrid's face as I turned away.

Her face then became sober, "Mary, tell Dr. Phillips I need help. Mr. Williams, we will need to sedate Walter. His wound isn't serious, but we will need to keep him quiet for a couple of days. We can't have him picking at his bandages. You can stay during the procedure if you wish, or you can go to the lobby to wait."

She turned back to her patient, and gently ran those long fingers over his forehead, "You're going to be alright, Walter." Then she deftly began to work on his wound.

He rolled those deep dark eyes of his toward her and relaxed.

Walter liked Ingrid too.

I stopped at the mailbox on my way from the office to my apartment, carried a handful of envelopes with me, and laid them on the counter. The letter on top of the pile had that all too familiar return address. It was from my lawyer. *Another bill? Just what I need.* Before I could retrieve a beer from the refrigerator and sit to open my mail, I got the urge to go to the park. Walter was recuperating at the vet clinic and there was no need to walk him, but it had become a regular routine. But first, I thought I'd stop for frozen custard. It had been a long time since I enjoyed one.

I was stressed at work today and couldn't focus on anything but my injured dog. I missed those days when I worked from home. On trying days at home, I could carry my work to the living room or kitchen table. Small changes like that seemed to clear and refresh my mind.

Walter and I always get soft-serve custard at a cheaper place than Culver's because I always need to buy two.

It's not that I can't afford custard for Walter, but I can't justify it. He doesn't exactly savor his treat.

Walter always gets a big cone, and it only takes him an instant to devour it. I can't get a cone and leisurely lick it. I need to get mine in a cup and spoon it in as fast as possible because as soon as Walter is done with his, he's all over me for the rest of mine. But today was different. Yesterday I left my dog at the clinic to heal and was now alone.

I felt guilty as I strode along the pathway, taking one small spoonful at a time; swirling the cool mixture around my tongue before letting it slide down my throat into my belly. The sweet taste of frozen raspberry custard can lift anyone's spirits.

Suddenly, I heard a commotion in the leaves. I saw Mike scampering around, digging here and there, and chattering. Mike caught my movement as I lifted the spoon to my mouth for another bite of the delicious ecstasy. He froze, sitting on his hind legs, twitching his tail. "Hi, Mike," I said without thought.

Once he realized it was me, Walter's companion, he dashed toward the tree in front of me, scampered across an overhanging limb, and stopped. I sat on a park bench not fifteen feet from him. Then with Mike in front and just a little above me, and me sitting on the bench, we stared at one another. Mike was the first to break the silence.

I listened as he began a long unbroken dissertation of barking and squeaking. It seemed he was asking about Walter. *Was he asking if Walter was going to be okay? Was he apologizing for tempting Walter to run through the grass? Was he imploring me to pick up the broken glass?* I wondered.

I succumbed to my need to speak to someone, anyone, and spoke aloud, "Walter is going to be okay Mike. He needed to have stitches and will have to stay overnight at the vet's. It will be a few days before we come back to the park. Don't worry, you were just playing your game, it isn't anybody's fault Walter got hurt. Well, not anybody but the idiot who broke the bottle and then left the remains." I said. Then briefly thought, *I'm glad no one is close enough to hear me.*

Mike's answer seemed to say, "I'm sorry, I'll make sure I check that the path is clear next time. I won't get so far from the tree from now on either."

I smiled and said, "It's okay," and took three almonds from my pocket. I always carry almonds; in fact, they are my favorite snack. I laid them on the far end of the bench to see what Mike would do.

He suddenly became quiet, fixated on the nuts for a bit, then scampered down the tree. He paused a few more moments. He kept stopping to look around and to watch me, like squirrels do, before jumping onto the bench. After a brief sniff, he snatched an almond, sat on his haunches, and began to spin the nut with his front feet while taking bites until it was gone. He ate the second, then the third. Once the nuts were gone, he paused, looked up at me, gave me a pitiful look and began to bark, begging for more.

Slowly, enjoying the moment, I reached into my pocket and retrieved another nut, then extended my hand. Fear and anxiety were soon overtaken by desire. Mike snatched the almond from my fingers.

We sat there, Mike and I, enjoying our snacks as a woman and her young daughter passed, "Mommy, look at that man and his pet squirrel," the little girl said.

"I see it, honey, isn't it cute?" she answered.

"Mommy, can squirrels talk?"

"No honey, animals can't talk."

"Mommy, can I have a squirrel?"

"No honey, squirrels are wild animals."

"Mommy, can I have a kitten?"

"No honey, kittens are dirty. We don't want a kitten. We would have to clean up after it all the time."

I sat there watching them walk away, sadly thinking of what the little girl was missing by not having a pet.

Mike jumped down with the remnants of the last almond in his mouth and scrambled up his tree.

I vowed to be at the Fillmore Veterinarian's Clinic waiting for the doors to open in the morning.

"Good morning, Mr. Williams." Mary smiled. "Walter is doing fine," she said, as she opened the door for me, then turned the open/closed sign over. "Dr. Johansson is here. She told me Walter's wound would heal; it would just take time. You can go back if you like."

Walter was still drowsy from the sedative. When I opened the door, he could only raise his head, but his tail started flapping happily against the bed.

"Hi boy, how are you feeling today?" I asked as I stroked the smooth hair on his forehead.

Her fragrance enveloped the room before I could turn around. "Good morning, Mr. Williams. We didn't expect you to be here so early," Ingrid smiled. "Walter had a fitful night; I am sure he missed being at home. We have kept him sedated because he won't be still. I don't think you should spend a lot of time with him this morning. We don't want him to get excited, he still needs to be as quiet as possible. You can come back this evening and take him home if you like, but I think it would be best if he stays at least another day," she said.

"Whatever you think is best for Walter is what I want," I answered, struggling to speak coherently in her presence.

She brushed against me as she leaned in to pet Walter. Her palm ran over the back of my hand. She was startled when she noticed I was no longer wearing a wedding ring. "Oh, I didn't realize you aren't married?" she said.

"Yes, Theresa and I have been separated for some time, but now we have made it official. It's over between us," I answered, choking on the words.

I hadn't worn my wedding ring since our final breakup. Theresa came back to the city one final time to "pick up the last of her stuff and say goodbye."

We made a scene at a restaurant that night, arguing loud enough for all to hear. She got mad when I asked her if there was someone else, then dug her ring from her purse and slammed it on the table before stomping out. By then, everyone in the room was awestruck. In the silence, the ring careened off the table and bounded across the tiled floor. Our audience heard every clink and jangle it made until it finally, mercifully, came to rest. I sat, left alone, among a roomful of spellbound diners, refusing to acknowledge them. In what seemed a never-ending quiet, I stood, removed my wedding ring, and stuffed it in my pocket. Then with a face flushed by a rush of embarrassment and anger, I walked to where her ring came to rest. I picked it up, flung it in a nearby trashcan, and rushed out.

A smattering of uneasy applause followed me as I left.

The next day a silent, smiling server meekly handed me Theresa's ring when I returned to pay my bill, "I thought you might want this back," he said, "It's worth some money you know."

I kept both rings on the dresser for a couple of weeks before putting them in the bottom of my sock drawer.

It didn't occur to me until now that I never told Ingrid anything about any of my personal life.

Ingrid stepped back now from Walter's cage, nervously buttoned her lab coat, and turned away. "Maybe you could call me some time," she whispered.

Dumbfounded, I stood with my hand still on Walter, but it no longer moved. I knew my face was red and I began to tremble and perspire. I didn't dare turn to let Ingrid see my pitiful expression.

I waited until I could no longer hear Ingrid's footsteps, then hurried through the lobby to my car.

I drove to the office, desperately wishing I could have a second chance, a do-over of what just happened. But deep down I knew, *You'd just blow it again, dummy.*

Mercifully, my long and unproductive day ended.

Once home, I poured a glass of wine and turned on the stereo. *Maybe listening to Van Morrison will help,* I thought. But I just sat there thinking, thinking about Ingrid. *Why had she shown an interest now? Did it just slip out? Did she mean what she said? If I sit here long enough, will I be able to understand?*

I poured a second glass, a full one this time.

∽

"Good morning, Mr. Williams. Walter is up. We put him in a pen this morning. He's back there limping around, refusing to lie down. I know he is anxious to see you," Mary said.

"Hi, Mary. I wish you'd call me James," I answered.

My request fell on deaf ears, "Dr. Johansson is busy with a patient this morning, Mr. Williams. She won't be able to see you. She told me to tell you she wants to watch Walter today, but if all goes well, you may pick him up tonight. I'll call later this afternoon to let you know," Mary said.

Disappointed Walter wasn't ready to come home and devastated Ingrid was busy and I wouldn't get to see her, I walked to Fillmore Park hoping to find Mike and give him an update. I know it seems odd, but I needed to keep some normalcy, although I was now not sure what normalcy meant.

I began to realize the park meant as much to me as it did to Walter. Right now, I needed the park. I needed the escape. I wanted to talk to Mike.

"Mommy, there's that funny man again. Look, now he's chasing that squirrel."

It was the same little girl from the day before. *She must think I'm some crazy old man, playing in the park with a squirrel. I wish I could talk to her, tell her how wrong her mommy is about animals,*

I smiled and waved at her. She smiled and waved back. Her mother did neither.

Once I stopped chasing him, Mike waited on his limb until I made my way to the bench and sat. Then, without hesitation, he scampered down and jumped up beside me, expecting his treat.

He quickly grabbed the first nut I laid on the bench and once the little girl and her mother were out of hearing distance, I began to talk. "Walter is doing fine. He's up and walking around, he favors his leg by limping though. They let him out of his cage, and he has a blanket in a corner of the kennel to lie on, but most of the time he follows Ingrid whenever she lets him. They told me I could come to get him this afternoon, but Ingrid was busy this morning, so I didn't get a chance to see her. This is her half-day off, so I won't see her this afternoon either. I think I'll wait until tomorrow to bring Walter home. I guess you don't know about Ingrid. Well, she's about the nicest, most beautiful woman in the whole world," I told Mike. "And I think she likes me."

"Excuse me, sir, are you okay?" a male voice asked.

A uniformed cop stood over me. A big man, imposing in every way, with a black mustache, arms and shoulders bulging with muscles, and a gun. He was wearing a gun! A person with a gun always gives me pause.

Mike scampered up the tree with his last almond, leaving me alone to explain why I was talking to a squirrel.

"Just thinking out loud," I stammered and started to get up from the bench.

The cop stepped closer, making it impossible for me to rise. Towering over me with his gruff, imposing voice he demanded, "Do you live around here?"

I slumped back to the bench, "Uh, yes. About four or five blocks from here."

"We received a report of a strange man conversing with animals. You fit the description. I need to see some identification," he commanded.

I fumbled with my wallet and dropped a credit card and some money as I struggled to get my driver's license out of its slot.

"Remain seated while I check your information," he ordered, then stepped back and began talking on his phone.

I scrambled to retrieve the items I dropped before the wind scattered them, then sat, too afraid to even scratch my nose, which picked this most inopportune time to itch annoyingly.

I'll bet it was the nice little girl's mother who ratted me out.

"Okay, I didn't find any priors or outstanding warrants. You are free to go," he said, "but from now on, keep to yourself and stop acting strange. You're scaring people."

It was almost nine a.m. before I arrived at the vet's. I was nervous. I spent almost an hour selecting a proper outfit and checking my look in the mirror, changing my shirt, my shoes, my slacks, and my hair. The last time I felt like this was in high school before my junior prom.

"Go on back, Mr. Williams. They are expecting you," Mary said, as I burst through the front door. "We haven't been able to keep Walter down this morning, I think he knows today is the day."

Ingrid's perfume overpowered all the animal smells you associate with a veterinary clinic. Her hair flowed over her shoulders like she was facing a morning breeze. Her deep sparkling eyes shone more dazzling than ever this morning. *Was she happy Walter was healed sufficiently to go home? Was she happy to be here in her comfort zone? Or was she happy to see me?* I hoped it was the latter, but just being in the same room with her was all I needed.

"Good morning, Mr. Williams. It is nice to see you. We can't slow Walter down, he is up and eager, I think he knows he is going home this morning. He is even trying not to limp in my presence. Keep him as calm as you can, and don't take him outside. No walks for at least a week. Leave his dressing on for as long as he'll let you. If he tears at it, tape it up. We need to keep it covered until his first checkup. Bring him back in two weeks. We will examine it again and then decide what more might need to be done," Ingrid cooed softly.

"Come on boy, let's go home," I grinned sheepishly, as I took his leash, careful to brush her hand as I did.

I could see Walter's leg was still bothering him. He tried to hide his limp as we entered the lobby and turned toward the exit. "She says she wants to see him in ten days, mornings work best for me, the earlier the better," I lied to Mary on our way out. "Please email me with the time, Walter is anxious to get home."

It took some effort to get Walter into the seat, I walked around to the driver's door, slid in and paused to catch my breath before starting the engine. *This morning, I took extra time with my shave and used my favorite cologne and mouthwash. I spent almost a half hour in front of the mirror. After all that, when I was alone in the room with her, I couldn't say a word.*

As I sat alone with a fidgeting Walter, my mind began to spin. I thought, *Why can't I say something about our conversation from the other day? Why hasn't Ingrid said any more about my calling her sometime? Why haven't I followed up on her request? Will I ever get a better chance? Will I ever get another chance?*

Walter was agitated because I wouldn't take him to Fillmore Park. He was dying to run, kick up leaves, sniff and mark every tree he passed, chase Mike, and find the old man, but I fought his demands. I was glad he was close to being back to the Old Walter, but I wanted to hold him back, at least for a few days. If nothing else, I needed to keep his wound dry.

After three days of his constant moaning, begging, and following me around, I caved to his demands. We went to the park, but all Walter's antics were in vain, I didn't unhook the leash. Mike stood on his haunches next to his tree, waiting. Walter strained at the leash; I wouldn't unhook it. We hurried as fast as I could toward Mike.

He didn't move until Walter was unusually close before bounding to the trunk and scrambling up the tree. Then he sat on his favorite limb. Almost at once, he was joined by several other squirrels, all barking and squeaking at Walter.

I sat quietly on the bench, enjoying the barking and chattering of the squirrels and the whimpering of my dog as I watched for the little girl, her mother, and the cop, and thought about Ingrid.

Chapter 3
The Money

The next afternoon, as we walked again, I heard the commotion coming from behind us. Even before I turned, I knew from their noise what to expect. A half dozen boys, all about twelve or thirteen, bore down on us on their mountain bikes. Boys just beginning to be engulfed in the flood of testosterone, which happens to all males about that age. Changes in body shape, changes in voice, changes in attitude, changes they would all deal with for the rest of their lives. Changes that were beginning to alter their character. Changes some would deal with more successfully than others.

Walter turned, set his feet, and growled as they approached. This was a reaction I'd never seen before.

Here they came, cocky, rude, loud, and hoping for trouble. They were riding their bikes through the dirt, jumping mounds, splashing through the creek, climbing its banks, enjoying what they perceived as their new manhood. All were wearing baggy shorts, tee shirts eleven sizes too big, and sleeves cut off at the seam, exposing the last area the testosterone would affect, their bony frames, hairless bodies, and muscles. And (most intelligently), they all wore their hats backward. Their leader (there's always a leader) eyed Walter and me and began to charge.

Staring fiercely, he gripped his handlebars, stood up on the peddles, and pumped violently toward us. What began as a show of leadership on his part, instantly turned into a manifestation of cowardice. Walter jerked the leash from my hands and charged. I froze as the chaos developed in front of me. The bully biker's expression changed. The ferocity of his glare fell from his face replaced with an expression of terror. Walter, his ears lying sleek against his head, his teeth bared, was in full decimate and destroy mode.

The leader of the pack, in an act of complete cowardice, slid his bike sideways, almost laying it down, then frantically peddled to the safety of the herd as his buddies watched in awe. I will give the kid credit though; he didn't cry as he scrambled in retreat.

Walter, now satisfied he was the clear winner of the confrontation and content with the impression he made, finally heeded my screaming, and trotted back with his head held high, strutting as the proud protector of his master. I wished this hadn't happened. I was surprised at Walter and felt a little sorry he burst the bully's bubble, but I leaned down, hugged his neck, and said, "Good boy!"

With Walter's leash now firmly in my grasp, we watched as they peddled around us, kept a safe distance, followed the curve of the trail, and disappeared. We waited until we could no longer see or hear them before resuming our walk. I hoped we'd seen the last of them, but suspected we hadn't.

Walter had already forgotten them. I tried to walk slowly, hoping to control him. His leg was still bothering him, and this recent incident worsened his limp. Even though I coveted any excuse to go to the clinic, I didn't want him to reinjure his leg.

I watched, still amazed, as my friend and guardian explored. We moseyed easily, winding among the trees, Walter marking each as though he had never been here before. I tried unsuccessfully to keep him from the creek, worried about infection but enjoyed watching him frolic. He clambered up the bank and once out of the water, shook himself dry and resumed his exploration.

Something caught his eye. Slowly, Walter approached it. He stopped, circled, and inched closer until he could touch it with his nose. He stood frozen, staring, but didn't try to pick it up. My first thought was he discovered just a piece of paper and wondered why he was so intrigued; but once I got closer, I could see it was an envelope. Walter gave me a curious glance as I reached past him to pick it up.

It was an envelope, but it did not have a letter inside. It was the type of envelope banks give you when you withdraw money. I opened it and saw it held several crisp bills. Two twenties, a five and two ones, forty-seven dollars, with no change and no receipt. I didn't know what to do but knew if I put it back, anyone could pick it up and who knew what would happen to it then, so I stuffed it in my pocket.

We walked on as I pondered what to do. Forty-seven dollars was not a lot of money, but still a significant amount. It was an odd amount of cash to carry, and why in an envelope, why not in a wallet or purse? Someone was carrying this money with a purpose. The amount had to have significance.

I heard them again. They approached, less rowdy now, spread out, riding slowly. I wrapped Walter's leash around my wrist and waited. At first, they paid no attention to us as they neared, their focus was on the ground in front of them. I smiled as their leader caught a glimpse of us and turned his bike away.

One of the quieter gang members rode toward me and as he approached, asked, "We lost some money. Have you seen it?

I stared at him but didn't speak.

"Danny had some money for his mom. We were riding to the store to give it to her, but he lost it," he said.

I was wary of their intentions, so I still didn't answer. Walter stood at my side, growling low, but loud enough to demand the boy's attention.

"It was in an envelope. Danny had it in his pocket and now it's gone," he said.

"How much money did he lose?" I asked, still not sure what I should do.

"Danny didn't know. He just got it from the bank. They gave it to him in an envelope. He didn't count it," the kid went on. The rest of the bullies stopped to watch our conversation, but none came close, especially their leader, Danny, who now hunkered behind the others.

I wondered how you could get money for your mother from a bank and not know the amount. But still, it was only forty-seven dollars. I asked the kid, "How can he not know the amount?"

"I don't know, but he doesn't. His mom was really mad when he told her he lost it."

"Can you identify the envelope? Did it have the name of a bank on it?"

"It was yellow, that's all I know."

The envelope in my pocket was yellow. Printed on the front were the words, US Bank, in a big enough font that you couldn't miss the print. I was sure the story he was telling me was not true, but he knew the envelope was yellow but didn't know it only held forty-seven dollars.

"Do you know where you lost it?" I asked.

"Not for sure. Somewhere in the park," he answered.

"My dog found it in the grass," I said, as I handed the money to him. "Tell Danny he needs to be more careful, and respectful."

"Gee thanks, Mr.," he grinned as he waved the envelope for the others to see. Then they all sped off in the direction from which they came.

"Come on Walter, let's go home. We've had enough excitement for today." I tugged on his taut leash, but Walter wasn't yet ready to leave his park.

As we neared the exit of the park, I saw an elderly lady wearing a worn green sweater, a floppy brown hat, and worn-out tennis shoes, sitting on a bench. As I got closer, I could see she was in tears. Walter saw her too and dragged me toward her.

"Do you mind if we share your bench?" I asked. "My dog has worn me out."

She merely nodded and continued to sob without looking up.

"Is something wrong? Do you feel all right? Is there anything I can do to help?" I asked as Walter moved closer to her, demanding her attention.

"I lost all my money," she sobbed. "Some boys on bicycles knocked me down and took my purse," she continued.

"Damn it," I blurted.

She gave me a stern rebuke, "Please don't use such language in my presence, young man," she said.

"I'm sorry, it just came out," I apologized. "My name is James. I'd like to help you."

"I don't know what you can do," she answered. "Those boys stole my money. It was the last of my savings, and I need it for my medicine."

"I'll call the police," I said, digging my cell phone out of my pocket.

Walter began nudging her, his way of comforting her.

"I like your dog," she said, forcing a bit of a smile.

It was the same cop from a few days before, the one who asked for my identification. The one who thought I was some kind of a sicko.

"Is this man bothering you?" he asked her, snarling at me.

"No, this nice young man is trying to help me. He's the one who called you."

"What's the trouble, ma'am?" he asked.

"Those mean boys on their bikes knocked me down and stole my money," she cried. "It was all the money I had in the world. It was the last of my savings. I was going to the pharmacy…"

Unsympathetically, he interrupted, "How much did they get?"

"It was forty-seven dollars and fifty-three cents."

"I'll file a report," he said. "Probably isn't much chance of catching them though," he went on.

"Don't you need a description, officer?" I asked.

"Yeah, I suppose. Not much chance we'll catch them, though," he answered coldly.

We watched from the bench as the cop walked away. He put his notebook back in his pocket and was not on his phone. I knew this was 'case closed' as far as he was concerned.

"Come on, Walter and I will walk you," I said, trying to assure her.

"I was going to the pharmacy, but since I don't have any money, I may as well just go back home now."

"Let's go on to the drugstore anyway, maybe we can work something out," I pleaded.

"Okay, but it won't do any good," she said.

***

"That will be sixty-eight thirty-two," the pharmacist said.

She started to sob again, "I'm sorry," she blurted.

Before she could turn away to leave, I handed him my charge card, "Take it out of this," I said.

Surprised, she exclaimed, "Oh no, you mustn't."

"It's all right, I'm just happy I can help. Please take the prescription, and come on, I'll walk you home."

We walked quietly to a run-down apartment complex about three blocks from the park. I held her package as she fumbled with the lock. "I'm sorry, I forgot to introduce myself. My name is Effie. You are such a nice young man; how can I ever thank you?"

"It is so nice to meet you, Effie. I'm sorry this has been such a bad day for you. I hope to see you again," I said and forced three twenty-dollar bills into her hand as I gave her the pharmacy bag.

Walter licked her hand as we turned to leave.

"You are so lucky to have such a nice owner," she told him, as she rubbed his neck.

Chapter 4

The Transfer

It has been months since I met Henry, months since Theresa left, months since Walter hurt his foot, months since those boys stole Effie's savings, and months since Ingrid expressed an interest in me. My divorce from Theresa still wasn't final. I wanted to visit Henry but felt uneasy about coming between him and his daughter, my soon-to-be ex-wife.

I posted a note on the bulletin board at work about Effie, and as a result, several fellow workers agreed to join me and start a group to help her. Soon the group grew to include almost everyone in our department. Even a few of the partners chipped in. Now, every other weekend, one of us delivered a box of items we collected, some groceries, and always a monetary donation. Her monthly pharmacy bill was now sent directly to my credit card account. I asked one of our researchers at the office, Olivia, to see if she could find any of Effie's relatives who might help her. Olivia found a niece who lived in Western Pennsylvania. We were now trying to convince Effie to move.

For some reason, which I refused to think about, Mike no longer visited us when Walter and I went to the park.

The bicycle gang had moved on. My hope was their experience with Walter influenced their departure. I doubted it though.

Walter's leg has healed. Once the hair grew back, his scar was barely visible. Walter has long forgotten about his injury and no longer favors his foot. He runs and explores as if nothing happened.

My only contact with Theresa now is through our lawyers.

All this, and I still haven't asked Ingrid for a date.

I plodded through the front door of my apartment, dropped my briefcase on the couch, and punched the message button on my wall phone. Only one message and I recognized the voice. "Mr. Williams, Walter has a check-up scheduled for next Tuesday the fifth at three p.m. Please call back or press one to confirm or two to reschedule," Mary's voice announced.

It's been three months since I last stepped foot into the veterinarian's office. In that time, coward that I am, I haven't mustered the courage to ask Ingrid for a date. I couldn't even bring myself to do something as safe as calling her when she wasn't working. Stupid excuses like, *What would such a smart beautiful woman see in a dolt like me?* plagued me.

When thinking about how Theresa and I got together, I realized she practically threw herself at me at the beginning of our relationship. Will and Rose invited me to go with them to an off-Broadway show. At a party following the show, we met Theresa who was a friend of one of the cast. A few days later, out of the blue, Theresa called me. *Hasn't Ingrid done the same? What have you got to lose? Suck it up and do something, Buddy. Suppose she's found someone else to spend her time with. Suppose they aren't very serious yet. Suppose they are. You only have six days until Walter's appointment.*

I spent the evening thinking of opening lines, practicing in front of the mirror, and looking through my closet for the most proper outfit. Tuesday was bearing down on me.

Walter knew, he always knew when something was bothering me. Our walks to the park became longer. I spent more time sitting on a bench watching him frolic than walking. Evenings, I searched for love story movies on the television and watched for the best ways to talk to a girl. Walter stretched out on my lap, watching with those moon eyes, encouraging me. This, like everything else in our lives, was a team effort.

My Tuesday deadline approached quickly with an ominous sense. If I botched this with a case of nerves, I might have to wait three months for another chance. A lot can happen in three months. *How can a grown man stumble through the trials of life without any attempt to control either its direction or destination?*

"Good afternoon, Walter. It is so nice to see you again," Mary said. Her greeting didn't help. It was just another example of the space between me and Ingrid. And Walter was in the middle of it. It was his visit they looked forward to, not mine. They would have been just as happy to see him, no matter who the bumbling idiot was who walked him through the front door.

Mary sprung from behind the counter and rushed toward Walter like a lost relative home from the war; she hugged, and he wagged. In their excitement, the two bumped into me, causing me to stumble. I felt invisible.

The commotion and anticipation in the lobby brought Ingrid from the back. She rushed toward Walter and began hugging and petting him until finally she acknowledged me and said, "Hand me his leash, James. I'll take him back."

She called me James. She's never called me James before, I happily thought.

I watched as Ingrid and Mary led that traitor, Walter, to an examining room, leaving me standing alone in the center of the lobby. *Why can't I have big sad eyes like his?* I wished.

An eternity passed before Mary returned, "You can go back if you'd like, Mr. Williams."

God, how I wished she would call me James, or Jim, or Jimmie, or even Hey You. Anything but Mr. Williams, but we had been through all that before and this was not the time to bring it up again. So now, completely devoid of any practiced approach or even an ice breaker I might use, I shuffled toward the examination room and what most certainly would be disappointment.

I watched silently as the woman I cared for deeply lifted the paw and examined the old wound. My legs were unstable; I needed to sit but didn't dare. If I were to muster the courage to make an advance, I needed to be standing, face to face.

Finally, not with courage, but urgency, I spoke. "Ingrid, I…"

Our eyes met, but they didn't sparkle as before. She began, "Mr. Williams…"

I worried, *Oh, not again. I thought we were well past all formality. This can't be good. She's found another. I know it. I blew it. If I just did something, anything….*

"I'm sorry, I mean James," she went on, "I hoped to see you sooner."
Oh God, I'm going to die.
She continued, "I wanted you to be the first to know."

This is the end, I know it.

"I am leaving my practice. I have an offer to move to a clinic in the suburbs, closer to the country."

I fretted, *Oh no, I'll never see her again. But at least it's not another man. Or is it?*

"I always wanted a rural practice. One where I worked with farm animals. A practice with more variety, more challenges."

With a squeaky voice, I managed, "When are you leaving?"

"I have given notice. A new doctor will take my place on the first of the month. Doctor Fredrick Schmidt is his name. He will take over the care of Walter and my other regular patients. He has already been introduced to Mary and the rest of the staff. You will like him."

No, he is taking Ingrid's place, I won't, I can't like him!

My world just crashed in on me from all directions. My pulse raced, my heart felt like it was going to explode, the air was rapidly escaping my lungs, and my legs were wobbling much worse than before. With a flash of courage buffeted by the lingering urgency, words in a surprisingly sensible order escaped my mouth, "For the last three months, I have struggled with what you said during my last visit. You said, 'Maybe you could call me sometime.'"

"Yes, I remember."

"Well, I came here today to ask. Could we have dinner before you leave, someplace nice, quiet?"

"It would be nice, but I just can't. Not now. I have so much to do, so much to plan, and so many things to brush up on."

"But…," the old insecure me blurted.

"I'm sorry, James. I just won't have the time. You can call me once I get settled," she smiled and handed me her new business card.

A knowing Mary glanced uncomfortably as I returned to the lobby. As I passed her, focused only on the exit, she forced an appointment card into my hand, "We will see you in three months. If the date and time on the card don't work, call me, and I'll be happy to reschedule. You will like Dr. Schmidt; he is a very nice young man."

An understanding Walter paced slowly at my side, tail hanging limply between his hind legs. I let him in the back seat, then sat behind the steering wheel without starting the engine. I'm not sure how long I sat, but when I saw Mary leave her desk and begin walking to the door, probably to ask me if anything was wrong, I hurriedly started the engine and backed from my parking spot. I didn't want to talk to anyone. Not Mary and especially not Ingrid.

Once home, the same insecure and now despondent me opened the door and instinctively walked to the refrigerator. Soon, over a microwaved ear of sweet corn and a warmed-over slice of meatloaf, the same old me appeared and began to mumble. *How could you be so dumb? Your cowardice is amazing. See what your procrastinations did. See what happens when you don't act on your thoughts. You knew this would happen. She turned you down, what are you going to do now, dummy?*

~

"Dr. Schmidt will see you now," a quietly composed Mary said.

Walter and I rose apprehensively and walked toward the examination room.

Chapter 5
The Suburbs

Three weeks later, I found a strange letter in the pile of mail as I dumped it on my desk. It wasn't official in appearance and the return address was not familiar, so I threw it in the trash can with the rest of the junk mail. It landed on top, face-up, and seemed to stare at me as it lay, so I thought I should at least open it.

It was just a thank you card with my name handwritten on the front.

Inside, I read a printed message sent to many former customers, I'm sure. Printed on the page:

I would like to thank all my former customers at the Fillmore Veterinary Clinic for your kindness and loyalty. It was signed, *Sincerely, Ingrid Johansson.*

I held it for a moment, thinking, remembering, and regretting. Then, through teary eyes, I saw the word *Over* handwritten in the lower right-hand corner.

Eagerly and apprehensively, I turned the note over.

Handwritten, it began, *Dear James,*

Terrified, I thought, *Oh God, it's a Dear John letter.*

But there was more.

I like my new job. My practice is growing faster than I imagined and I am making many new friends. I like it here. The air is fresh, the sky is clean and clear. I can watch sunrises and sunsets. I miss you and Walter. Please call me sometime, my new number is on my card.

I folded the card backward and stood it in the center of my desk.

But I didn't act. Every time I sat at my desk, I peered at her note. Sometimes I paused as I passed, picked it up to look at, but I would lay it down again.

What is the point? She's so far away now, how could it work? Would I drive over there, then stay alone in some God-forsaken motel, after a date? Why didn't she stay here?

There was a point. No matter the distance, I could make it work. And why would I think a night in a motel, alone, would be a hindrance? And most importantly, she found an opportunity, and took it, like any normal person would.

Chapter 6
The Firm

Odd to get two personal letters in one week. I don't think it ever happened before; personal letters have a way of bringing bad news.

All last week rumors floated around the office about possible changes within the firm. Our senior partner announced his retirement earlier this month. And, while no one thought much about the possible effects, or at least verbalized them, I wondered early and often about what might be going on. While this might not affect the partners, it could easily affect the office personnel because everyone knew who the new senior partner would be - his son.

As the junior of the four legal assistants, I felt my position might be the least secure. Not that we didn't have enough work, we did. My concern was the son, who was known for his disdain for the help. Although never stated, we all knew his philosophy was, 'The more the business expenses, the less I pocket.'

The end of the month was upon us, and the announcement was about to become official. Tuesday was the deadline, the day the name of our new boss will be announced. This was going to be a week of worry.

As usual, Walter met me at the door. He stood with his leash in his mouth, ready for his walk to the park. Walter followed not more than a foot behind me, as I threw my mail on the desk and hurriedly went to the bedroom for a change of clothes. He continually nudged me as I sat on the chair to put on my running shoes. "Be patient, boy," I smiled. The words fell on deaf ears, Walter was not patient.

As I watched him move from tree to tree, marking each as he did so many times before, I wondered about work.

It was a cool, breezy evening. No one came to Fillmore Park tonight, so we had the place to ourselves. I sat alone on what had become "our bench" and watched him explore. He didn't have concerns about job security, the cost of utilities, or even the source of his next meal. Walter knew I would be there to take him on his walks, open the door to a warm house when we returned, fill his water bowl whenever it was low, and refill his food dish.

I envied him.

Once we returned to the apartment, I did just that; I fulfilled my Walter commitment. Then I poured a glass of wine, sat in the Barcalounger, removed my shoes, and began to go through my mail. Items like the weekly blurb from a hearing aid company (I am not growing deaf - yet), an offer for term life insurance (I know better than to waste my money), an ad for cable TV (my apartment complex supplies cable), and a notice my auto warranty was about to expire (I don't have an auto warranty). Near the bottom of the pile, I found a small envelope, the size most greeting cards come in. It had a North Carolina return address. *Is it from Henry? What could he want?*

Inside I found a letter written with a shaky hand. I unfolded the wrinkled paper and read,

Hello James,

I wanted to write to thank you again for your help in finding my daughter, Theresa. Even if it was coincidental, if you hadn't realized the connection, I might never have found her. I will never forget the way you opened your home to me for those few days. I should tell you that it hasn't worked out the way I hoped. Theresa tried, but my farm was not the place for her. She has given up on her hope for a career in theater and has found a compromise she thinks might make her happy. She took a job as the entertainment coordinator on a cruise ship. Her job will take her on cruises in the Caribbean and her home base will be in Tampa, Florida. I doubt she will ever return to North Carolina.

Thank you again for your caring and friendship,

Sincerely,
Henry Crane

PS If you are ever down in this direction or wish to take a vacation from your city life, please come visit me. You will always be welcome. And you should know, there are jobs down here.

I read it a second time, laid it on the end table, picked it up, and read it again. *What a nice man, he didn't need to do this.*

When I walked into the break room my fellow employees were huddled around the message board. I knew this meant the long-anticipated notice was posted. None of the faces in the group showed signs of relief or elation as I approached. I inched close to the posting and read. It was the classic, "This announcement is to let you know we have nothing to announce." It merely said an announcement about the direction the company would come at the beginning of the new fiscal year.

"Great," I mumbled sarcastically, "At least this means they will pay us all through the holidays."

My comment was not well received by those around me.

Now, faced with the uncertainty of the next two months, the impending semiannual check-up by the new vet, who neither Walter nor I would like, the absence of Ingrid from both our lives and the filth that is New York in the winter, I fell into the inevitable despair.

I should cut expenses, no telling what the next year might bring. I could get along without my car; driving to work was more trouble than it was worth; then finding a parking spot close to the apartment when I got home was always an issue, and poor weather worsened it. But if I gave the car up, trips to Ingrid's new job would be difficult at best. I turned the thermostat down; *I can always wear a sweater,* I rationalized. Trips to restaurants became more infrequent, to the point of never. Rather than eating so many prepackaged meals, I began to cook and then eat the leftovers. I hadn't eaten leftovers since I moved away from home. The only place I couldn't bring myself to scrimp was on Walter's food. *No reason he should suffer too.*

Through all this, I thought more about Ingrid and Henry. Both their notes lay open on my desktop. I picked them up often. No need to read them though, I knew their every word.

My phone buzzed. I read the text; it was from Mary. "Mr. Williams, Walter's appointment is this coming Tuesday at one p.m. If you need to reschedule, please let me know before the end of Friday's business day."

When we arrived at the clinic, Walter was reluctant to leave the car. I purposely didn't tell him we were going for his checkup, but he knew. Somehow, he always knew. Ingrid would not be the one who examined him.

I probably looked like an orphan with an abandoned dog as I dragged him through the doorway.

"Good afternoon, James. Hi, Walter. It is so nice to see you both," Mary said. Her greeting was sincere, but the joy was gone from her voice. *This was the first time she called me by my given name. Why now?*

She petted Walter's drooping head, then returned to her desk. I quietly waited, hoping to see Ingrid appear from the back room, knowing full well she wouldn't.

"Dr. Schmidt will see you now."

Walter and I silently plodded to the open door as Mary watched. I had to lift my reluctant dog to the examination table. In the past, he would have dragged me to the table and jumped up without my asking. Anything to get closer to his vet. Now the eager anticipation was gone.

"Good morning Mr. Williams. This must be Walter. Hi Walter, I am Dr. Schmidt. I am going to be your veterinarian."

A tall slender dark-haired man leaned stiffly over my dog. He moved awkwardly; his every movement seemed calculated. I watched as he went ahead, prying Walter's unwilling mouth open to examine his teeth, looking into his ears and eyes, prodding Walter's stomach for abnormalities. "This is a nasty scar," he said as he examined Walter's paws. "Someone did a fine job repairing this."

Walter jerked his leg from Dr. Schmidt's hand.

Once we returned to the waiting room, Mary asked, "Your next appointment will be in May, would you like to schedule it now?"

"I'll call you later."

As I opened the front door to leave, she called after me, "Say hello to Ingrid for me. Tell her I miss her. Tell her we all miss her."

Why would she think I talk to Ingrid?

Chapter 7
The Drive to Henry's Farm

I planned to take my remaining vacation time because we couldn't carry any over, and since I was near the bottom of the pecking order, those last two weeks of the fiscal year were all that was available to me. I still didn't have any clue as to whether I would be employed after the first of the year, and if I was, I didn't know if it would be in the same capacity or even at the same salary.

I texted Henry; I thought it would be more considerate than a phone call. I didn't want to make him uncomfortable if he needed to deny my request. I told him I needed to use my last two weeks' vacation before the end of our fiscal year; I was going to take a road trip, and would it be an inconvenience if I stopped for a visit as I passed through. I said it would be during the last two weeks of September. I didn't mention Walter.

My phone beeped during our walk home. "James, I would love to see you, show you the farm, and the great state of North Carolina. I will be here all through those two weeks. Stop anytime it is convenient and plan to stay as long as you like. And please bring Walter."

I copied, pasted, and printed Henry's note and Ingrid's card, then put them on my desk at work.

These last few weeks at work were made much easier by an occasional glance at them throughout my day. True to form, only one more notice was posted. It was on the wall when we returned from the Labor Day holiday and true to form it didn't hold any answers.

It read,

Ladies and gentlemen,

As you have already been informed, the firm will restructure at the end of this new fiscal year. A meeting will be scheduled for nine a.m. October 1. At that time, all decisions will be completed, and you will be informed of your new status, and we will resume operations.

Separation packages will be offered where applicable.

Signed,
The Partners.

I now had less than one week to work before vacation. It finally began to sink into all employees that changes were imminent, and some of my colleagues might not be happy with the reorganization. Tensions rose. Even friendly relationships within the firm were strained. I began to see my forced vacation in a new light. I would not be around as the bickering and speculation grew because very little work would be needed in those two weeks. Traditionally, only some tax information, some final decrees, estate issues, or divorce papers would need to be finished. All other work would be left for the new year.

I texted Henry to ask if the week from this coming Monday would work.

"Absolutely," he wrote back. "Plan to stay a few days. And don't forget to bring Walter!" he reminded me.

I finished the last of my work by noon on Friday. All that was left was to wait until five o'clock, and then finish packing. It was a two-day drive to Henry's, and I didn't want him to think his place was the only destination I had in mind, so I texted, "I will arrive sometime Monday if it is okay?"

In seconds he responded, "I am looking forward to your visit."

Walter never hesitates when I get his leash. He doesn't know where we are going or how long we will be gone, and he doesn't care. Going is all that matters to him. Today he sensed this was to be the beginning of a new adventure. He sat patiently - well, patiently for him anyway while I carried one bag after another to the car. He fogged up the window in the front door as he sat and watched me load the trunk. From the street, I could hear his tail thumping on the floor. When he saw me carry his carrier on my last trip out, his ears drooped. Walter was always up for an adventure; he hated having to ride in the carrier though.

"It's just 'til we get out of town, I promise," I said as I held the door, then watched as he lumbered toward the car, wondering if the trip was going to be worth being in the carrier. I chose Interstate 81 to begin. I didn't want to drive through Baltimore and Washington DC. I would have liked to spend time in DC but having a dog with me would make it undoable.

So once my car was loaded, I begged and pushed Walter until I got him into his carrier so we could start. "It's only temporary," I apologized to those big sad eyes and started the drive.

He lay in his carrier, whimpering and giving me moon eyes until I caved and pulled into the first rest stop we saw. Here he explored an entirely new group of trees, inspected each until he was satisfied, then peed on it and moved on to the next one. This went on for several minutes. He was taking up time I didn't want to spend, so I tied his leash to a picnic table while I rearranged my car, putting the carrier in the back seat in case we needed to stop and be legal again, then dragged him back and shoved him in.

By noon it warmed up enough for me to crack the window for him. He was now ecstatic but could only get his nose out into the air, as it was all I dared allow him. I pulled my hood up, zipped my sweatshirt, and tied the drawstring. People grinned, especially kids, as cars passed us. Eager but not hurrying, we motored on.

This was Walter's first extended car ride. Every time I acted like I was about to leave the apartment, Walter would fuss and carry on, wanting to go with me; his favorite outside adventure was exploring Fillmore Park. But if I even got close to my car, he wanted a ride. He didn't care where; he just wanted to go. Cracked window weather was his favorite. But this trip was different. Walter soon realized we were going farther than ever, so before long he became fixated on all the trees we passed. Trees that needed to be marked. It only took one pause at a rest stop for him to realize rest stops meant trees.

After the second one, he recognized the roadside sign. Every time we passed a big blue rectangular placard signifying, "Rest Stop Ahead," he began begging, whining, and tormenting me until I couldn't ignore him and caved (again) to his pleadings.

I didn't expect this. I wanted this to be a leisurely drive, even when on the freeway. I thought I allowed more than enough time, telling Henry we would arrive on Monday. But I soon realized that traveling with Walter was full of detours, even if just to the edge of the interstate.

I envisioned him breaking the window in his haste to get out, so I closed it each time before we began to slow. Even then it was a struggle to calm my frantic dog enough to grasp his collar and fasten the leash. Our second rest stop was a learning experience for me too. Sixty-five pounds of airborne black Lab was more than I could hold. This time, he jerked on the leash so hard getting out, that he hurt both my elbow and shoulder. Running to those first few trees he found needing his mark nearly upended me. The jerk when the leash went taut almost caused me to fall.

Once every tree was inspected at least twice we found a pet-friendly drinking fountain. I eagerly drank some much-needed water, while Walter refilled his bladder for our next stop. Then I wearily dragged my still-excited dog to the car, where after loading him, I sat motionlessly in the seat, trying to catch my breath.

A person traveling with a dog soon learns rest stops are not restful, and traveling from one to the next wasn't easy because Walter's panting between stops fogged the windows.

I started the car, backed from the parking spot, and eased back onto the highway. As I came up to speed, I thought of the day I bought my car. The dealer had two similar Camrys, one with an automatic transmission, the other with a manual. I considered the manual because the price was lower, and it would get better gas mileage. After pondering though, I chose the automatic, thinking of all the gear changes I would have to make driving in the city. Now I was happy with my choice. The unanticipated advantage of not having to shift gears repeatedly with a sore arm and shoulder because I owned a well-muscled dog, made my earlier decision far better.

Chapter 8
The Lost Dog

I didn't realize there were so many rest stops in Pennsylvania. I was not prepared for this constant stopping.

One summer when I was in college, I went to Colorado with three friends. We flew to Kansas City, where one of my buddy's folks lived, then drove his dad's car on to Estes Park to hike in Rocky Mountain National Park. On the way out we drank so much soda and water that one of us was in constant need of a restroom, only to learn there aren't many places to stop on Interstate 70 in Kansas and Colorado.

Interstates in the East aren't like those in the West. Or maybe it was just my perception, because now traveling with a dog with a constant need (or wish) to stop, it seemed like there was one around every curve. So, despite the fuss from the back seat, I began to ignore those big blue signs. I knew once we got to Henry's farm, Walter would forget the freeway rest stops. But this was knowledge I couldn't share.

After skipping a couple, my dog settled in the back seat. He lay back there on his blanket dreaming about whatever dogs dream about, until the urge struck. Ironically it was me who was struck. I watched for the first place to stop, which took an uncomfortably long time. Finally, I spotted a sign near the top of the next hill, and I needed to change lanes before the off-ramp. Walter felt me tap the brake pedal and rose from his nap instantly. As we drove into the parking area, he was up smearing his window with his nose, panting and whining. Eagerly he turned to me as we came to a stop. He now understood we wouldn't leave the car until his leash was attached, but waiting was not something Walter did well.

As we stepped out, the first noise I heard was that of a crying child.

Not crying because she wasn't getting her way, or because she was scared. She was frantic about something else. Walter and I both turned our attention to this little girl, wanting to see if we could help.

Standing by their rickety old camper, a bewildered and anxious mother and father faced us, restraining their little girl.

"Molly ran away," the girl sobbed. "Please, can you find her for me? Please?"

"What do you think, boy? Do you want to try to help these nice people find their dog?" I asked Walter.

Walter's solemn expression pled, "Can't we go see the trees first? We have been riding for over an hour and I drank all my water at the last break. And besides, there are so many trees here."

I leaned down, patted him on the side, and said, "Let's help this little girl find her dog first."

Then I asked, "What's your name, young lady?"

"Amy."

"Well, Amy, if you could get us one of your doggy's chew toys, we could let Walter sniff it, and then we could go try to find Molly."

"Her favorite is her teddy bear, Sam," she sniffled.

"Will you go get Sam and bring him to Walter? It will help him find Molly."

"OKAY, but Sam is a girl, just like me. Her real name is Samantha, I just call her Sam."

I watched as Amy's mother helped her up the steps and into their camper. "Sir, if you could hold my dog's leash for just a minute?"

He smiled knowingly, "Sure, but please hurry."

I made a quick trip to relieve myself and hurried back. By the time I got there, a hopeful Amy was standing in the doorway of the camper. She jumped down, and ran to me, with her arm extended, holding a tattered brown teddy bear.

"Let's just let him sniff it," I said, then turned to the father and asked, "Can you tell me what happened?"

"We opened the camper when we stopped. As soon as I opened the door, Molly saw a rabbit. The rabbit saw Molly and ran. She started chasing it. I yelled; we all yelled at her, but she wouldn't stop. They ran that way," he said, pointing. "We saw them run past that picnic table then out of sight. I ran to the edge of the hill and yelled, but Molly wasn't anywhere in sight. I came back to the trailer to help Angie try to calm Amy and get Molly's leash. That's when you drove up. I sure appreciate this," he said.

"We'll try our best. Walter has a good nose," I answered.

"Come on, boy. Let's see if we can find this nice little girl's friend."

We hurried through the scattering of cars and trucks parked in the lot, asking. No one noticed little Molly or the commotion she caused. The tractor-trailer parking was behind us, and the highway was on the other side of them. *At least the dog ran away from the highway*. But the image of a little dog squished on the highway wouldn't escape my mind.

So, fixated on the urgency, I coaxed Walter, "Come on boy, we can do this."

We clambered up the rise toward the picnic table.

Black Labs aren't known for their tracking ability, but mine could do anything. Beyond being my best and most loyal friend, I knew he was exceptional. I knew if any dog could follow Molly's trail, it was Walter.

So, full of hope, confidence, and adrenalin, Walter dragged me as we followed his nose. At the picnic table, he paused, sniffed, then turned. *Thank God we are turning away from the highway*, I thought, as we rushed through a patch of weeds toward a fence in the distance. I wondered about Walter's decision to hurry through the weeds. *Would he lose the trail here?* I worried. But Walter seemed intent and confident, so we hurried on.

I could see some commotion in the distance near the fence, but I was gasping for breath so hard I couldn't hear any sound. Walter's taut leash strained against my grasp. If I hadn't looped it around my wrist, he would have torn it from my hand. "Slow down, boy," I begged. But to no avail. He sensed he was close and wouldn't heel or heed.

I could hear yapping now, not far from us. As we neared the fence, I could see something moving. As we got closer, I saw it was a small dog.

Hung up about a foot off the ground, we found a small shaggy puppy caught in the fence. The loop on his collar was caught on a broken strand of the fence. The poor dog hung there, feet flailing, unable to free itself. When I leaned down to grasp the collar, she tried to nip me, but the presence of another dog calmed her. And when I said, "Easy, Molly, you are going to be okay," she let me touch her.

It took a bit to release Molly. I had to bend the fence to unhook her while reaching over the top to prevent her from running away when she was free. Once I freed her, I held her for a moment, trying to calm her racing heart, but knew we needed to get back to the camper and Amy as quickly as we could. I wasn't concerned Walter would run off, so I unhooked his leash and attached it to Molly's collar. He did have to mark one tree as we hurried back, but I waited as he did. I felt he earned the right to mark just one. I watched as he dallied, then called, "Come on Boy, we need to get back."

The instant we were in sight of the camper, Amy and both her parents saw us and came running.

With tears of happiness, I watched the reunion. Amy hugged her dog, her mother hugged both Molly and Amy, and the father hugged Walter.

"That's a great dog you have there," he said to me. "I don't know how to thank you."

"It was all Walter," I smiled.

"But you and your dog were a prayer answered. My name is James and this is my wife, Alicia," he went on. "We are so grateful."

"Ha, that's funny. My name is James, too."

"Hello, James," Alicia smiled. "It is so nice to meet you. This means so much to us. How can we ever thank you?"

"It's Walter who deserves the thanks. All I did was tag along. He did the work."

"We are so thankful you both happened along. Can you sit with us a while?"

"Yes, it would be nice. But first, I need to let Walter run. We stopped for him, and he still needs to see all these trees."

She smiled, "Okay, but we'll still be here when Walter is finished."

For such a small rest area, this sure has a lot of trees, I thought as I happily watched Walter do his thing. He earned this break, so I just followed along, thinking how lucky I was to have such a good dog. But thinking about Walter got me thinking about Ingrid, which got me thinking about Henry, and that got me thinking about Theresa, which got me thinking about my job, and that got me thinking about living in a big city, which got me thinking about my future. I pulled on Walter's leash until I got him close enough to sit and hug him.

At first, he gave me one of those "What was that for?" expressions, then we sat quietly, his paws on my lap, my arm around his neck.

My mind was swimming. We sat there for several minutes before I realized people were waiting on us, "Come on, boy, we need to get back."

Alicia, James, and Amy were waiting anxiously when we returned. Amy was holding Molly. Molly was wearing her leash, and it was tied to the picnic table next to the camper.

"Come, sit," James said.

"Can I get you something to drink? We have sodas. Won't you eat with us? I made my special potato salad for our trip home. I have ham sandwiches too; won't you please try one?" Alicia asked.

"Can I pet Walter?" Amy begged.

We spent an hour with them. The Whitneys told me all about their home in upper Pennsylvania. They were traveling home after a week of visiting her family in Virginia. Alicia had a sister there, Connie. Connie raised dogs and had a new litter of puppies. And after a week of relentless begging, Amy was coming home with a new puppy.

Alicia told me, "Amy has been begging for a dog for a long time. We just couldn't put her off any longer. If we lost Molly on our way home... well, I don't know what we would have done. It hurts to even think about it, but as they say, 'All's well that ends well' and thanks to you. We can't thank you enough."

"It was all Walter," I repeated.

In those silent moments, when no one spoke I sat and watched Amy sitting cross-legged next to Molly and Walter. The two dogs had already formed a bond. Once the getting-to-know-you sniffing finally subsided, they lay next to each other, each with a head on Amy's lap, each with Amy's hand rubbing their bellies. They were the image of innocence and contentment.

"This has been a good day, but I need to get going." I finally said. "Can I help you put your things away before I leave?"

"This has been more than just a good day," James answered. "This has been a great day. To meet and make a new friend; you are such a nice man. We will never forget you and your kindness, and Walter. We will never forget Walter."

Alicia drew her phone from her purse, "I'd like a picture of you and your dog. I want to always remember you."

"Mommy, can I be in the picture too?"

"Just a minute," James said and walked to a car stopped not too far from us.

I watched, guessing what he was doing. Shortly, he returned with the woman. "This is Charlotte, she is going to take pictures of us in a group. James, do you have a cell phone, we'll get her to use both yours and ours."

Charlotte gave me back my phone. It had at least twenty new photos of our group. Some with the parents and me, some with Amy and me, some with Amy holding Molly. Walter was in every picture.

"Here, take this," Alicia said as she handed me a scrap of paper with their names, addresses, and phone numbers. Then she handed me her notepad. "Please write your name, address, and phone number for us. We want to keep in touch."

"We'll find a nice place to stay tonight. A place close to a park or stream. You've earned a special night tonight, boy," I told Walter as we drove away.

He already had his nose pressed against the window, watching for more trees to mark.

Chapter 9
Virginia

It was dusk when we stopped in a little town in Virginia.

I parked in the lot of a large motel complex, cracked the window enough for Walter to stick the tip of his nose out, and walked inside. There I was greeted by a nice-looking young lady dressed in a company outfit and well groomed. She seemed out of place; not your average motel help. She glanced through the window of the lobby and saw Walter's head.

"How big is your dog, sir?"

I wished she hadn't seen him. For an instant, I wished I hadn't parked so close to the front door, but I was a proud dog owner and wasn't going to sneak him in the back.

"I don't know, probably twenty or twenty-two inches."

"No, I don't mean how tall, I mean how much does he weigh?"

I knew where this was going. I picked this motel because it was close to a park with a stream. I wanted to reward Walter for a good day with a walk in a park, to remind him of home, but I wasn't going to lie to her. "About sixty-five pounds I guess," I answered.

"I'm sorry sir, the motel's policy is no dogs over fifty pounds.

"Can you overlook it this one time?" I asked. "My dog and I have driven a long way today, and I wanted to reward his patience with a walk in the nearby park. That's why we stopped here, and really, he's just fifteen pounds over. Who will know?"

"I'm sorry sir, it's company policy."

"You aren't busy. Walter is a good dog; he won't be any trouble."

"I'm sorry, sir."

"My car is just outside, why don't you come out and say 'Hi' to him before we move on?"

"Okay, I guess it would be all right. I like dogs. It's just that...well, you understand."

Walter was sitting alone in the front seat wearing his most mournful expression. I had left him alone in the car for no more than three minutes. Three minutes can be a lifetime to a dog.

"Aww," she smiled when she saw those big anxious eyes.

I knew Walter and I just scored a room.

"I guess it will be okay," she said. The manager is gone and won't be back for a few days. Just don't parade him through the lobby, okay? Oh, and if you leave him in the room alone, he is supposed to be in a cage."

Once we took our stuff to the room and got settled, Walter and I drove to the nearby park. The map showed it as a dog park, so I thought it would be a perfect place to end a perfect day.

It was.

It was not as big as our park back home. It had a fence all around with a gate at each end, so nothing like the Fillmore. Both gates were open and no one was around to supervise. I wondered, "What's the point?"

A worn sign engraved with the likeness of two dogs at the entrance read, "In memory of Sammy and Pearl."

"At least they got that part right," I told Walter.

Sammy and Pearl's park was liberally sprinkled with a variety of pre-visited trees. There were trails and benches throughout, but no swing sets, slides, or merry-go-rounds. Walter was so excited about this newfound treasure he didn't notice their absence. We spent an hour, thoroughly examining each tree, marking it repeatedly before dashing to the next. I wondered if I was beginning to resemble a professional tennis player, with one arm bigger and longer than the other. But I smiled, *No, tennis players don't have an extra ring around their bellies.*

Within a few minutes, other dogs began to arrive. Dogs that needed to be "examined." Several times I felt compelled to introduce myself to other owners as we stood uncomfortably waiting while Walter and the other dogs acquainted themselves.

After twenty or thirty new trees and a half dozen canines, I dragged my reluctant friend to a nearby bench and sat. It was under protest, of course. *Where does this dog get all his energy?* I wondered.

Funny about dogs, they live only in the moment, no matter the circumstances. I had to drag Walter from the park, listening to his incessant begging and whimpering until he spotted our car. Then he dragged me the rest of the way, hoping for a new adventure.

Once we returned to the room I ordered pizza–pepperoni, of course. When it arrived, I took my half, set it on the desk near the television, and laid the box with Walter's half on the floor next to his water bowl. I gobbled mine as quickly as I could, not wanting to share. We both ate until we were full.

I spread Walter's blanket next to the bed, and collapsed with the remote in hand, finished my soda and let dinner settle. As luck would have it, we found a re-broadcast of a kennel club show, and with Walter's approval, I moved his blanket to the end of the bed, and we watched it again. My head was propped by a pillow against the headboard, fighting sleep. Walter's front paws were hanging over the end, fixated on the screen.

My watch alarm woke me at nine p.m. Time for Walter's final visit outdoors before we settled for the night.

Against house rules and without worry, I unsnapped his leash as soon as we walked out the back door. I sat on a patio chair to watch as Walter roamed the yard. The door suddenly opened. I called for Walter to come. We watched with anticipation as our motel clerk appeared.

"Time for a break. Mind if I join you?" she smiled.

I fumbled, trying to reattach his leash as Walter tried to sniff her leg.

"Don't worry, it's late, so no one will bother us," she said. "Remember, I told you I like dogs. Come here, Walter, let me pet you. Oh, you're such a handsome boy."

"We came out for one last inspection," I said.

"I've never heard it called that before. It fits though. I came out for one last break," She laughed. "Ronny comes in at six. We both work until ten and then I'm off for the night. We trade breaks before I leave. I take mine first, then he takes his, and after that he's here alone all night. My name is Elizabeth. You can call me Lizzy."

"It's nice to meet you, Lizzy. My name is James, I like Jim or Jimmie, but for some reason, people have always called me James. Thanks again for letting us stay. I know you took a risk doing it and we appreciate it."

"It's okay. I'm not worried. This isn't my real job anyway, and they're not about to fire me over something like this. I have taken some time away from college to catch up with my expenses, and honestly, they have a tough time finding people who will take this job and do it well."

"Well, thanks. Walter and I appreciate the gesture. What are you going to school for?"

"I want to be a veterinarian."

"Really? That's nice. My girlfriend is a vet." I fibbed a little, I should have said, prospective girlfriend or my wannabe, but that wasn't the point. Lizzy's mention of her aspirations brought me back to reality and got me thinking again about all that was going on in my life and Ingrid. Mostly I thought about Ingrid.

"I wish I could have a pet at school. I get to be around cats, dogs, and livestock all day, but I can't have a pet. I don't get it. I'd love to have a dog like yours. They are so well-mannered."

"Be patient, you'll be able to have one after you graduate. Just think, once you are a vet, you can take your dog to work with you every day."

She scribbled something on a piece of paper, folded it over, handed it to me, and said, "Remember to take Walter out the back when you check out in the morning. Ronny's a good kid and won't say anything, but I wouldn't want him to get into trouble either. Here's my name and address. I'd like to be friends with you and Walter."

"That's nice," I said. "I don't have anything to write on or I'd give you mine. I can leave it with Ronnie in the morning."

"Don't bother, I can get your information off your check-in paper if you don't mind. We are not supposed to do that, but if it's okay?"

"It's fine," I answered. Then I thought, this would be a good time to move my car away from the front door. "Would you watch my dog for a minute? I'll go move my car so we can be less conspicuous in the morning."

"I'd be happy to," she grinned, scootched closer, and began rubbing his ears.

When I returned, she swallowed the last drink of her soda, reached down for one final shoulder rub, and then excused herself, "Nice to meet you, Walter. Nice to meet you too, Jimmie."

"Thanks, I like that. Good luck with your schooling. There's a big need for vets. It's a great field."

After she left, I opened the paper, read her name, number, and comment, and then stuffed it in my pocket, "Come on boy, we need to get to bed."

I opened a beer, turned on the television, and lay against the headboard. Walter crawled up beside me, turned, hung his feet over the end, and waited for the set to warm up.

The kennel show had ended and a western was in its place. Walter turned his head and with begging eyes, "That show is over," I told him. "Give me a minute, I'll see if I can find something else."

His ears perked when I found a *Turner and Hooch* rerun. Not something I would watch in his absence, but he was happy. Within minutes I lost interest, picked up my phone, and began to browse through my Twitter page.

I couldn't focus on that either, so I laid the phone on the nightstand, took a long pull on my beer, leaned back again, and pulled the covers up.

Lizzy seems like a nice girl. I like people who have their heads on straight. She's not very old but knows what she wants and what it takes to achieve. Many of the kids I know her age are still oblivious and have no idea about the real world. I thought about her boyfriend. I wondered what he was like, and did he know what a good catch she was? Wondered if they had a good relationship. Wondered if he shared and supported her goals. My thoughts turned to Ingrid again, *Surely the new veterinarian in town already has a lot of admirers. Has she responded to any of their advances? Does she like her new job or location for that matter? Does she ever think about me? I should call her.*

As I reached past my beer for my phone, I noticed the alarm clock. It was 10:30 already. *It's too late to call.* I laid the phone back on the stand.

Maybe tomorrow night? I rationalized.

Chapter 10
North Carolina

We left early the next morning. Well, as early as a guy traveling with a dog can leave. Walter needed to patrol the backyard one last time before we started. Then, respecting Lizzy's wish, I took him out the back door, around to the end of the parking lot, and put him in my car. I walked back around to the back door, went in, came down to the lobby, settled my bill with Ronnie, and drove away. The windows I cleaned before loading my dog were already smudged.

My computer map said we were almost seven hours from Asheville, and from there it was still another hour farther to Henry's farm. Traveling with Walter meant there was no way I could make it in one day. We weren't too far from Gettysburg, but stopping there with Walter in tow, trying to see the sights wasn't possible, and since it would be crowded, it was out of the question. So, we motored on. First through the corner of Maryland, then down the interstate toward Henry's farm.

When we entered the Appalachian Mountains, Walter got excited by all the trees and wanted to stop, It didn't matter that we just left one of his roadside explorations. I smiled at his constant begging. If he could just understand, all the black Labs in the entire country couldn't mark all these trees in their lifetimes.

Futility was not a concept Walter understood.

As we drove along, the two of us admiring the scenery, I began to wonder. *With all this wide-open space, these picture-perfect locations, and the clean clear air, why do I live in a big city? Here I am, worried about a job that I don't want or like when I could be living in a place like this. I'm still young enough to change my direction. My only responsibility now is Walter, and wouldn't he be happier living in the country? But then there's Ingrid. Or is there Ingrid? She's moved away. Has she moved on? I don't doubt the local single men have discovered "the new vet in town." Is she being courted? Does she like someone? Have I missed my chance? Am I too late? What the hell am I doing to myself? My God man, get a grip. You are having the same thoughts as last night. You need to either do something about it or put her in the past and move on."*

Suddenly, Walter barked at a car that cut just in front of us. I jumped, panicked, and slammed on the brake. We came too close to being in an accident, yet the guy driving the other car was honking at us, even though he was supposed to be the one to yield. This wasn't a time to argue traffic rules though. If I hadn't been daydreaming, I would have seen him coming onto the highway from the on-ramp. I was in the right, but we easily could've been dead right.

"Sorry, boy," I said as I reached to pull him away from the window.

It was too soon to stop again; we'd only been driving for about an hour, but I needed to get out, calm myself, and stretch my shaking legs. I took the first off-ramp and stopped in the back lot of a filling station.

Walter was up in the seat, ready to explore, but I wasn't. I stood for a few moments, holding the leash, and waiting for my legs to work, but it was too much for him. He gave me two choices; move, or I'll drag you. I nearly fell, but we were off, nearly running. This was not a place where I could let him run free, so I needed to keep up. He found a small grove of immature trees in the far corner of the lot. Since it was fenced in and no one was around and it had obviously been visited by other dogs, I felt comfortable unhooking the leash to let him explore and do his business.

I waited impatiently, wishing this was the last day of our trip.

"Come on boy, we need to get going," I yelled.

He trudged back to me with his tail down, head drooping, wearing his best forlorn expression; the one which always made me feel guilty, but it wasn't working on this trip.

"I know, I know, but we need to get going," I told him.

I hooked his leash, and we began toward the car. Each time he stopped to sniff something, I had to drag him away.

Funny, this happens every time, he drags me out, and then I drag him back.

I didn't need to buy gas yet but thought since we had already stopped, I might as well fill up. Then, on the slim chance we didn't need to stop again for anything else, I would have enough gas for the rest of the day.

As soon as he realized we were not getting back on the highway, Walter climbed into the back seat to pout.

There was a vehicle at every pump, so I picked the one that I thought was about ready to leave, pulled in behind an old rattletrap of a car, and waited. A Chevy, maybe a Plymouth or Pontiac, I didn't know which. I noticed the man was standing by the driver's side door and talking to the woman on the far side of the front seat. I couldn't hear their conversation over the two kids scuffling in the backseat. The gas nozzle was still in their car, but I could see the handle wasn't up, He wasn't pumping gas. I could see he had a few dollar bills in his hand though he must be asking her for more money.

Then I realized they were using the last of their money on this fill-up.

Walter sensed the delay and was now smudging the inside of his window with his nose.

"Come on boy, let's see if we can help."

"Nice dog," the man said uncomfortably, trying to mask his predicament.

"Are you having trouble with the pump?"

"No, it works, we are about done. We'll be out of your way in a minute."

"No hurry, I just thought…"

"Get back in the car kids, we need to get going," he yelled.

Two freckle-faced kids, a boy and girl, probably twins, managed to get the door open and were struggling to get out of the back seat so they could pet Walter. His wagging tail only encouraged them.

"Get back in the car kids. Leave this man's dog alone."

"It's okay, he's friendly and he likes everybody, especially kids. His name is Walter, you can pet him."

Both kids leaned out of the back to pet an eager dog, who now had his paws on the car and was trying to stick his nose in the window. Once again, Walter rescued me from an uncomfortable situation.

I looked at the gas pump, pretending to notice it for the first time. "You only bought six gallons. Do you live around here, close?"

I reached over and head-rubbed the boy so I could let him answer without making eye contact.

"Things are kind of tight right now," the man stammered.

"Six gallons isn't going to get you very far."

"I know, we'll find something up the road."

"I'd like to help."

"We'll be okay," he answered. But didn't protest further.

"What's the trouble here?"

I turned to see a big gray-haired man, about sixty smiling down at me.

"No problem," I answered. "I'm helping these folks out, is all."

"Tough times, huh? I've had some myself," the big man said.

"It's okay, I've got it. We'll be out of your way in a few minutes," the dad said.

"Alright, just thought I'd check," he said. "I was just going in to get a snack, you kids hungry?"

The children looked to their dad with anticipation. He didn't object.

"Name's Gary," he smiled, now facing the dad. "Like to buy the kids a soda if you don't mind."

The dad struggled for words, but they wouldn't come, so he just nodded uncomfortably.

"You kids get your mom, we'll go inside. They've got vending machines. I'll buy you a snack and a drink. Why don't you come too, sir?"

"It's okay, I'll wait here with the car."

Just as the pump stopped and I finished the payment, Gary came back with the twins and their mother. Those two kids, who moments before were scuffling and arguing, were now skipping along, a soda in one hand, and a sandwich in the other. The woman carried two bottles in one hand and a sack in the other.

The man extended a callused wrinkly hand, "Thank you, gentlemen, I can't tell you how much this means to us."

As they drove away, I could see her taking something from the bag, unwrapping it, and handing it to her husband. She put her hand on his shoulder as he took the first bite. I sensed the smile they shared and patted Walter's head.

I was about to get back into the car when I felt a slap on my back. I turned to see Gary, hand extended, grinning.

"Glad to see you help those nice folks out," he said.

"It was the right thing to do," I answered.

"I know what it's like, folk's just trying to get by, hoping to find something 'just down the road.' Lost my farm over twenty years ago. Only job I could find was janitoring out here. I used to spend all day here, cleaning up after folks, keeping water in the windshield buckets, emptying the trash, and doing anything that needed done. Got to know some of the regular truckers. They told me I ought to get a truck of my own. Like I said, that was twenty years ago. I own a bunch of trucks now. Don't need to work anymore, so I come out here, clean up the place, empty trash barrels, fill the windshield buckets, and talk to the truckers like I did twenty years ago. I'm gonna keep paying it forward until I'm gone."

I couldn't think of anything to say, so I just nodded.

"Nice dog, mind if I give him a treat?" Gary asked as he rubbed Walter's head. "Every man should have a dog," he said.

I watched as he shuffled over to the next island to check the windshield washing bucket and talk to the fresh customers.

Walter lay in the back seat, chewing on Gary's treat. I sat in front, both hands on the wheel, smiling, trying to concentrate, but thinking about the family at the truck stop, and what a good day this was so far.

It's Sunday, I wonder what Ingrid is doing today.

A sobering thought spun round and round in my head and wouldn't leave. The satisfaction of helping another had faded now. Gradually, I settled into the drive.

I planned to drive on scenic roads on my trip and absorb the beauty. I'd never been to this part of the country before, but I soon discovered it was hard to make any time on the curvy, hilly roads of Virginia. So, reluctantly, I got back on the interstate and fell in line. Now with Walter lying in the backseat quietly gnawing on his treat and me contemplating my future, the miles began to blur. Somewhere near Roanoke, I plugged my thumb drive music into the USB port and set it to browse. But after three or four blues songs in a row, I decided I'd rather have the silence.

The miles passed. Walter was quiet. He even fell asleep on his blanket for a while. The landscape remained much the same all day. I drove along admiring the small towns, the pretty farmsteads, trying to prioritize thoughts and worries. Little by little, my list grew into an order. Some of my issues moved around the list in my head; my job, my need for a newer car, where I live; and things like that. But as the list took shape, I began to realize Ingrid was always at the top. Much as I needed changes, my biggest need was to find a way to have her in my life.

I drove on, thinking. I turned back to check on Walter, asleep. He lay there curled up on his blanket, nose on his front leg with his chew treat next to his nose. *What a life, I'd love to be like him.*

We stopped just short of Asheville for the night. It was late and we were tired. I called Henry, "Traveling a long distance with a dog takes a lot longer than I realized, it will be Monday afternoon at the earliest before we arrive," I told him.

"Take your time," he laughed. "The farm will still be here when you get here."

Chapter 11
Henry's Farm

Henry had sent me directions to his farm before I started. I had printed and folded them and laid them on the console. I checked the printout and did the math in my head. I figured we only had an hour and a half left to drive. Even with the anticipation of getting there, I had trouble getting out of bed. Somehow, I felt today was going to be a big one, maybe a turning point. Would it be a good day? Maybe, maybe not.

Before we left, we took advantage of the motel's backyard again. I opened a gate at the far end of the yard and let Walter run through some trees in the vacant lot next door. Another dog, a little toy poodle, was there, running free. Its owner was standing a few feet away. Walter ran to check it out.

"His name is Cooper," the owner said as he walked up.

"Mine's name is Walter," I answered. "I see Cooper and Walter are already friends."

"Yeah, Cooper likes to be around other dogs. Sometimes I think about getting him a friend, but I don't need a second dog. I am Owen, by the way."

"I'm Jimmie."

Funny how it sounded, I never called myself Jimmie even though I wanted others to. It caused me to pause. Today is going to be a nervous day; meeting Henry again, staying with him for several days, sleeping in a strange bed, maybe in Theresa's old room. *And here I am, calling myself by a name I have never used. I have only been away from the city for a few days, am I already changing?*

We stood for a bit, each watching our dogs before Owen broke the silence, "We need to be getting on. We are driving to New York City. I have a job interview there."

"We need to get started too; we are going the other way. We are on vacation. Good luck to you, by the way."

"Safe travels," he smiled as he picked up Cooper.

———❧———

Shortly after one p.m. I braked at the end of Henry's lane. What seemed like a long trip while we were driving, in reality, flew by. I had arrived.

A long well-kept lane lined with a freshly painted white rail fence stretched toward an old white farmhouse with a bright red tin roof. A shiny white mailbox stood at the entrance. Red block lettering on the side read, Henry and Emma Crane. Just below in a child's cursive was the name, Theresa, painted in pink. A "Welcome Friends" sign stood on the other side of the entrance.

Here goes, I thought, as I let off the brake pedal and started to ease down the lane. First, I encountered a small dip, then a slight curve, and then the yard in front of the farmhouse came into view. To one side sat a newish two-car garage, on the other was an old barn. All were freshly painted with bright red tin roofs. I slowed to admire.

Big, purple-flowered bushes, weigela or rhododendron, framed a porch that covered the entire front of the house. Two rocking chairs sat side by side on the porch. An elderly white-bearded man sat in one.

Walter jumped from between the seats and pressed his nose against the window.

I reached over, rubbed the back of his head, and quietly said, "We're here buddy. Remember that guy?"

Henry rose from his chair, ambled down the steps with the help of his cane, and stood smiling as I stopped.

"It is so good of you to come," he said. "I am so looking forward to sharing the place with you. I see you brought Walter with you; good."

He extended his hand, such a firm handshake. I didn't expect it from him.

"How was your trip?"

"It was great. I got to see a lot of country I'd never seen before. I didn't have any idea how pretty it is here in the mountains."

He turned to Walter, who by now was so excited his tail was wagging his entire body. "How about you, Walter? Did you enjoy it too?"

Henry dropped to one knee, and I could only step back and admire the hugging, licking, and petting which ensued. "Come here, boy, I've got someone to show you."

I followed as the two of them walked to the back corner of the house, where Henry whistled one time, and then waited.

"Walter, this is Winnie. Winnie, meet Walter."

A beautiful shiny-haired golden retriever and a coal-black Labrador became new best friends instantly.

"Come inside, we'll get a glass of tea then sit out front a spell. After, I'll show you the house and barn. We'll get you settled in tonight, then tomorrow, I'll give you a tour of the place. I think you'll like it here."

I turned to call for Walter. He was nowhere in sight.

"Don't worry about them. Winnie won't leave the yard without me. Let them go, they'll eventually be out there on the porch with us. I am so glad you decided to come. I want you to relax and enjoy your stay."

I studied him as he fixed the tea. He was the same bearded man I met in Fillmore Park, yet somehow, he wasn't. He had the same beard, but it wasn't scraggly now. He wore the same type of black pants and brown jacket, but now they were clean, wrinkle-free, and tailored. He wore a new leather fedora now, not the worn tweed one he wore when I first met him. Mostly though, the biggest change was he no longer wore a tired worried expression.

"A penny for your thoughts?" he asked.

I didn't answer. I wasn't comfortable talking to him yet; so I couldn't answer a personally loaded question like this.

"I hope it's not too sweet for you. You're in the South now. You'll have to learn to like sweet tea, or you won't ever fit in."

I followed him out of the kitchen, through the dining room and living room, then onto the porch.

The inside of the house was just as I pictured, only cleaner. Ornate furniture, some probably original to the house, sat in the same spot where they had for years, decades maybe. Pictures, mostly of people, surely family, lined the papered walls. There were coffee tables and end tables, all in their perfect positions, made from real wood, covered with books, doilies, and an occasional potted plant. His house was perfect.

He must have a housekeeper. I thought, then smiled to myself. *What a strange reaction!*

Henry held the front door open, and I walked out.

"Take a load off," he smiled.

I hesitated. I knew one of these chairs was his and the other, his wife, Emma's. I didn't want to sit in his and wasn't sure I should sit in hers. Either choice would be wrong, somehow.

Henry sensed my problem. "I'll sit here, you can sit in Emma's rocker. She wouldn't have it any other way."

Walter and Winnie came bounding up the steps, panting from their exploration.

Instinctively, I reached to pet Walter, but he flashed by me and headed straight for Henry. Winnie then laid her head on the arm of my seat, demanding attention. In a few moments they settled. Walter lay next to Henry and Winnie was next to me with her head nudging my leg, demanding more. "Did I just lose a dog, gain a dog, lose two dogs or gain two?" I laughed.

~

The view from the porch was spectacular. The lane from here seemed to lead to another world. The whiteboard fence disappeared at the curve. The hedge that lined the lane was enveloped by a variety of larger trees, mostly maple and white oaks. Near the perimeter of the grove, I saw two trees covered with yellow flowers.

"What are those?" I asked.

"Those are tulip trees, son. There are lots of them here. People plant them in their yards, but they don't grow as well as the native ones. Mother Nature planted those two trees long before my family came here. Tomorrow we'll walk out there. Emma loved the smell; she would break a couple of twigs and put them in a vase in her kitchen. I know it seems odd, two twigs in a vase, but she loved the smell so much. Would you like more tea?"

Winnie raised her head and watched him go back into the house but did not try to follow. I rubbed her head again, and she laid back down.

I sat silently with two contented dogs enjoying the cleanest clearest air I ever breathed.

~

"James."

"Huh?"

"You've been asleep."

"Huh?"

"You've been napping for over thirty minutes. I would have let you sleep longer, but Winnie and Walter are getting restless. Winnie wants to show you more of the farm."

"Really, I've been asleep?"

"Yes, North Carolina has the best naps in the world. Come on, let's walk the dogs. I heard Hannah's mail truck. We'll walk down the lane, then I'll show you the barn."

The lane was just as picturesque walking out as it was when I drove in. As we rounded the curve I could see the white fence converge with the mailbox in the distance, *This could be a cover on a book. I could picture Ansel Adams with his huge view camera and tripod set up in the middle of the lane, waiting for the instant the light was perfect.*

Walter and Winnie jogged past us. Winnie knew the routine. She stood patiently with her new friend waiting for Henry and me to reach the mailbox. I learned that each day Winnie got a treat at the end of the lane. Today, Walter got one too.

As we started back, Henry began to reminisce, "My great-great-grandparents came here from Germany in the early 1800s. They came from poor farm families and followed the news of free land for everyone here. They sold their little farmstead over there and used most of the money for fare to the new world. The story is they bought a horse and wagon when they arrived, put all their belongings and their baby boy, my great grandpa, whom I am named after, in the wagon, and then started west with no real destination. Somewhere back in the mountains, they got off the main road. Whether they did it on purpose or by accident has never been clarified. Supposedly, as they rode down the trail, which is now the road you came in on, Great Grandpa stopped and said, 'This is our new home.' My dad used to laugh when he told me, 'This was nothing but trees and brush then, and Great-great grandma was not at all happy with the choice.'"

"But Great-great-grandpa was a stubborn old German, so getting him to change his mind was out of the question."

Henry stood quietly for a moment, remembering, and smiling. The contentment on his face was something I never experienced before, on any other human anyway. *How can you not envy a man who is so at peace?*

"Come on, I'll show you the barn," he said.

We walked back along the edge of the lane. As soon as Winnie and Walter realized we were headed back, they took off. Running side by side, jumping on each other, they disappeared around the corner of the house. Henry saw the concerned expression on my face, "Don't worry," he reassured. "Winnie won't let Walter leave the yard."

We stopped short of his barn. Its size was overwhelming now that we were close. Beaming with pride, he said, "Great grandpa built it in eighteen seventy-five. He and some neighbors all built barns about the same time. They all worked together. They'd build a barn at one place, then another at a different farm until everyone had a new barn. Grandpa told me he and some of the neighbor boys got to help. He said they helped with some of the framing, carried a lot of the lumber, even got to pound some nails. One of the boys, a good friend of Grandpa's, got hurt. Somebody dropped timber. It hit him on the head. At first, everyone thought he was dead, but he regained consciousness after a few minutes. But he was never the same after that. Grandpa said the boy's mom wouldn't let him come outside very often after that and never allowed him in the barn.

"They did a good job though. This old barn is still standing.

I thought we'd go into town for dinner tonight. We've got a café that serves real good meatloaf. Tomorrow, I'll show you around the farm. You'll have to get up early, I have a surprise for you."

It was a long time ago when I last ate real country cooking, so meatloaf after the last few days of eating out of vending machines and fast food appealed to me.

Henry was right about the meatloaf. My mom made good meatloaf and so did one of my aunts, but what they served in The Family Café was better than either of theirs. The mashed potatoes had just enough texture to tell you they were homemade, and whoever was married to the lady who made the gravy was a lucky man.

"I ate too much," I groaned.

"I thought you might," Henry smiled.

It was dark by the time we started back. I couldn't see much of the country as we rode and was so uncomfortably full that I didn't feel like talking. We rode in silence, each with something occupying our minds.

As we pulled up to the front of his house he said, "I'll show you to your room. You will need to get some rest; we'll leave before sunrise. Do you have any warm clothes?"

"I have a jacket."

"It won't be enough, I'll get a heavy coat from the closet, a pair of boots too. You'll be getting your feet wet."

The wonder of where he was taking me and why so early took my mind away from what I was thinking, *Please don't put me up in Theresa's old room.*

As we climbed the stairs, I saw the first sign; a pink heart stuck to a closed door to the side of the hallway. I knew it was the door to her room.

"This is Theresa's old room. We kept it just like she left it, just in case," he said as we walked past. "I'll put you up in the guest room. It has fresh sheets and its own bathroom. I think you'll be quite comfortable there."

I hoped he took the relief on my face as an expression of gratitude.

"There's no clock in there, just come down when you first smell the coffee."

He stood over the stove with his back turned to the door as I entered. The table was already set, two pieces of toast lay on a plate, a steaming cup of coffee sat in front of one chair, and a second cup was on the counter next to him as he worked. "Sit yourself down," he said without turning.

He smiled as he set down a plate with two sausages, two fried eggs (over easy), and some hash browns. "Eat up, we need to get going. I have a thermos and two mugs fixed. I hope you don't think it rude of me but I've already eaten. I'll get the Mule and let the dogs out. Come out back when you're done. Don't worry about the plates, we'll do the dishes when we get back. I hope you like your coffee black. I don't keep cream anymore. You'll find a coat, gloves, and a pair of chore boots by the door."

A mule, we're going to ride a mule?

I bounded down the back steps, struggling with the gloves with the last of the toast hanging from my mouth. There he was, under the yard light, sitting in one of those farm all-terrain vehicles. It was painted green and black, with the words "Kawasaki Mule" printed in large letters, grinning. "You didn't think we were going to ride mules, did you? You are in the country now, son, but we aren't hicks."

Walter and his new friend Winnie were in the back, in a homemade pen. Walter was both eager and perplexed. Being in a pen meant going to the vet to him. He thought he was going on an adventure and was eager to go but riding in a cage on the back of this strange vehicle, he wasn't so sure.

"Climb in, the sun is going to be up in no time," he smiled.

Once we left the barnyard, it was pitch dark. Only the lights of the Mule gave me a hint. We were on a path, well-traveled but not smooth by any stretch. The bouncing over big rocks flashed the Mule's lights on the trees and brush. The path was narrow and I could tell that even though we were weaving back and forth, we were constantly going up. After about five minutes, which seemed like a half-hour, Henry abruptly stopped.

"We have to walk from here. Give me a minute to let the dogs loose. Here's a flashlight. Watch your step, the ground will be rough and slick."

Winnie bounded ahead, sure of our destination. Walter stayed at my side as we followed Henry through the weeds.

"Just a little more. Stay behind me, it's steep. There's a big drop off up ahead."

His light shone on a well-worn wooden bench. A simple thing, just a thick plank, about six feet long and a foot wide, sitting on four short legs with no back.

"Careful, it's a long way down."

I cautiously followed him around the bench and sat next to him.

Now with Walter at my side, Henry sitting next to me and Winnie on the ground laying against his leg, we waited.

"Pour yourself a cup while we wait," Henry said.

I sat, fondling my warm coffee with my cold gloved fingers and wondered, *What are we doing here? Why so quiet? Does he have some big secret he's about to tell me?* But he didn't speak.

The sky gradually began to lighten. First gray, then it began to turn a dark blue; then oranges, yellows, purples, and reds appeared. *He brought me here for a sunrise. Why?*

Still, neither of us spoke.

Light began to fall on the tops of the mountains in the distance. Clouds appeared–huge, puffy cumulus clouds. Farmsteads started to show themselves in the hills below. Small plumes of smoke rose from chimneys in the distance. Birds began to appear, flying through our view, carefree, singing as they flew. As the sky brightened, I soon realized how special this place was. Here we sat, no more than six feet from the edge of a cliff, several hundred feet above the valley below. Just me, Henry, and our dogs.

"This is our spot, Emma's and mine. We've come up here more times than I can count. Most times together, sometimes alone, either her or me. We sat here and watched some of the most beautiful sunrises imaginable. We've sat here under our umbrella in the rain, cuddled under a blanket, wearing our winter coats. We've solved many of our problems up here. We've come here to be renewed. We've come here for guidance, for clarification, for peace. I've come here to ask for Theresa, to guide her, to help her, and then to find her. I was led to an abandoned park in New York City, from this spot."

Henry fell silent.

I didn't have any proper words for a response.

I saw tears forming in his eyes, so I turned away, to not embarrass either of us.

"I call this Emma's Point," he said. "I come here now to talk to her. She hears me. I tell her about Theresa, about Theresa's new job. I tell her Theresa is happier now.

"I've told Emma about you."

I leaned down and laid my hand on Walter's back. He gazed at me with those deep dark eyes. Tears gave the valley below a misty, reverent glow. Walter seemed to understand.

Henry and I sat together, each immersed in our thoughts. Thoughts neither of us shared.

"We should be getting back. We have a kitchen to clean and chores to do. Then we can go to town."

Most of the dew was gone when we walked back to the Mule. Somehow, it was harder to walk down than it was to walk up. The trail was steep and littered with rocks of all sizes, and though it was light now, it was harder to focus. Our minds wandered quietly.

"We could never get Theresa to come up here much. I thought

listening to the wind and watching the light change might help with her music and dance. Maybe it was the trip up and down she didn't like? Subconsciously, I think she didn't want to like it. Maybe she feared it would make it harder for her to leave when her time came."

The dogs jumped in the back of the Mule, and we began the ride back.

"I have a lady, Bess, who cleans, does laundry, and cooks some, but I always try to wash dishes and clean the kitchen. I do some of the things around the house too. I always helped Emma and feel I should do the same for Bess.

"Tomorrow, I need to go to town to see my lawyer. We can leave the dogs here. Winnie is good by herself. I can leave her in the backyard, she won't try to get out. And if we leave Walter with her, he'll be okay too. My lawyer's name is John Gray. I'll introduce you. Afterward, we'll stop at Joy's Diner for coffee and pie. They have the best pecan pie. Then I'll drive you around, to show off our town. We like it here. It's not very far, I'd like to take the Mule and feel the fresh air, but we have a new police chief and I think he has watched too many episodes of *Gunsmoke*."

Henry chuckled at his own words. This was the first time I saw him laugh. I was beginning to feel at ease. My earlier apprehensions were unwarranted. There was a lot more to this man than I first guessed. The overused, trite, corny expression, *you can't judge a book by its cover,* flashed through my mind.

The ride to town was much shorter than I expected. Henry's farm seemed so isolated, so rural; it surprised me we were so close. The scenery changed so quickly from rural to small town. This was nothing like New York.

Downtown seemed warm and friendly, in no small measure because I was riding with Henry. People smiled and waved, he smiled and waved in return. I caught myself joining, waving at total strangers. I turned to Henry, "I like your town."

"I've lived here all my life, know most everybody; good people live here. I remember once when I was in grade school stopping at Joy's with my dad for pie and a glass of tea, an older lady came in and sat with us. Dad introduced me. She ran a local motel, one that had been in her family for years. I still remember their conversation.

"Dad said, 'Marge, what with this new Super 8 and now they are building a Holiday Inn, why don't you close the motel and travel? See the world.'

"Marge answered, 'Where would I go that would be better than right here?'

"That has always stuck with me–where would I go? I think that's why it was so hard for me to understand Theresa. We think we have it all here. Why did she want to go somewhere else?" he asked.

An uncomfortable air came over us. I couldn't think of anything to say so I turned to the window and went back to smiling, waving, and wondering.

"Here we are. This won't take too long. I'll introduce you to John, then you can visit with Ira, John's legal aid. John has some things to go over, I just bought the little place next to me I've wanted for years."

"Good morning, Ira, is the old rascal in?"

"Yes, he's expecting you. Who's your friend?"

"This is James Williams. He's from the big city and knew Theresa when she lived there."

It startled me at first that Henry didn't introduce me as Theresa's ex-husband, but as I thought about it, I realized Henry meant it as a courtesy. *No need to make me feel uncomfortable.*

"Good morning, Ira," I said. "Henry has told me about you. Did he tell you we are fellow combatants in the world of law? Legal aids that is."

"Yes, he told me about it. He seems to have a lot of respect for you," Ira answered.

"Come with me, James. I want to introduce you to John, then you and old Ira here can exchange stories."

"Come in Henry. It's good to see you. Is this your friend from New York?"

"Yep, this is James. He's the one who helped me find Theresa. Remember, I told you all about it."

A tall, slender, well-groomed man with just a touch of white hair around his ears, extended his hand, "Hello, James. I'm John Gray. Henry and I have been friends since the time I first moved here. I was leery when I first came to town, but Henry here convinced me to stay long enough to give his town a chance to grow on me, and it did. This is a great place to live."

"Hello, Mr. Gray. It is a pleasure to meet you."

"James, why don't you step into Ira's office? You two can visit while John and I finish some paperwork. It won't take long."

"Again, it was nice to meet you, Mr. Gray."

"John, please. Everyone calls me John."

"We're probably a little more informal here than you are used to, but we get things done just the same. John is meticulous, and that's a good thing. It didn't take me long to learn his methods, but that was almost thirty years ago, sometimes I forget. John took over from another attorney who retired. He and his assistant both left at the same time, so John and I grew into this firm together. I've never once regretted working here. He's a great man, honest, open, and fair. Tell me a little about yourself," Ira said.

My answer was to be both brief and vague. I was away from my job, primarily to consider my future. Spilling my story on an unsuspecting man, whom I just met, didn't seem proper.

"I've been with the firm slightly more than three years. My intent has always been to become a lawyer, but my mom got sick. I dropped out of school to help Dad care for her, and once it was time to go back to school, I needed to work, so I took this job as a legal aid. I might yet go back to school..."

The door opened and Henry reappeared, "I'm ready for a steaming piece of pie, James. How about you?"

I thanked Ira for our visit, happy we didn't have to delve any deeper into my personal life.

"John seems like a very nice man," I said to Henry. "Ira is nice too. We had a good visit. Our jobs are similar, Ira's and mine, except he is researching and writing for a rural area and I'm working for a big firm, and huge contracts are at stake. I doubt Ira makes many mistakes, and if he does, I imagine he and John work them out together. Me, on the other hand, I work for several lawyers, and we legal aids work in a high-pressure atmosphere. Any mistake we make can be our last."

"Yes, in my mind, there is no doubt the perks of living here far outweigh the advantages of the city. I don't know if John told you, but Ira wants to retire. You might think about that."

"Morning Henry, who's your friend?"

"Morning Liz, this is James. He's down here from New York. James, this is Liz; she's been serving me pie for what seems like forever."

"It's a pleasure to meet you, Liz; Henry's told me about your famous pies."

"So, Liz, do you have any pie today?" Henry grinned.

"Henry, you teaser, you know we have pie. Joy's always has pie."

"Jim, do you mind if I call you Jim? James seems formal and everyone in here is a friend."

"Jim is fine."

"Good, there's the list up on the wall. They're all homemade, fresh this morning. The ones crossed out are sold out. What's your pleasure?"

"It says up there you have gooseberry. Do you really have gooseberry? I've never eaten gooseberry pie before."

"Best in the state. One gooseberry al a mode coming up. Usual Henry?"

"No, I think I'll have rhubarb today."

"Ooh, venturing into the unknown, huh? We must be feeling spunky today," Liz said.

Several mouthfuls later Liz returned returned to our table.

"Good pie, huh?"

"Mummph," was the only sound I could make with a mouthful.

"Yes, nothing like a piece of Joy's warm pie, on a warm plate with ice cream melting over the top."

"Mummph."

"I'll bet this is better than your mom used to make."

"Mummph," I answered and managed to give a thumbs up while holding a forkload of gooseberries and crust, watching the melted ice cream drip from it.

"Slow down," Henry cautioned. "Savor it. This won't be the last time you eat pie here."

I wondered if this was prophetic. I expected to only stay a couple of days, but I think Henry supposed I would spend my entire vacation here. *Was there more to this visit than I originally thought?*

"Come on back," Liz smiled as we left. "We've got lots more kinds to try."

"I'll show you more of the town, then I'll show you the little place I just bought before we go back and check on the dogs."

The dogs: I completely forgot about the dogs. This was the first time since we left New York that I left Walter alone. *Is he okay? He's not used to being alone. What if something happened? Even with another dog to watch him, he's in a new place.*

Henry read my face, "Don't worry, Walter is alright."

Driving around Henry's town was like driving back in time. I remembered watching *The Andy Griffith Show* with Dad when I was little. It was like that here, only the cars were newer. More waving again. Everybody seemed to know everybody.

We drove into the driveway of Henry's new place. The lane was like Henry's but needed some attention. Several potholes made the ride bumpy. There was no white wooden fence, just some woven wire guarding the edges. The house was smaller than Henry's but was in the same style. It could be in a rustic scenic painting or photograph, black and white, like some of those Dust Bowl photos from the '30s. It was clear the house sat empty for a while, but it wasn't beginning to deteriorate yet.

"Always liked this place. I thought I might retire here; you know, downsize, but with all those memories of Emma, Theresa, and my family before me, it wouldn't seem right to leave the home place. I used to try to buy it from the widow lady who lived here. She'd say, 'Henry, you can have it when I'm gone' but she didn't put anything in writing, so I needed to wait on probate. That is what I needed to see John about today and complete the purchase.

"John laughed about me buying it. 'What are you going to do with it, Henry? You don't farm the place you have anymore.'

"So now it's finally mine. Don't know what I'll ever do with it, maybe fix up the house a little bit, but I don't want to rent it. Renting can be an inconvenience; you never know what you are getting for renters. Come on, we'll walk around the place. It's cozy and nice."

The dogs came bounding to the fence as we drove back to his home. You'd think we'd been gone for a week the way they jumped on us once Henry opened the gate. They followed us into the house, where Henry and I each got a glass of sweet tea and a couple of warm chocolate chip cookies Bess baked and left for us in our absence. In a few short moments, we were back on the porch, my new normal - sitting in the chairs, hearing the breeze rustle through the trees, with a dog resting beside each of us.

"I get a little lonely sometimes, but I don't want to go anyplace else," he said.

~

My week passed too quickly. Long breakfasts each morning, early afternoon trips to town for coffee and pie, occasional odd jobs (Henry liked to feel needed here) in the afternoon, sweet tea and cookies later, then a quiet evening.

It was so different here. Henry had a television, but he seldom turned it on. Occasionally, we watched an old movie or TV show (*Gunsmoke*, the black and white ones) or an old comedy like *Leave it to Beaver, I Love Lucy* or *The Honeymooners*.

We rose early and went to Emma's Point just one more time, it seemed so special to Henry. I realized why he didn't go often; he used these trips for special times with special needs.

Walter was at home here now. He was always at someone's side, more often Henry's or Winnie's than mine. If Walter wasn't following one of them, he was lying next to Henry, or more often, he and Winnie were exploring together. He was never alone and certainly never lonely. Thoughts of New York, my apartment, and my job were distant – but not forgotten.

Chapter 12
Our Last Day With Henry

"I wish you didn't have to go," Henry said.

"I know, me too, but it's almost seven hundred and fifty miles, and with all the times I'll have to stop for Walter, it may take three days. And no matter what the message, I need to be there when they post the notice on the board at work."

"I understand. I have enjoyed your visit so much, promise me you'll come back. And if I may say so, I think you should get up early tomorrow morning and go to Emma's Point one last time. I want you to go alone, well without me at least. I know Walter will want to go, and anywhere Walter goes, Winnie will want to go too. But go without me, you have a lot to think about, and one last sunrise will do you good. You can take a lot of questions up there and come back with almost as many answers."

Again, the smell of coffee woke me from a restless sleep.

The kitchen table was already set. Steaming biscuits lay in a basket beside a sausage and egg casserole. Henry told Bess this was to be my last day, so next to the tub of butter was a dish of her homemade Pawpaw jam. "Bess wanted you to try her jam. She figures it will be enough to bring you back."

We ate quietly. I wanted to ask him about his thoughts but didn't have the courage. Besides, I had enough of my own.

"The heavy coat is hanging by the door. You'll find gloves and a cap on the bench. Your boots are underneath. The Mule is sitting out and Walter and Winnie are already in the back. Stay up there as long as you need."

The trip up the hill was hard. Not that I didn't know the way; I was conflicted. I needed to hurry but also wanted to make this morning last. Each time I hit a rock or caught a tire in a rut, I thought, *This will be the last time this happens.* But once I got to the turnaround and opened the back for the dogs, a sense of urgency swept over me. Walter and Winnie sprang from the Mule; I could hear them scrambling through the brush ahead of me as I flashed the light from side to side, hurrying to the bench.

Henry and Emma's bench.

The sky was just beginning to turn from its deep black to the first hints of gray as I sat. Although I was completely alone, we must have been a sight, me at one end of the bench, with Walter next to me with his head on my lap, and Winnie snuggled next to him, the three of us watching what might be our last sunrise together, ever.

I thought about Henry, *That first impression of a poor old man from a black-and-white movie could not have been more wrong. Despite the difference in our age and our uneasy relationship because of Theresa, he could not have been a better friend. My original suspicions of what his motives might be were wrong, just plain wrong. How lucky I was to find such a kind man to mentor me. Not consciously, but by example. I wanted to be like Henry without taking anything from him. Does he know how much I respect and like him?*

My hand slipped around Walter's neck. Much like it did that day at the veterinarian's office, that day when Ingrid's hand slipped over mine, that time when she discovered I wasn't married any longer. A sliver of orange appeared in the distance, the official beginning of this new day. I moved a little closer and petted Winnie (without his objection). Thoughts raced, crawled, and sometimes paused. *Ingrid, my job, New York, Ingrid, my apartment, Henry, Ingrid, North Carolina, Ira, Henry, Ingrid, the firm, my job, Ingrid.*

The sun warmed my face now. A gentle breeze forced the tears from the corners of my eyes. The clarity of the morning air penetrated my brain.

I made some promises.

I called and called before Walter and Winnie finally loped down the path toward the Mule. Neither wanted to get in the back. *How could they know?* Finally, I gave in and the three of us scrunched into the front and began the ride down. I was so conflicted. I wanted this morning to last forever but knew it wouldn't – and couldn't.

Henry said goodbye inside but came out onto his porch as I loaded Walter. This only upset Walter more, and then Winnie began to howl. I was trying too hard to hurry and the dogs only made the situation worse. My hands trembled as I tried to open the trunk and put my bag in. Things I normally do without thinking became enormous struggles. I finally got Walter in my car by shoving on his hind end, but once he was in, I had to roll up the window because I was afraid he would break the glass. Winnie was on her hind legs, scratching at the opening, trying to help Walter escape. Henry came off the porch to help, but this only made leaving harder.

I didn't need this. The thought of leaving a place I had learned to like was hard enough, but to have all this commotion – I nearly broke down.

The drive down the lane was heartbreaking. Walter now pressed his nose hard against the back window, barking, and howling. Winnie was whimpering as she tried to break Henry's grasp. Any calm and determination I felt as I left Emma's Point earlier was gone. There I felt resolute, now I was sick with sorrow.

When Henry and Winnie disappeared from my mirror, an emptiness swept over me. The turn onto the highway only made it worse.

Chapter 13
The Drive Back

Long after Henry's place was out of sight, Walter continued his pitiful moaning. We drove for a while, but I hadn't filled my gas tank before beginning the drive back to New York. I didn't think about filling up before I got on the highway, and since my car was parked all week, I hadn't thought of the need. Everywhere we went, Henry drove his old pickup or the Mule. There was a car in his garage, but he didn't drive or even mention it; I assumed it was Emma's. I drove on for a while, hoping Walter would settle down and the endless whining would stop. But he didn't calm, and the needle was getting uncomfortably close to empty, so I pulled into a station.

I stood by the pump quietly, hoping no one would notice, but it didn't work. I watched a lady sitting in the passenger seat of an SUV on the other side of my pump. She opened her door, got out, and began to walk around.

I knew what was coming.

She tried to be inconspicuous as she peeked in the back of my car, but upon seeing it was a dog making all the noise, she spoke, "Is your dog hurt?"

"No Ma'am."

"What's wrong with him?"

"We've been visiting a friend who has a dog. He's mad because we left."

"I've never heard of such a thing," she said.

"This is a first for me too," I answered.

We stood for a moment, me concentrating on the gas pump, her not knowing what to say or do next.

The pump finally stopped. I quickly put the nozzle back, took my receipt, and as I opened my car door, said, "Have a nice day," to her. Then I drove away, still with the incessant moaning coming from the back seat.

He was getting on my nerves, so I turned on the radio, something I rarely do in the car. I turned the volume up, but it didn't help. Walter wouldn't stop. I'd never seen him act like this, and my patience was growing thin. I began yelling at him, also something I rarely did, but it didn't help either. I hoped all this noise would make him hoarse. It didn't. I wanted to roll down a window but didn't dare, fearing he would jump out.

I couldn't stop him and needed to continue driving. At least it was still chilly so no one else was driving with their windows down. Getting pulled over by a police officer because someone called to report, "The guy in that blue Toyota must be killing a baby," and having to explain "It is just my dog," would have been uncomfortable, to say the least.

It was quickly approaching noon. It already had been over seven hours since I got up. The stress of going back to my real world, with all its unknowns, and the constant moaning from the back seat, got the best of me. I needed a break, so I pulled into the next rest stop.

At first, Walter must have thought we were back at Henry's. He shut up, jumped up, and was ready to bound from the car until he saw we were at just another rest stop. I struggled to fasten his leash, then dragged him from the back seat. It is surprising how hard it is to move a sixty-five-pound dog who doesn't want to cooperate. Once out, he did stand, and when I jerked his leash, he did follow. We grudgingly headed toward the nearest tree. Once he finished, he just stood with his head and tail down. Normally, we would have been checking every tree in the area, but not today. I needed "a tree" as badly as he did, so I fastened his leash to a post, watched him for a moment, and then walked to the building.

The quiet in there was comforting. People coming and going, not speaking, just attending to business as travelers do. Couples entering, splitting up, heading to their respective doors, then reuniting, and walking down the path toward their vehicles. I envied their solitude.

Once back from the restroom, I browsed the map and brochure section on the wall of the lobby, found a map, found an empty bench, and sat. *A little alone time might help us both.*

I must have dozed off. Unfamiliar voices startled me awake. I looked at the big clock above the exit, twelve-forty. It didn't mean much because I didn't notice the time when I came in, but I knew several minutes passed, maybe as much as a half hour. *Oh, crap, Walter!*

I wadded the map that lay on my legs, hurried past the vending machines I intended to peruse, pushed past a young couple entering, and ran toward the yard behind the building, looking toward the area where I left him.

Walter wasn't there!

Panicked, I ran to the post where I thought I left him. Nothing. *Was this the right post?* I looked in every direction. No Walter. *Maybe he got loose and went to the car to wait.* I ran to the car. He wasn't there. *Maybe he followed me to the restrooms?* I ran back to the building. *No! Is he with another dog?* I searched everywhere. Still nothing. *Did he break his leash?* I checked all the posts where I might have tied him. No broken clasp or frayed rope anywhere.

Frantically, I ran from one end of the property to the other. I went from car to car, looking in windows, asking if anyone saw a black Lab, frightening the people inside, beating on truckers' doors, waking some, annoying most. I tried stopping cars and trucks as they pulled on the onramps, hoping to catch one leaving with my dog. Drivers were yelling obscenities at me, but I could only think of Walter.

Did he run off? Did someone steal him? Did he get hit by a car?

I saw a man in a blue uniform standing next to the building. I ran to him, thinking he was a cop, "Officer, I can't find my dog. Have you seen him?"

When he turned toward me I could see the logo of his trucking firm on his shirt. I was too frenzied to be embarrassed, but I did manage, "Sorry, I thought you were a police officer."

I saw another man, this time in a brown uniform. But before I could get to him, he set one of those yellow barricades in front of the women's restroom and disappeared inside, pushing his mop bucket.

I collapsed on the same bench I was sleeping on just minutes before.

I hurried through the entire perimeter of the rest stop a second time, calling Walter's name as I went, looking in every car and truck - again. This time I apologized if it was someone I had annoyed before. People asked me who I was looking for and wanted a description once I explained it was my dog. Some even helped, calling Walter's name.

Slowly, I began to realize what I was doing was futile. It was clear Walter was not here. What wasn't clear was whether he ran off or was stolen. I went back inside, found the brown-suited custodian, and said, "I've lost my dog. Is there someone here who can help me?"

"Sorry, this happens sometimes, but there isn't anything we can do. People lose a pet, most times a dog, but once they give up and move on, we never hear any more about it. I work for a company that contracts with the state, so we don't have many people who do that sort of thing. You could call the highway patrol, but I doubt they will help. You could call a local TV station, I don't know. There's a humane shelter back in town, they might be able to help. It's probably too soon for your dog to show up there though."

I ran back to my car, opened the back door, then got in the front, hoping Walter might jump in at any moment and we would be off, down the road, going home like nothing happened.

But something had happened. I lost my dog. It didn't matter whether he was lost or stolen; what mattered was that he was gone, and I didn't know what to do.

I had a sobering thought; *You've got to do something! You can't just sit here. Nothing good is going to happen if you don't make it happen.*

I dug my phone out of my pocket and dialed. "911, what is your emergency?"

"I'm out here on the interstate at a rest area and I've lost my dog."

"Could you repeat that sir?"

"Yes, I'm out here on the interstate at a rest area and I've lost my dog."

"Sir, this is an emergency line. I'm sorry, but we don't deal with lost dogs."

"But this is an emergency, I've lost my dog."

"I understand sir, I can take your information, but we don't send emergency vehicles to look for pets. If you were in town, the fire department might help you, but if you are on the highway, you are not in their service area." "But..."

"I'm sorry, sir, I can take a description and put it on file. If you have a picture of your dog, like on your phone, you can send it to us."

"Okay, but isn't there anything else?"

"Well, you could call the TV station up in Roanoke, they have a spot on the evening news where they tell about people who are lost or missing, they might do pets too. There is a veterinarian clinic not too far from you; you can find their number on your phone. There might be a humane society in Red Bird or Christiansburg. I'm sorry, sir, but I really must end our call. It's Friday afternoon and we are flooded with calls."

"But…"

The phone went dead. I stood holding it, listening to it beep.

"Hello, Red Bird Veterinarian Clinic, may I help you?"

"Yes, I hope so. I'm out here at the rest stop on the interstate and I have lost my dog."

"Oh, I'm sorry, that's terrible."

"I know, I'm sick about it, can you help me?"

"I'm sorry, sir. If your dog was injured, we could send our truck, but we don't have a search team. Can you send us a photo of your dog? We can post it on our website and pin it on our bulletin board. You should call the humane society, I can give you their number."

"Just a minute," I said and rummaged through my console for a scrap of paper and a pen.

"Please hold for a second, I need to write down another number before I forget it."

My hands shook so badly I could hardly scribble legible numbers on the paper. "Okay, now what is the humane society's number?"

I tried to hold the paper still, brace my arm against the console, and write slowly; still, the letters and numbers were close to gibberish. I would have to memorize.

"Sir, are you still there, sir?"

"Yes."

"I need some more information. What is the dog's name, species, color, and age? Is it a male or female? Was he wearing a collar? Is he chipped?"

"His name is Walter. He's a four-year-old black lab. He has some white on his left front paw and the back of his left leg. He was wearing his collar, but if he was stolen…"

"Thank you, sir, but I also need to know, was he chipped?"

"Chipped?"

"Yes, did you have him microchipped?"

"Oh, yes, chipped. Ingrid insisted I get that done."

"Ingrid, sir?"

"Sorry, Ingrid is my vet's name in New York."

"Yes, so I also need your personal information. What is your name, address, and phone number? You know, so we can reach you if we find out something."

"Okay, My name is Jim Williams, it'll be James on all my information. Walter (it gave me chills to even say his name) is registered at the Fillmore Veterinarian Clinic in New York City."

"Okay, Mr. Williams, I'll post Walter's information on the lost and found network and pin it to our website. I can call the local humane society for you if you'd like."

"I have their number; I can do it myself. They might have a question you can't answer. I can't thank you enough for your help. I didn't get your name."

"Laura, sir. I wish I could do more. Good luck finding Walter, we all know how hard this is."

"Thanks, Laura. Thanks."

"Red Bird Humane Society."

"Hello, my name is James Williams. I've lost my dog out here on the interstate at the rest area."

"What kind of dog was it, Sir?"

'Was it?' Why would he say, 'Was it?'

"He *IS* a black Lab. His name *IS* Walter. I am out here at the northbound rest area. My dog has run off, or someone has stolen him."

"We have one black Lab. I don't know if it is male or female. It came in a couple of days ago."

"NO, you don't understand, I just lost him about an hour ago."

"If it just happened, we wouldn't have him yet. Is he chipped?"

"He's a male, and yes, he's chipped."

"Well, if he is chipped, and the information on file is correct, we will contact you if he is brought here. Is there anything else? We are closing soon."

"No, nothing."

He wasn't any help. He wasn't anything like Laura. He probably doesn't even have a pet.

I leaned back in my car seat, closed my eyes, and tried to put all this in some sort of order. It was Friday afternoon, almost five p.m. I was on the road, in a place I'd never been before, over three hours from Henry's farm, with about eight hours left to drive to my apartment. My dog was gone, either lost or stolen, I didn't have a way to find him, and he was alone. All alone. For the first time in what seemed like forever, I was all alone too.

Before, being alone meant being away from other people. Now that Theresa was gone, being alone was when I was the last one to leave the office, or when I was driving, or watching a movie, or walking in the park, or waiting in the Fillmore Street Veterinarian's office. In all those alone times, Walter was either with me or waiting for me. Now, I was alone, in an unfamiliar place and Walter wasn't waiting.

I forced one last walk around the rest area, but it was futile. Any hope I had was quickly disappearing.

~

"Son, is there a problem?"

A blinding light shone in my eyes.

"What?"

"Are you okay?"

I could see he was a highway patrolman. "I'm sorry, officer, I'm not thinking clearly. I lost my dog here earlier."

"Well, you look out of place sitting here in your car with the door open in the dark, and it's my job to check. Please step out of the car, I need to see some identification."

"I...I lost my dog."

"I'm sorry about the dog, I need to see your driver's license and insurance card."

"I'm sorry for the bother, sir. But..."

"License and registration," he insisted.

I got back in my car, dug the papers out of my glove box, and handed them to him.

He walked back to his car and sat for what seemed forever before returning.

"Your papers seem to be in order. You need to move on," he growled.

"But sir."

"You can't stay here!" he said, firmly, then walked back to his squad car. But he didn't drive away. It was clear he wasn't going to move until I did.

Reluctantly, I put my license back in my wallet, my wallet in my pocket, climbed into my car, closed the door, started the engine, and started to drive away slowly.

He followed me on the highway until I reached the first turn-off then stayed behind as I drove down the ramp, stopped at the light, and then turned. In a way, I knew he was right. In his opinion, I didn't have a reason to stay at the rest stop. Walter would have returned by now if he could. He was gone, whether lost or stolen didn't matter now. Just that he was gone.

<hr>

I stopped at the first motel I saw, walked to the desk, registered for a room, and then returned to move my car and get my bag. The squad car still sat in the street as I walked back to the lobby.

I didn't sleep. I didn't undress or even open my bag. I lay on top of the covers for a while. Nothing on the TV could distract me, so I turned it off. Sometime in the middle of the night, I looked out my window to see if the patrolman's car was still there. It wasn't. So I drove back to the rest area to search again. It was hauntingly dark; a few semis were parked with their engines running. A couple of cars sat dark, away from any lights. Occasionally, a car would come in and stop and the occupants would quietly walk to the restrooms, return to their vehicles, and then drive off. I stayed as long as I dared but didn't feel safe and didn't want to face the patrolman again. I drove back to the motel.

The morning light woke me. I scrambled downstairs just as they were closing the breakfast nook. I took a biscuit from the tray before the helper could carry it away, then scooped the last of the gravy from the bottom of the crockpot. I took two pathetic boiled eggs from the refrigerator, got a container of yogurt, filled a coffee cup, and found a table in the corner out of the way.

I answered a stern glare from one of the helpers with, "Don't worry, I'll clean up when I'm done."

My thoughts didn't even come as complete sentences. *Walter. Lost. Work. Saturday. Henry. Ingrid, Walter. Lost.* My mind was in a place it had never been before.

Just over twenty-four hours ago, as I walked down the path from Emma's Point toward Henry's Mule, I felt a sense of ease. I thought I had formed a workable plan. A plan that would lead to happiness and contentment. A plan that would include Ingrid. Now, I sat at a corner table of the breakfast nook in a motel in a small town a long way, both in distance and time, from what I left and what I faced. I never felt this low; my life was in total chaos. I wanted to just sit here. Or check out, find a bar, and drink until my money ran out.

But I had to find Walter.

Chapter 14
Facing The Future

Fighting the urge to shun this day, I gobbled the last of my breakfast, hurried up the steps to my room, gathered my belongings, checked out of the motel, and drove to the rest stop, hoping Walter had come back. I pictured him sitting, shivering, lost and lonely, apologetic for his actions the day before. It was quiet and desolate there. Travelers were not yet out. It was too early to have been on the road long enough to need to stop. A few semis sat with their engines idling, their exhaust melding into the misty air. I walked the dewy grass from one end to the other, calling his name, but no answer. My fantasy reunion didn't happen. My hope was destroyed.

How will I live my life without him? Can I live my life without him? Do I want to?

I couldn't sit here and mope though. *This is Saturday. I need to get to the Red Bird Humane Shelter and the veterinarian's office before they close at noon. Maybe there is a humane society in Christiansburg too, if I could get there before it closes.*

I drove to the Red Bird Humane Shelter. "Hi, I called yesterday evening. I am looking for my black Lab, Walter. He was stolen or ran away from the rest stop just south of town. Has anyone turned him in?"

"Oh, you are the guy I spoke to last night. Hi, I'm Laura."

"Has my dog been brought in?"

"I don't think so. It would have to have been this morning. I wasn't the one to open today and our vet didn't say anything about new arrivals. Normally, people don't bring lost pets here. Usually, they go to the humane center."

"Could we check?"

"Sure, come on back. We can go by the pens, but like I say…."

There were only a half dozen dogs, some being held for vacationers, others healing from surgery. Anyway, they didn't have any black Labs, let alone Walter.

"I could call the clinic if you'd like."

"That would be nice. You've been a big help, but I am going to drive over there right now. I want to see for myself, so you don't need to call."

"I understand. Well, good luck. I hope you find your dog."

"Thanks," I answered.

"We open at ten tomorrow morning if you still haven't found your dog," Laura called as I hurried to the door.

A petite, dark-haired girl opened the Red Bird Clinic's front door, "May I help you?"

"Yes, I called here yesterday about a lost black Lab."

"Oh, yes, I found a note. It was Ernie, our custodian who talked to you last night. Hi, I'm Ellen. I'm pretty sure we don't have your dog but let's take a look."

"Are all these dogs homeless? There must be thirty dogs here."

"Yeah, it's depressing, isn't it? People buy pets, then soon learn that for one reason or another, they are not pet people. They don't realize all the work and time involved in keeping one. Sometimes we get expensive ones, dogs and cats who cost them a lot of money, then they don't want it. It's such a waste. They bring them in and just leave them. We have people who don't even tell us their pet's name, let alone do the paperwork. It's so sad. I wish there was more I could do for you. We don't get enough like you in here; you know, people who care."

"Thanks, I'm glad you tried."

"What are you going to do now?"

"I don't know. I want to get to Christiansburg before their shelter closes, then I guess I'll go back to the rest stop where I lost Walter again. But I live in New York City, and I have to be back to work Monday morning."

"You'll never make it to Christiansburg in time. They close at eleven on Saturdays. I could call them for you. My friend Amy works there, she'll be happy to help."

"That'd be great."

I fidgeted while she called. I made small talk with Ellen as she waited. I pictured Amy walking to the cages and hoped for good news. Ellen grew quiet; her expression changed. I knew the answer.

"Sorry," she said. "I was hoping."

"I know. Thanks."

I turned my car toward the interstate and hurried south, drove past the rest stop, turned around at the first overpass, drove back, pulled in, shut the engine off, walked to the park bench close to where I left Walter yesterday and sat.

Chapter 15
Trying to Move On

Much as I wanted to stay, I knew it was futile, It just didn't make sense. Sitting here in this rest stop for the rest of my life wasn't going to fix anything. All those plans I formulated two days ago on Emma's Point now meant nothing. I had to move on. I had to drive north.

I don't know how many times I started the engine and then shut it off. How many times did I back out of my parking spot only to pull back in? How many times did I get close to the on-ramp then turn back through the truck parking and return to the same spot? Or how many times did I walk back to the same picnic table, then walk the perimeter calling Walter's name?

Too many times, but deep down, I knew I wouldn't find him. *I don't think I can do this - abandon the search.*

But I couldn't leave. I went back to Red Bird to spend the night. *I'll search one last time in the morning before going on.* I needed someone to talk to, but I didn't want to call anyone. I wanted to talk to someone in person but didn't know anyone here. I wanted to call Henry, but it wouldn't be fair. He'd want to come up and help me search or insist I came back to his farm, but neither was a possibility. I called the humane society, hoping for some reason Ellen might still be there, or the message would give me her number.

She wasn't and it didn't.

~

I showered and went to bed, but I didn't sleep. After tossing and turning, switching the TV on and off several times in frustration, I checked the clock. Still only 8:30. *I should call Ingrid. I need a familiar voice, and she should know about Walter.*

The phone rang several times. I was about to hang up when I heard her voice, "Hello."

"Hello, Ingrid, this is Jim."

"Jim?"

"You know, Jim from the Fillmore Street Clinic."

"Hi?"

"James Williams, Walter's owner. You remember him."

"Oh, yes. Sorry, I wasn't expecting your call, we haven't talked for such a long time."

"I wanted to call and catch up. I…"

"I'm sorry, but I can't talk right now. Could you call maybe tomorrow afternoon or some evening next week?"

"Have I caught you at a bad time?"

"Yes, right now isn't good. You can call another time if you'd like."

She is seeing someone! I know it. On top of everything else, She's found someone else!

I pushed the red circle on my phone and dropped it on the floor, put my head on my hands, and broke down. *I've lost my dog, I've lost my girlfriend, and I'm about to lose my job. Why is this all happening to me?*

⁓

The traffic was heavy by the time I finally got on the highway. People were hurrying to their Sunday dinners with family or a day at the lake. Travelers were coming back early from vacations, picking up the pets they boarded for the week. But me, I couldn't hurry. Every mile on the highway took me further away from Walter and closer to my apartment and my job. I once knew what I was going to do when I read the announcement at work, but now it was hard to think. I felt helpless. How could I manage without Walter and Ingrid?

Cars honked. Some drivers flipped me off as they passed the slow car in the right lane. A long drive still lay ahead of me, and it would be late when I got home. I would be tired in the morning when I needed to be fresh and alert, but my Toyota just wouldn't speed up.

Scenery that a week ago would have captivated me now went unnoticed. I drove by rest stops, knowing I needed to stop, but the thought of a rest stop only made me think of Walter. I drove on, only stopping twice for gas, to use the restroom, and to buy a snack and a drink. It was almost nine p.m. when I found a spot nearly two blocks from my apartment. *Sure, why not? Everything else has gone wrong today.*

I unloaded my bag and gathered the trash I accumulated on the drive back, then trudged down the darkened street toward my building. Once inside, I threw my clothes in the hamper and opened the refrigerator for a beer (thankfully, there were only two, or I would have drunk myself into a stupor). I thought about calling Ingrid in the morning, but I knew it wouldn't be a good conversation, and I just wasn't up for it.

I took off my shoes, socks, shirt, and trousers; then fumbled in the bathroom cabinet until I found my sleeping pills, took two and laid on top of the covers. My last thought before a fitful night, *Maybe Monday night after work? Once the air clears.*

In what seemed like only minutes, my alarm startled me. After laying there for a few moments, I knew I had no choice. It was Monday morning, I had to go to work. After a quick shower, a cup of yogurt, and an apple, I stood in front of the mirror. Still a wreck from the weekend, I adjusted my shirt and gave my hair one last try before heading out the door, not fit to face the day.

I purposely arrived just before nine. I didn't want to be early and be a part of the uncomfortable, 'hanging around until the other shoe drops' crowd and I certainly didn't want to be late. Anyone who came in late today could well have their name added to the list.

"Good morning, James." It was Will, my only real friend here. "Are you ready for this?" he asked.

"As ready as I can be," I mumbled.

We all knew when Young Eric took over as managing general partner from the old man, things would change. We expected the atmosphere to be less friendly, the new approach would be a squeeze-every-dollar-we-could company, but we never expected this.

"You picked a good time to take your vacation, a bunch of us wished we'd done the same. You sure didn't miss anything these last two weeks, not much got done. People walked around in trances or sat at their desks peering at black computer screens or playing video games. Occasionally, someone would start yelling. A couple of times, I thought there was going to be a fight. How was your vacation? Could you relax?" he asked.

I didn't want to talk about my lost dog now, "It was good," I answered. "It was nice to get away. Some days I didn't even think about the firm or the list. You know, a guy could be happy living in North Carolina."

The list. I hoped it would already be posted, so as not to postpone the agony of making small talk with someone I might not be working with in the future while we waited.

But it wasn't. In fact, not only was there no list posted, but none of the partners were in the room. It didn't take us long to realize they were still meeting.

So we stood around, everyone from lawyers hoping to be partners someday to clerks and gofers, all waiting. No one wanted to talk, not even small talk. It reminded me of all those people lining a hallway, waiting to testify in a trial. It struck me that several were holding coffee cups, but the pots were all empty. No one was even willing to start a fresh pot, thinking this was the end. *Come on people, this is a notice. We aren't going to be ushered off the property today, or are we?* I could use a coffee after yesterday but gazed wistfully at the empty carafes. *Amazing how easily we all fell into the same funk.*

The elevator door opened, and the CEO's secretary appeared carrying a single sheet of paper. She was like Moses parting the Red Sea, but the waters didn't stay parted. We filled in behind her. *This would be interesting to see from a camera in the ceiling.*

Without comment, she took a stick pin from the bulletin board, stabbed the paper she held up in one corner, then searched for a second, before finding, sticking, and walking away – strutting if you will. It was obvious; her name was not on the paper.

Since this wasn't the most important item in my life right now, I stood back and watched the throng crush against the message board. The pushing and shoving soon led to harsh words and jousting, and then, within seconds, employees began to push back through the crowd and made their way to the workstations. Some intended to go back to work because their names were on the paper. Others shuffled back toward the windows or empty coffee machines with no intention of ever working again.

My name was on the list. I was safe. But I read the disclaimer at the bottom of the paper, something most of the others missed, and it wasn't encouraging. It read, *"The company will review this decision quarterly and revise it as necessary."*

One small sentence with life-affecting meaning. A sentence none read, but all were affected by. Its meaning was clear: <u>No One's Future Is Safe Here.</u>

At that moment, I vowed to no longer be at their mercy. *Three months from now, I will not care whether my name is on the next list or not, I will have changed my path.*

Chapter 16
The Interim

"Hi Ingrid, it's James. Can you talk?"

"Hi, James. I was expecting your call yesterday."

"I know, but I was driving home from vacation; the traffic was bad. I was on the interstate and needed to concentrate, there were so many dangerous drivers out there. And today was an important day at work."

"Oh, where did you go?"

"North Carolina."

"I've heard it is pretty down there. Did you like it?"

"Yes, I have lots to tell you…"

"James, I'd like to go first if you don't mind."

She paused, and for a moment I thought she might have ended the call. Then I heard her take a breath.

"I need to tell you something. Back when I was at the Fillmore Clinic, I felt an attachment to you. I saw how much your dog Walter meant to you. I saw what a deep and caring soul you are. I thought we might start a relationship. But you were strangely reluctant, and I didn't think I should force it. Several times I thought we were close, but nothing ever happened. I was never happy in the city and always dreamed of working in a more rural location. When I learned of this position, I was torn. It seemed perfect for me, but I wanted to stay because of you. But nothing was developing, so I decided to move on.

"After I moved, I thought you might want to see me away from work, but you haven't called or even brought Walter out here. I have a friend now; his name is Dylan. He runs a small distribution company that sells medical supplies for animals. Our clinic is one of his customers. He's a nice man, you'd like him. I thought about telling you about him and would have if you ever called. I think we may be serious. He brings me flowers, and when he is in town, he takes me to dinner. I feel bad, telling you this over the phone, but this is my first chance.

"Tell me about your vacation."

"I've lost Walter," I blurted.

"What? What do you mean?"

"I've lost him. There was going to be a big shake-up at work. The firm announced it was going to become leaner, meaning some of us were going to lose our jobs. They said they were going to announce it at the end of our fiscal year, which was today. They said those whose names were not on the list of employees would continue with the firm and be granted sixty days severance and would be paid for any vacation that remained. I decided to take the rest of my vacation anyway. You remember me telling you about Henry, my ex-wife's father, Henry, who lived down south? Well, Henry invited me to visit him in North Carolina, and I couldn't think of anywhere else to go, so I went. Well, Walter fell in love with the place, and I did too, and on the way back Saturday, he was having a fit about leaving, laying in the back seat, whining, and howling, so I finally stopped at a rest stop.

"We both needed to get out of the car, and I needed to get away from him for a bit. I tied him to a light post next to a picnic table to go into the restrooms and when I came out, he was gone. I looked all over; I couldn't find him anywhere, I called the highway patrol, and checked with the closest clinic. I checked the humane shelters but couldn't find him. I didn't know what else to do, where else to check, or who to contact, and I had to be at work today because they were going to post the notice, so I left.

"I don't know whether Walter broke free and tried to find his way back, or someone stole him. You know he was too friendly for his own good. Now I don't have any vacation left, so there's no way I can go back to hunt without asking for unpaid leave. And if I take some now, I won't appear to care, and I don't have any other job options so getting a blemish could be disastrous, so I don't know what to do."

My phone went silent.

After what seemed like an eternity, I blurted, "Ingrid, are you still there?"

"I don't know what to say. I felt so bad about having to tell you about Dylan. Now I feel guilty, telling you at such a bad time."

Her voice changed. In a more reassuring tone, she went on, "You know there's hope though. When Walter gets turned in to a veterinarian or humane society, they will check to see if he has a microchip, and when they find it, they will contact you."

"You mean 'if,' don't you?"

"No, I mean *when,* not *if.* I am trying to tell you that there is always hope. You need to try to be positive and do all you can. You need to focus on the 'there's always hope,' part," she said.

Chapter 17
Starting Over

Talking to Ingrid helped a little. I was still in a deep dark place though. Despite knowing I lost her, hearing her voice and her positive attitude slightly eased my pain. For the first time since I lost Walter, I felt like I might be able to control my future by doing something. It might not work out the way I wanted, but now it wouldn't for lack of trying on my part. In just three days I lost my dog and lost the girl I wanted. I didn't know where Walter was but hoped if he ran away, he would somehow find his way back to Henry, or turn himself into some kind person who would contact the right people. Or if he was stolen, please let it be by someone who wanted him and would give him a good life. I couldn't stand to think something tragic might have happened to him.

It was funny, not funny ha-ha, but odd to rationalize this way. Walter and Ingrid each deserved a good and happy life; I wanted the best for them, even if their lives didn't include me.

I called Henry.

"I will leave in the morning. I have another appointment with John tomorrow, but it can wait. I'll leave first thing. We'll find him."

"No, it won't help. I just wanted you to know. There is nothing more to do, just to wait. He'll either show up someplace or someone will contact me. Or something happened to him. We just have to hope it isn't the latter."

***

The atmosphere at work had changed radically. The idle talk ended. Employees no longer gathered at coffee machines. People who were friends before now passed each other without acknowledgment, let alone a friendly greeting. Work gradually began to resume, although without enthusiasm. Voices were grim. Exchanges were often heated. Our futures were all in limbo and we were uneasy at best. Now all those names who were on the list began to realize their employment still could be temporary. I didn't want to be here anymore. I needed to find a future somewhere else, even if it was in another field.

Will's name was on the list. I secretly thought he would be one to leave. He was talented but didn't care for the drudgery of office work and everyone knew it. His paperwork stood out above the rest of us. He could write a brief that made the recipient glad he was being sued - almost. I guess someone upstairs noticed.

Despair and indolence were sweeping the office.

Will and I decided to make a pact. We promised to help each other stay positive and do our jobs the best we could. Whether we left or stayed with the firm at the end of the next quarter or the quarter after, or even the quarter after that, as long as we were both here, we were not going to let the grumbling and sabotage affect us.

"You need to get another dog," he said.

"I don't want another dog. I want Walter."

"Okay, then let's figure out how best to go about finding him. You aren't helping yourself by moping about him. And it's not going to do any good to search for him on weekends. Hurrying down there where you lost him as soon as you get off work on Fridays, driving around without a plan until noon Sunday, then driving back that evening isn't going to find him. I mean, think about it. What are the odds? The best way to find your dog is to get as many people helping you as possible."

"And how do you intend to do that?"

"The internet?"

"Exactly, why didn't I think of that? So do you have a plan?"

"Yes. You need to get the word out. You need all the help you can get. You have pictures of Walter, don't you?"

"Well, yeah."

"Good. How about coming up to my place after work? We'll order a pizza, drink a couple of beers, and see what we can come up with - and bring a photo of Walter."

I knew Will's idea was a good one, certainly the best way to reach the most people but I couldn't calm my mind enough to work out any details.

I lay in bed running ideas through my head until finally, and mercifully, I fell asleep.

"Come over after dinner and we'll start," he told me at the coffee machine.

Still, without working up a scenario, I drove to his apartment, "Hi, Rose, is Will here?"

"Hi, Jim. Will told me all about everything. I feel so bad for you. You had such a nice dog. I hope he's alright and I hope you guys find him. Will's in his office, go on back."

"Okay, first, let's pick a favorite picture," Will said. "We should choose one which shows your dog's face. What do you think, happy or sad? Happy might make someone who finds him want to keep him, or maybe it would show how much you miss him and they'd turn him in. Sad would show how much he misses you, or maybe make anyone who finds him want to keep him. Either way, whoever finds him may not know about microchips in pets. I know I didn't until you told me about them. What do you think?"

"Let's go with happy. Walter was always happy, even when he was begging to go for a walk, he was giddy at the idea of getting out of the apartment."

"Okay, happy it is. Now we need to come up with a poster. One we can send as an email and post on whatever social media you use."

"You mean like, 'Lost or stolen, a black Lab named Walter?'"

"No, we can do better than that. How about something like this?"

I've lost my best friend
He's a seven year old Black Lab
whose name is Walter.
He's friendly and has all his vaccintations
and has a microchip.
He was last seen wearing a red collar

He dissappeared on September 28th
from the Northbound lane
Rest stop on Interstate 81
Near Radford, VA
Call or text 555-555-1234
Anytime!

"That's perfect, you've been thinking about this, haven't you?"

"Yeah. I've listened to you talk so much about your dog, and I knew this sulking about at work wasn't about the job. If we put it out as an email to all the sheriff's offices, humane societies, and veterinarian clinics within a couple hundred miles of there, and post it on the web, maybe someone will find him, or if they already have, maybe this will encourage them to turn him in. I think this is your best chance."

Will and I worked deep into the night on separate computers, finding email addresses, sending messages, and listing my ad on the web. I wanted to call Ingrid and Henry with my news.

"I've already told our sheriff, the police department, and everyone I know," Henry said. "This will find him, I'm sure of it."

"That's a great idea," Ingrid answered when I told her. "I have contacted all the clinics in our network and told Dylan too. He said he will tell all his customers."

Oh great, there's that name again. I wonder if she knows how I feel. I wonder if she cares. She must care, otherwise…

James, focus man. You're trying to find your dog, remember?

Days later as we sat together at lunch I told Will, "I was hoping to hear something by now."

"It's only been three days. Try to think of it this way, if something happened to your dog, you know, been injured or something, you would have heard about it. For now, no news should be considered good news," he assured.

"I guess you're right, but it's hard."

"Just be patient. There isn't any more you can do."

Two weeks passed and I began to give up hope. I checked my computer every morning first thing, even before I fixed my breakfast. At work, every chance I got, I was checking for emails. Nothing, not a single response from anyone, anywhere. I'd been calling Henry almost every day to give him an update, but I never had anything to report. As soon as he realized nothing had changed, he would change the subject. Talk about what he was doing to his new place, what was going on in town, the most recent sunrise at Emma's Point, or what kind of pie he had at Joy's that day.

It was harder now than ever to call Ingrid. Our conversations always began with talk of Walter, but she began to tell me about Dylan like I was a friend who wanted to know. But I wasn't that friend and I didn't want to be. I never could be.

—◦—

Evenings alone were harder than ever now. I wanted to go for walks, but there wasn't any place I could go without being reminded of my dog. I went past Mike's tree on those few times I walked in Fillmore Park, but Mike disappeared months ago. I sat on the same bench with a pocket full of almonds hoping for someone to talk to, but neither Mike nor any other squirrel came. I tried not to think about it but wondered if Mike ventured into a street somewhere and got hit. That of course made me wonder if something similar may have happened to Walter. Vivid sickening images formed in my brain. Images I couldn't unsee, Images I couldn't stop them from forming. It didn't make any difference if I went out or stayed home. I thought of nothing but Walter.

Weeks went by. My depression and loneliness kept getting worse. Most weeknights and weekends, I sat in my recliner, eating a never-ending bowl of chips and drinking one soda after another. I made a promise to myself not to drink alcohol on the off chance someone called about my dog, (it was hard to even think of his name) I wanted to be aware and literate. I knew if I started, one beer or one glass of wine would only be the beginning. I was tempted, every weekend and most weeknights but knew I didn't dare.

To their credit, Will and Rose tried to help. Will and I used to play racquetball on Sunday mornings, but over the last few months, we seemed to always find a reason we couldn't. Rose started playing pickleball with some of her friends. I wondered if this was a result of Will's being home, bothering her during her "alone time."

Then, out of nowhere, and without asking me first, Will reserved a court. "Man, I don't know. There is so much going on right now, I think I'll pass," I told him.

"What is so important that you can't play? You can't do anything about your dog, and work shouldn't be a problem for you now. You certainly aren't going to be bringing anything home to work on in the next few months. You don't have any decisions about the future which have to be made on Sunday mornings. You need to face your future. A game of racquetball is as good a way to start as any."

"Okay, I guess you have a point."

I thought one of the reasons we quit a few months ago might be

I was beating him regularly, but when we started, he was a different player. Better, much better.

"You've been practicing, haven't you?" I asked.

"A little, but you aren't concentrating. If you don't start focusing on your game, I will have a lot of bragging to do at work. When I tell them what a pushover you are now, guys and even some of the girls will start lining up to beat the great racquetballer, James Williams."

"We'll see about that, don't get your bravado speeches ready just yet."

Over drinks in the gym's lounge (water for me, Will knew about my beer-drinking promise) a defeated, but not demoralized Will started. "I knew the good player was still in there somewhere. It didn't take much to bring him out. How about one night this week? It's established now, the real racquetball player is back."

"I admit, it felt good. Not beating you, you understand, just playing again. I guess I should thank you for that," I said.

"I'm glad, I thought it might. What you need is to focus on what you can change in your life. And on that subject," he grinned. "Rose has this new friend, Abby."

"No, don't even go there. I am not interested."

"Just listen for a minute, will you? Abby recently started playing pickleball with Rose. She and Abby want to play doubles. I told her okay, but not as a regular, and of course, I need to find a fourth. And it's not what you think."

"Yeah, right."

"Okay, you've got me. It is what you think, but Abby is a real nice girl, and face it, man, you need to get out and get on with your life. You know you can't stay like this forever. All you have to do is play pickleball and be nice. No strings. No pressure. Oh, and I know you can be nice."

"You tell Rose this is a dirty trick."

"It's no trick, man. Just a buddy and his wife trying to help a friend. Admit it, you'd do the same."

"So when is this big match?"

"Wednesday evening and don't tell me you have plans, I know you don't. You were going to play racquetball with me. Now you are going to play pickleball with us. And don't say anything about reserving a court. We already have a court rented."

"Kind of sure of yourself aren't you?"

"I know you better than you think I do. It'll be fun – if you let it be."

"Okay, but no promises."

"No promises and no strings. Just show up, be nice, and let yourself have a good time. It will be okay, you'll see."

I went through my gym clothes, took out the newest shirt and shorts, and put them in the laundry with all my white socks. I thought I should at least smell good at the introduction. I didn't want to do this, but after I thought about it, I couldn't blame Will and Rose. And yes, if I were in their position, I would probably do the same for one of them. Yet Wednesday came before I was ready.

I planned to not be my usual punctual self so we could get the uncomfortable introductions out of the way easily.

Rose smiled as she approached me, "Jimmie, this is Abby, she's going to be your partner tonight,"

"Hi Abby, it's nice to meet you. Will tells me you and Rose have been playing together."

Abby wore a charming smile. Such glowing cheeks and dark sparkling eyes. Her shiny brown hair was tied back into a ponytail. She was petite, grinned easily, and thank God, didn't remind me of Ingrid.

"Hi, it's nice to meet you too, Jim. I haven't been playing long, I'm not very good."

"Don't worry, we'll just play. We don't care who wins."

"Okay, we know who the teams are. Will and I will take the far end. Want to volley for serve?" Rose asked.

"Hey Jim," Will yelled as he and Rose trotted to the far end of the court, "Rose and I'll be shirts, you and Abby can be skins."

"Will Lamb, that'll be enough out of you. These two have just met and you've started already. Stop it. Just stop it right now," Rose scolded.

She turned to her embarrassed opponents. "I'm sorry Abby, I can't take him anywhere."

"It's okay Rose, we'll play fully dressed this time, then next time you and Will can be skins," Abby answered.

Nice, a girl with spunk and a sense of humor.

With tensions eased, our evening began.

"Rose has told me a lot about you," Abby said.

"Has any of it been good?" I asked.

"Come on, let the drubbing begin, losers buy the pizza," Will yelled from the other side of the net.

I was surprised, Abby was pretty good for a beginner. We played for a while, not keeping score, and truthfully, I was okay with it. I didn't want to get serious. But it wasn't long before Will was saying, "Come on, we're talking bragging rights at work tomorrow."

Rose and I tried to talk Will into playing for fun, but he insisted. I didn't argue because we were having a good time despite Will's shenanigans. Abby was nice, she was nervous at first, but I was too. We forced ourselves to laugh off our misses, but soon the laughter came easier, almost naturally. I didn't hog the court. I let her play, unlike what was happening on the other side of the net. I was surprised at Will; he didn't act this way when the two of us played racquetball. I wondered what he was doing, was he showing off for Abby?

They won the first game, but we rallied to make it close after falling behind early. The second game was more of the same except Abby and I started our rally sooner and won. I tried to get him to call it a night, "Okay, we've each won once, how about quitting while we are even?"

"Nope, we have to have a winner. Besides, we still have almost forty-five minutes of court time left," he said.

Abby and I were now in a groove and much to Will's disappointment, we smoked them. Abby told me sausage and mushroom was her favorite, I told her I liked it too. "Make it sausage and mushroom," she yelled as the ball swooshed by Will for the final point.

After a slightly nervous start, our two hours of court time were over in a flash. We found a table in the lobby, Will said, "I'll go order the pizza."

"No, we are not eating here, you are taking us to a real restaurant," Abby answered.

I liked this girl.

Once we finished and it was time to leave, Will drove us to Abby's apartment. I walked her to her door. "I enjoyed this evening, I hope you did too," she said.

"Yes, it was nice to get out. I'm glad you had a good time. I know I did."

Back in the car, Will wanted to know all that was said at Abby's door. Upon hearing my simple honest answer, he groaned, "That's all you said to her."

"Yes, that is all I said. I told you I am not interested in a relationship. I have too many things going on right now, and I'm still only interested in Ingrid."

I did have a good time with Abby, but it felt good to speak Ingrid's name again.

—⬦—

At work on Monday, none of my colleagues asked anything about pickleball. I knew Will told a couple of mutual friends about the big match. But neither asked and Will didn't volunteer. I thought it best not to bring it up either; these things have a way of backfiring.

I expected an update about the firm's restructuring this week. But it didn't happen. All week my fellow workers, even Will and I, went through the motions. No laughter or even idle chatter; we were just a bunch of robots going through the motions, most doing the least amount of work to get by. Some were doing less. I didn't think this could go on much longer. *How can two incidents, the death of our CEO and the ascension of his son have such a profound effect on our company?* Six months ago, this firm was well-established, well-run, with a very good reputation. I wondered how long it would be before our reputation would be tarnished beyond repair.

"Rose talked to Abby yesterday," Will said. "Are you up for another round of pickleball? The girls want to play."

"We discussed this. I thought you understood."

"You made your point, but the girls want to play. What harm is there in a few games of pickleball? And yes, I understand where you are coming from, but still, I think it will be good for you. Besides, Rose says Abby likes you."

"This is precisely what harm it can do. It isn't fair to Abby. She's a nice girl and I like her, but she has no future with me. She deserves better and should be looking for someone else."

"So it's settled, you'll play. I'll tell Rose."

It wasn't settled. Will put me in an uncomfortable situation. He either didn't understand or didn't care what he'd done. I suspected the latter. I wished I knew what Rose and Will said about this. And knowing Abby was also a victim made me feel worse. I didn't know what she thought of me, it was too soon for her to know, but her willingness, maybe eagerness, was going to make it hard for both of us. I couldn't see an easy way out.

～

"Hi Jimmie, I'm so glad we are playing again. I am looking forward to this."

"Hi, Abby. Will tells me you and Rose have been practicing."

"Yes, this is fun. I've never been athletic. All through school, I didn't join any teams. Most of my friends played volleyball or basketball. I didn't even try to be a cheerleader, but this is fun," she grinned.

"Well, don't get too serious about it, you can quickly take the fun out of playing if you try too hard. See how serious Will is; do you think it's still fun for him?"

"Best two out of three, you two better be ready," Will shouted from his side of the net."

"See what I mean," I said to her.

We had fun, maybe relaxed too much. I didn't help as much as I could have, and we lost. We won the first match, then lost two of the next three.

"We're tied, three each. There's got to be a winner. One more."

"What do you mean, three each?" I asked.

"Carryovers, we are playing carryovers. You won two out of three the first night, we won two of three tonight. We are tied," he said. "We need to have a winner. Bragging rights are at stake, you know."

"No, Abby and I have played enough," I said.

"Nope, we have to play one more," Will answered.

"Okay, but let's switch partners," I said.

"You mean the boys against the girls?" Will asked.

No, I mean you and Abby against Rose and me," I smiled.

Abby turned toward me, her face went sour. Will seemed to be caught off guard but Rose grinned about it. Once Will and I swapped sides, Rose smiled at me, "Let's tromp those two wannabes."

Now I was the uneasy one. I understood where each was coming from. "You've got it." I smiled.

"Alright suckers, but the game is fifteen instead of eleven this time," Rose grinned.

Out of the goodness of my heart, and to be nice to Abby and Rose, I split the cost of dinner with Will, the big loser.

"Rose and Abby have a court rented for Saturday morning," Will said.

"This is getting to be too often. I told you I don't want to lead Abby on, I am not interested in a relationship, and you know it. And I've noticed, you keep bringing these discussions up at work where we can't have a proper discussion."

"Oh, come on. You need to get out of your funk. This constant dreariness of yours isn't good, and frankly, it is getting old. It's time you get on with it. Rose told Abby you would pick her up. She said we are not going to keep bringing her. It's three against one, buddy. You may as well surrender."

We played, I guess they won. I wasn't into competing today and Abby was nursing a sore wrist. By the time everyone was tired, Will and Rose won three straight games, but only by a little each time. I could see Abby was beginning to tire of Will's constant banter and competitive attitude. She just wanted to play pickleball with either Rose or me.

But me. I was becoming the problem. She liked me and I liked her, but in different ways. Pickleball was fun, I enjoyed it. Playing with someone who just wanted to play for fun was nice too. All those times Will and I had played racquetball were refreshing, and I confess, bragging rights were fun (for me), but I never came away from a game with Will happy, only exhausted, and a little more fit.

I knew our relationship couldn't go on like this. It would have to change, but the change I knew was inevitable, couldn't be satisfactory for both of us. *How did I get into this situation, and how do I get out?*

"A penny for your thoughts," Abby said.

"Huh?"

"A penny for your thoughts," she repeated. "I know your mind was wandering, I just wondered where."

"Oh, I was thinking about my dog, Walter. Where he is. How is he doing? Who has him? You know that sort of thing."

Suddenly, I felt ashamed. I knew I was allowing our relationship to continue without commitment, which was unfair, but this was the first time I told her a lie. It didn't seem like much, but I wasn't thinking about him, at least not directly.

"Let's go for a walk, Will," Rose said. I think she sensed the beginning of an uneasy moment.

"I'm tired, I spent a lot of energy beating the rookies. Let's sit here for a while, order another drink; maybe one with a little kick to it, if you know what I mean," Will answered.

"Will Lamb, you bounced around the pickleball court all morning, carrying on. You mean to tell me you don't have the energy to walk around for a while? And it isn't even noon yet. You are not going to have a drink 'with a little kick to it' this early! You have things to do this afternoon."

This was the first time I'd seen the forceful Rose. I suspected she had a controlling streak but I hadn't seen it before. I was glad it surfaced at such an opportune time. I guessed it was purposeful because I was sure she had an idea of what was about to happen between Abby and me.

"A walk is a good idea, Rose. Come on Jimmie, the fresh air will do us good," Abby grinned.

We must have walked for an hour, the girls in front, gazing in store windows, giggling and talking about nothing in particular. Will and I dutifully followed behind, he probably hoping Rose wouldn't find anything to buy, and me – me thinking the usual – Walter, Ingrid, and what to do about the situation I was in with Abby.

"Oh look, a pet store. Let's go in," Abby grinned.

Oh, please, no. Anything but a pet store.

"Yeah, I love going into pet stores," Rose answered.

What? Wait a minute? Earlier you were on my side, rescuing me from an uncomfortable situation. Now, you are dragging me into a pet store!

"Rose, we are not getting a pet. First of all, we don't have room for an animal, and second, you know my situation at work, we don't need the extra expense, and we might have to move if I lose my job," Will said.

I followed silently, as the automatic door opened to the sounds and smells of a pet shop.

Birds in cages, all making some sort of bird noise. Fish in aquariums, thankfully, not making any noise at all, which caused me to wonder, *why would anyone want fish for pets?* The store had all the pet trappings too: birdhouses, scratching posts, and every type of play toy you could imagine. Several cats walked among the menagerie, strutting as if they were the owners of the place.

"Let's go to the back where they keep the cats and dogs," Abby grinned.

Cats and dogs. My worst fear. God, I hope they don't have any black Labs!

"We don't need a pet," Will reaffirmed.

The girls weren't listening.

They found the cats and kittens first–cages and cages of them.

This is the primary reason I avoid these stores. All these animals waiting and hoping for someone to adopt them. Many have already been someone's pet, but for some reason, not known to them, they aren't anymore. Dogs and cats who have been abandoned, left, or dumped by their earlier owners. Puppies and kittens are taken from their mothers because – there are so many different reasons and none of them are good. Some were lost, then found by good Samaritans and brought here for a chance at a second life. Not claimed by their owners for any number of reasons. Reasons like their owner left them tied to a picnic table leg at a rest stop on an interstate highway so their owner could go to the restroom. I pictured Walter in a pet store somewhere, waiting.

"Come on Jimmie, let's go peek at the puppies, they are always so cute. Maybe they will have a black Lab like the one you used to have," Abby said.

Thank God they didn't.

Everything about the pet store depressed me. I couldn't bear it. My stomach began to churn, and sweat was forming on my forehead. "Can we go?" I begged. "I don't feel good."

I felt bad about leaving so abruptly, but I had to. Much as I wanted to explain, I couldn't. I left without even saying goodbye.

I had a long, fitful night. I knew I hadn't managed it well, and I felt terrible about the way I acted. My phone rang early. Caller ID told me it was Rose. I dreaded the conversation which was about to ensue, but I knew it was unavoidable.

Is this about Abby saying she wanted a dog?

"Jim, can I meet you somewhere? We need to talk," she said.

Over a cup of coffee in the breakfast nook across the street from their apartment, she began, "I'm sorry about yesterday. I should have known going into a pet store was not a good idea. I wasn't thinking. One thing about it though, it lets me understand how much you miss your dog. I realize now how important he is to you, and I think I know how much you miss him. I wish I had minded my own business, and not interfered with your personal life. I understand a girlfriend is not something you want right now; I shouldn't have shoved Abby into your life. I see how uncomfortable you are. I know you want out of your relationship with Abby. It is too bad though, she is such a wonderful girl and would make you or someone else a great partner, but I understand now it is not going to be you, at least not right now anyway. If you want, I will talk to her about you. And if there is anything I can do for you about your dog, please ask. I am so sorry."

I didn't see this coming. I didn't realize my discomfort was so clear.

"Jimmie?"

"I don't know what to say, just that Will is a lucky guy."

"What about Abby?"

"I think I can manage. It is something I should do alone."

I left the coffee shop feeling somewhat relieved. At least Rose now understood, at least to some degree, but I still needed to make it right with Abby. It wasn't going to be easy.

———

"I have a court. Saturday morning, eleven a.m., bring your 'A' game. I didn't get an earlier time because the girls are going to some kind of women's group breakfast. Rose is going to bring Abby," Will said the next Thursday.

Rose hadn't spoken to Will about our little talk the other day, or maybe she did, and he didn't get it, or ignored her like he often did with bad news. Anyway, there wasn't any point in arguing about it. I would have to explain it all to him in good time, and it probably would be better if Rose told him about Abby. I didn't need him botching my attempt to end my relationship with Abby.

"I'll come, but don't count on an 'A' game. I'm losing interest in pickleball."

"What's the matter, Buddy? Tired of losing?"

———

I was the first to arrive at the court. I knew I needed to control the beginnings of any conversations.

I hoped to be the initiator this morning, but I didn't. Abby looked oblivious, even happy as we came together. I struggled for words.

She was the first to speak, "Hi, Jimmie, I feel good about my game. I'm glad we are getting to play again so soon."

"Hi, Abby," I answered, without enthusiasm or interest.

"I enjoyed our walk last weekend. I wished you felt better, wished you didn't have to leave the pet store so soon. I wished you would have come with us to the back where they kept the cats and dogs. I've been thinking about getting a pet. They had some cute kitties there. I thought I'd like to have a cat; they're so cute and cuddly. But when we saw the dogs, I started to change my mind. They have lots of them, some cute puppies too. We should go back. If I had a little dog, we could go for walks on the weekends, just you, me, and my new puppy."

I was afraid something like this would happen. I so dreaded this. It was nice, having a friend like Abby, but I know this can't be.

I looked at Rose, but she wouldn't let our eyes meet. I wanted to be mad but knew she knew what I was thinking and felt as terrible as I did. *If only I hadn't let this get out of control.* But I did, and I needed to face it, it was my problem to solve, no one else's.

"Let's just play pickleball," I said.

———

It was an uncomfortable morning. Everyone was in a curious state. Abby was upbeat but sensed she wasn't connected to the game or its participants. Rose was distracted; she knew what was happening on the other side of the net and felt in no small way responsible. I was conflicted; my past and the present were at war and I was stuck as the mediator. Will wanted to play pickleball and wondered why everyone else was not competing.

There was no joy in Mudville this morning. Three of the four of us were striking out, and the fourth was oblivious to the real game.

"Can we go for a walk?" I asked Abby. "I have some things I need to say."

I didn't start this well. Abby's face drooped as if she seemed to suspect.

"Sure, if you think we should," she answered.

Outside, she reached for my hand as we started.

My first instinct was to draw back, but thought it was the wrong reaction. I knew this couldn't be pleasant, but I liked her and the thought of hurting her feelings was sucking the will out of me. My dad used to tell me, "Son, do the right thing for the right reason." His saying went on; "and don't worry about the consequences," but that part wasn't right for this situation. I was worried about the consequences, at least Abby's. This wasn't fair, and nothing she had said or done caused it.

"Abby, I don't know how much Rose has told you about me. First, she probably told you about the law firm where Will and I work. Our jobs aren't stable and it appears as if they won't be in the foreseeable future. Will has family here and doesn't want to move, so he has decided to weather the storm, so to speak, do his work to the best of his abilities, and hope for the best. Our company said they are going to reevaluate at the end of each fiscal quarter and they told us the reevaluations would last for at least a year. A year that is going to be miserable. Morale will be low, and friendships will be tested. I don't want to be a part of any of it. I don't know what I am going to do yet, but I plan to resign at the end of next term.

"I don't think you know, but I lost my dog. He has been my best friend ever since I got him, and we have been through so much together. I left him tied to a post at an interstate rest stop about two months ago and he got away, or someone took him. I am devastated by his loss and can't focus on anything else. Every day, I hope this will be the day someone calls to tell me they found him.

"And there is a girl. I met a veterinarian a couple of years ago; she worked at a clinic where I used to take my dog, Walter. She moved to a suburban facility about a year ago. I didn't realize how much she meant to me until she left.

"I know you know Rose got the two of us together, hoping for the best for both of us. I like you; I like you a lot, but not in the way you want. I wish it wasn't this way, but it is. I'm sorry!"

I watched her facial expression change as I spoke. She suspected at the beginning, and by the time I was done talking, I could see the heartbreak in her eyes.

"I will take you home if you like, or I can have Rose take you."

Her head fell and she began digging for a Kleenex in her bag. As she tried to remain composure, she only spoke one word, "Rose."

⁓

Sunday was the saddest day I can remember. The second saddest, I guess, the saddest was the day I lost Walter. I had never been this despondent before. I'd lost Walter, my best friend. I'd lost the girl of my dreams, Ingrid. I'd lost what might have been the girl of my dreams, Abby. And I was about to lose my job.

Everything I touch, I ruin!

There was nothing on TV that interested me. I couldn't even find anything on the National Geographic or science channels to watch. I picked up a book I'd been trying to finish and put it down several times. At noon, I jokingly told myself, it was time to start drinking, but when I opened the refrigerator, I knew it was a bad idea and closed the door. I wanted to go for a walk, but I knew I would end up in Fillmore Park. I even tried to take a nap but couldn't even close my eyes. I wished this day and this night could be over.

For the first time in months, I looked forward to work in the morning.

⁓

Will burst into my cubicle, " You SOB! What did you do to Rose?" he screamed.

"What?"

"What did you do to Rose? She spent all Sunday morning in her room crying. With the door locked damn it! She wouldn't come out, even to get something to eat, and wouldn't talk to me through the bedroom door."

"I ....."

"Yesterday afternoon, she left with a bag of clothes and didn't come home. Last night, after nine, she called and said she was staying at Abby's. She wouldn't tell me why, just hung up the phone. What the hell did you do?"

"I …"

"This better be good. What the hell, man?"

"Can we go to the conference room? We can talk there."

"Damn right, we can talk. You've got some explaining to do."

"I know, I know."

"Yesterday, after pickleball, Abby and I went for a walk," I started.

"Yeah, I know, get on with it man. This better be good."

"If you'd just let me talk. I can explain."

"Like I said, this better be good cause you are screwing up my life."

"Abby and I went for a walk so we could talk – alone. I broke up with her."

"You did what?"

"I broke up with her. I saw where our relationship was going, Abby and me, and I needed to end it. It was inevitable. Waiting longer was only going to make it harder.

"You idiot. She was perfect for you."

"Yeah, I know, if only the circumstances were different. She was getting too serious, she wanted us to get a dog; I couldn't deal with that. And there's still Ingrid. Rose is upset and feels guilty for what she tried to do. She tried to fix me up. She wanted to help. She had the best intentions, I don't blame her for trying.

"God, you're dumb."

"I know, but I have to do what I think is right. And it wasn't going to work and the sooner it was over, the better. My dad always said, 'Don't put off till tomorrow what needs to be done today.'"

"Yeah, you and your dad's sayings. I'm fed up with them too."

"He was right and they work for me, especially this time."

Will and I received a lot of inquisitive glances as we returned to our cubicles. We weren't arguing anymore, but we weren't wearing happy faces either.

The air in our workroom was icy the rest of the day. Colleagues exchanged with a minimum of conversation and phone conversations were all quiet and subdued. It was a day of nervous glances and whispered comments.

I needed to talk to Rose. But not with Will around. I dialed her number.

"Hi, Jim," Rose sniffled.

"Is Abby okay?"

"Abby called in sick and I'm on my way back to the apartment. How was Will this morning?"

"He's better now. We talked. I'm not sure he's forgiven me yet, but he will, eventually, hopefully. Can we talk? Meet for a coffee somewhere?"

"I don't think we should. This is not a good time. I'm not sure what Will is thinking, but I'm pretty sure he's not happy with you and me. I think he wonders if something is going on behind his back"

"Really?"

"Yes, really. Maybe I could call you during lunch," Rose said.

"Lunch won't work. I'm going to the lunch room with Will. I'm sure he has more to say," I answered.

"Okay, then. First chance we get. But I don't want to appear to be secretive. Will is already suspicious. When he calms down, he's going to understand, but it might take a couple of days, so I guess maybe right now, on the phone will have to work," she said.

"I wanted to tell you, I understand what you did and why you did it. I know your motive was pure. You saw what you thought I needed and tried to help. I don't blame you, you were a friend trying to help a friend. And you made a good choice. Abby is a nice girl, a special someone. Just not my someone now. Another time, another circumstance, another me; I see how you thought it might work. Thanks for that.

"Someday you, Will, Abby, and her new special someone will be playing pickleball on Saturday mornings and having fun. I hope it's soon, but I won't be there," I said.

"Oh, Jim, you are such a good guy."

Our law firm was beginning to approach a new normalcy. A part of our old efficiency returned and our new president began to spend more time in his office, letting those who knew how to manage run our business. Our workloads increased. Seeing this, employees gained a sense of ease, a feeling of security. Still, I was resolute. I made a promise and intended to keep it.

I signed on to a headhunter website and began to search. There seemed to be a multitude of opportunities, but as I researched them, I always found a disqualifier.

I began to reconsider. *Working here isn't so bad. I like what I do. I am more comfortable with our new boss and mesh with him much better than I expected.*

Will and I found a new normal. No more pickleball now, only racquetball – just the two of us. An occasional Friday evening together for pizza was comforting, if not comfortable. Rose was uneasy. She wished she could undo the Abby scenario, they were still close friends. But sometimes, when I looked into her sad eyes, I could see she was still hurting.

Today was unusually stressful. Halfway through the document I was building, one of our lawyers asked me to aid his assistant in drawing up a brief. Both items needed to be completed by the end of the day, so I worked well past the end of office hours. When we finally finished, I offered to take Will home. I spent the long ride home thinking about work. I was still daydreaming as I stopped in my lobby, got my mail from the box, and trudged up the steps to my apartment. I struggled with an unusually large bundle of mail, the newspaper, and my briefcase as I fumbled for my key.

Once inside, I dropped my load on the couch, then walked to the kitchen, and opened the refrigerator, hoping for inspiration.

It came in the form of a ham sandwich, half a bag of waffle potato chips, a chocolate pudding cup, and a glass of skim milk.

I returned to the couch with my dinner to read the paper.

A terrorist attack on a train station in Paris covered the front page. The second page reported Iran was still resisting the inspection of their nuclear facilities and another new case of Chinese computer hacking was discovered.

I was not in the mood.

I opened my briefcase and began going through papers, work a dedicated employee would spend his evenings going over, but I wasn't in the mood for work either, so I began to sort through the mail.

A legal-sized envelope, rather thick with extra postage caught my attention. It was addressed to me. A letter from John Gray in North Carolina.

I shook it; nothing rattled. I slit the end with my opener and pulled out two sheets of paper.

What unknown messages could cause my hand to tremble?

The letter stared up from my lap, daring me to open it. It demanded attention. Slowly and carefully, I cut it open. I unfolded to the opening page. It was from Ira.

Dear James,

After much thought and consideration, and with John's blessing, I have decided to retire.

The date is still being discussed. In the interim, John has begun a search for my replacement. As we began our inquiry, your name has been at the forefront of our discussions. And once my decision became known to some of our clients, suggestions were being offered. Not the least is the friendly interest from our mutual friend, Henry Crane.

Attached, please find an invitation from John,

Sincerely,
Ira Jacobs.

I looked at the second letter:

From the desk of John Gray
To James Williams

Dear James,

As you just learned, after many years of faithful service, my associate and friend Ira Jacobs is planning to retire. I wish Ira all the best. This office will miss an invaluable friend and trusted employee.

I have begun a search for his replacement and your name appears in our list of candidates. I would like you to interview for the open position.

Enclosed you will find a voucher for airfare and expenses for your visit. Should you choose to accept, your friend Henry Crane has asked that you stay with him during your visit.

I know you are currently employed and are in a situation where it is difficult to secure time away. With that circumstance in mind, if you schedule round-trip travel, at your earliest convenience leaving Friday evening and returning Sunday evening, Ira and I will make ourselves available for your visit.

Please bring any documentation you feel is appropriate.

Sincerely,
John Crane

Also, in the envelope I found two vouchers, one for airfare and the second to cover expenses for the trip.

My hands had shaken before opening the envelope, and they trembled now. *So much, so quickly, where do I start? How do I respond? Where would I live? How soon would I have to move? What about Ingrid? What about Walter?*

I called Will and asked if I could come over.

"Something's come up, I need to talk." I didn't need advice so much as just someone to bounce ideas off of to see how they sounded verbalized.

"Sure, come over for supper if you want. Rose went to a play with a couple of friends from work, so the place will be quiet. I'll order a pizza. What time will you get here?"

Pizza and beer seemed like a good idea. It was a long time since just the two of us spent an evening together, and for the first time in a long time, a beer seemed right.

I almost wished Rose would be there, maybe even instead of Will, but it wasn't an option. Rose and I had grown closer and Will and I more distant as a result of the Abby fiasco. It pained me to think about it, but my best friend's wife understood me better than he did.

"So what's the deal?" he asked.

"I received a letter from the lawyer in North Carolina I told you about."

"Yeah, so?"

"He asked me to come down to talk about a possible job opportunity."

"Doing what, exactly?"

"I don't know, exactly, but it sounds like it would be similar to what I am doing here."

"So when are you going?"

"That is what I wanted to talk about. There are all sorts of complications. You know like..."

"What do you want me to say?"

"I don't know. I just need reassurance, I guess."

"Reassurance about what? This sounds like it may be a golden opportunity."

"I know, it is what I think too, but…"

"So you've lost your dog and it's beginning to seem like you will never find him. You've lost your girlfriend if you can call her that, and you may never see her again. You have a job which may not, no check that, which probably will not last. Now you may have an opportunity to move on, and you need advice? Really? Go listen to what this lawyer has to say. What have you got to lose? Sounds like a no-brainer to me. Unless of course, you want me to go in your place."

"I know, but."

"There are no 'buts' about this. None of your problems will be solved if you stay here. Besides, aren't you the one who said you weren't going to stay and be subject to the whims of our new boss?"

"Yeah."

"Okay, let's finish the pizza. Want another beer?"

～

I called John Gray's office. "Will the weekend after next work for you?"

Chapter 18
The Return to North Carolina

I felt a little guilty, using the voucher for the airfare. This was a position I secretly hoped for since I visited Henry several months ago. But this was a business opportunity, and I needed to think of it as business and nothing more.

I chose the six-thirty flight. I wanted to leave earlier but would need to ask permission, which was something I wanted to avoid. I didn't feel the need to hide my decision to move on from the firm and didn't want to make anyone aware of my intentions either. I could see no good coming from an announcement of any kind at this time.

Will and Rose drove me to the airport. Except for a few tirades at inconsiderate drivers who cut us off or honked without reason, it was a quiet ride. All three of us were anxious about what lay ahead, although our reasons were different. Will and Rose were sad about the possibility of losing a friend. I was venturing into a new world, one which was filled with fear of the unknown.

I regretted allowing Henry to meet me at the Asheville airport. When I first acquiesced to his offer, I hadn't considered how late it would be when I arrived and hadn't considered the length of the drive back to his farm.

I said goodbye in the terminal. Will insisted they come inside instead of leaving me at the curb. I told him this was just an interview, but he wanted to help with my luggage.

"Good luck, buddy," he said, as he shook my hand. "I hope this works out for you if it is what you want. I hate to see you go. I will have to find a new racquetball partner."

"Yeah, maybe you'll be able to beat the next one." I forced a grin and squeezed his hand a little longer than was comfortable.

It was Rose who affected me the most. We grew closer once she understood my side of the Abby debacle; close to the point where I thought of her as a best friend, someone I could confide in. Easier than with Will, but more awkward because he resented it.

"I am trying to wish what is best for you," she said. "But selfishly, part of me wishes you weren't going and hope you don't get the job, but deep down, I hope you get it if you think it will make you happy."

We hugged, probably too tightly and definitely for too long, especially since Will stood next to us watching. I kept a sort of manly decorum until I let her go and stepped back. Tears were streaming down her cheeks. Her mournful expression caused a moment of guilt to sweep over me. I smiled, said goodbye, and turned away before my eyes began to mist.

Once I got my ticket and checked my bag, I walked to my gate and found a seat.

I understood the need, but this business of having to arrive two hours before a flight was stressful. I wished I was waiting for a vacation flight to Mexico, the Dominican Republic, or one of those Caribbean islands, but as I thought about it, I would be anxious in that situation too. Whether eager to go on an expected vacation or dreading venturing into a life-changing moment, time in an airport has a way of dragging on.

A woman and a cute little girl shared my row on the plane. She and her daughter were flying back to Asheville on a connecting flight after a week with her parents. They were happy in their anticipation; one to see her husband, the other to see her Daddy.

"My grandma lives on a farm. She has lots of cows and cats. They have a tractor, a barn, and a big yard. The cows live outside in a grassy field."

"Susie, don't bother the nice man. He probably wants to rest," the mother said.

"No, it's alright. I don't mind," I answered.

"She's so keyed up. She's not normally this talkative. It's just because she had so much fun and can't wait to tell her daddy all about it," she apologized.

"I don't mind. My name is Jim. You have a cute little girl. It's nice to visit with children sometimes. It can be refreshing."

"My name is Elizabeth. I go by Beth."

"Beth is a nice name. I've always liked it."

The two-hour flight to Asheville seemed to last only minutes. I helped Beth get her bag from the storage bin above, then followed them into the terminal, waited with them, helped them retrieve their bags from the conveyor, followed them to the exit, and then watched as Susie ran to the open arms of her father.

It was only then I thought about Ingrid.

Chapter 19
Henry, John Gray, Ira Jacobs, and Winnie

"It's good to see you again. I've missed the sound of your voice. I was hoping we could go to The Family Cafe for meatloaf tonight, but we can settle for home cooking in the morning before I take you to see John," Henry smiled. "My friends have been asking when the nice young man from the city is coming for another visit. How long will you stay?"

"It's good to see you too, Henry. I can only stay through Sunday night. I need to be back at work on Monday morning. I didn't tell anyone at work what I was doing this weekend. I didn't want anyone to know. I don't want to burn any bridges," I answered.

"John told me why you are coming."

"I brought some papers, references, and the like. I hope I brought what he wants."

"Don't worry. John will be prepared; he always is. Throw your bag in the back and we can get started. Winnie will be happy to see you."

I realized he was uncomfortable and tried not to mention Walter. I knew it would have to be me who started the discussion.

It was almost dark as we began. I wanted to offer to drive as the thought of Henry driving all this way to meet me and now having to drive back bothered me. But he knew the way, and if I drove, he would need to navigate, so I didn't offer.

I was tired. It wasn't nine o'clock yet; this had been a long day. The thought of venturing into the unknown, a new job (if it was offered), a move from the city to the country, moving farther from Ingrid (if I moved), and the impending reunion with Winnie would bring back uncomfortable memories. All this, and I was alone with a relatively new friend at night, on the deserted highway.

"Would you like to talk?" Henry asked.

"I'm not sure I am up for conversation right now," I answered.

"I thought you might feel that way. But let me say a couple of things, then I'll honor your wish," he said. "First of all, you wouldn't be here if you weren't at least somewhat open to a change in your life. Second, this could be an opportunity to make some of those changes you feel you need to make. I know you aren't happy with your current work situation. I know your personal life is in disarray and you don't see a solution. And I know you miss Walter.

"Try to think of it this way. You could end up in a better work situation, you might see a path to a better life with change, and maybe most importantly, you would be closer to the place you lost Walter."

I gazed at him. He was still the same bearded man I first met in the park. His clothes were fresher, better fitting. He wore the same beard, only neatly trimmed now. The blue light emitting from the dashboard lights gave a hint of a gleam in his eyes. He seemed at ease.

There is so much more to this man than I ever dreamed.

"I think I will just ride, at least for a while," I answered. "And I am looking forward to seeing Winnie again."

I awakened when Henry slowed to turn into his drive.

"Your room is just as you left it," he said. "Bess is coming over first thing, we'll have breakfast here, then I will take you to town for your day with John. Get some sleep, tomorrow will be a new day, my friend."

～

Another sleepless night. They seem to come too often.

I was awakened by the gentle tap on my bedroom door, "You have an important day ahead," Henry said.

My fingers struggled with buttons and zippers. Then after checking my appearance in the mirror, three times, I came downstairs to a steaming breakfast and a smiling Henry.

"Just be yourself, you'll be fine," he said as I left.

Minutes later I found my way into the lobby of John Gray's law office, "Good morning, Ira," I said.

"Good morning, James, It is nice to see you again. John asked me to visit with you before he comes in this morning. He wants me to give you an idea about your visit."

"Okay," was all I could muster. This was a slightly unsettling development. I didn't know what to expect, I assumed I would immediately go into John's office for an interview.

"When last we talked, I told you I was contemplating retirement. There have been some changes which have forced me to make my decision sooner than I expected. I fell about a month ago. I didn't think much of it at the time; I thought I must have bruised my hip but the pain lingered until It finally forced me to seek help."

"I'm sorry to hear it," I said.

"Thank you. This has been a struggle," he said and went on. "They sent me to Asheville for x-rays and an MRI. The specialist there told me I cracked both my pelvic bone and femur. They told me I would have to walk with an appliance. Then they scheduled me for physical therapy. I had to learn to walk with crutches. After a month, they let me try a cane but it was too painful, so I reverted to the crutches. In two months, I go back for more tests, and if I haven't healed sufficiently, they hinted a hip transplant would probably be in my future. I hoped to retire on my terms at a time of my choosing, but these old bones seem to be deciding for me. John and I have talked at length about this. I am going to retire, but not until my health issues are resolved. In the interim, John is going to find a replacement, and once someone is on board, I will be available as much as my health will allow to help the new person learn."

"I assume then, I am here for an interview," I answered.

"Yes, we started with a list of names and gradually reduced the list until it was down to a manageable half dozen candidates. Your name survived because you made a positive impression on John when you were here last. You impressed me with your intellect and intuition. And of course, Henry has always been here to trumpet your case. He is so impressed with your compassion and honesty.

"Thank you, I appreciate your kind words, and am forever in Henry's debt."

"Odd you should say that; it is exactly what Henry says about you.

"John will be in shortly, may I get you a cup of coffee or bottle of water?"

"No, please don't get up, I will get it myself."

Ira smiled in appreciation.

John Gray entered the office, "Good morning, James."

"Good morning, Mr. Gray."

"Please, just John. We try not to be formal here."

"Thank you for your invitation," I answered.

"Come, step into my office."

He held the door for me and I entered. The office seemed bigger, imposing somehow; more official than I remembered. Maybe the reason for my visit made it seem different, more austere.

As he walked to his desk, he seemed taller, more distinct. His slender frame seemed more fit, his face chiseled and serious. *I wonder if he plays racquetball.*

He began, "I am sure Ira has brought you up to speed. We both knew the time would come for him to retire, but we hadn't expected it would be a result of health issues and inflict a sense of urgency upon us.

"When you first visited us, Ira hinted at his retirement. He has been a long and faithful employee, a vital piece of my business. More colleague than an employee and I hate to see him go; moving on without him will be difficult. I am searching for someone capable of filling his void.

"Over the last couple of weeks, Ira and I have worked to compile a list of candidates for his replacement. I should tell you, it hasn't been an easy task. We have pared our list to six.

"You, being in this office, shows you are one of those candidates. You made a positive first impression on both Ira and me on your earlier visit, and I will tell you Henry Crane has, in no small measure, been your advocate."

"Thank you, Mr. Gray. John," I corrected. I felt both honored and intimidated and could not think of more to say.

"I asked you to bring any recommendations and paperwork you thought proper. If you would give those papers to me now."

I fumbled in my briefcase, retrieved a handful of papers, tapped them on my knee to straighten them, and passed them over.

"Why don't you go back to Ira's desk, have a cup of coffee, and visit while I go through these," he said.

He wore a serious expression now; formalities were over. The weight of the situation swept over me.

"Ask me if you have any questions, John."

"I will, thank you," he responded, without looking up.

"May I get you something before I sit, Ira?" I asked.

"No, thank you, how did it go?"

"I don't know. Mr. Gray is going through my papers."

"Well, make no mistake. He asked you to visit because he feels you may be qualified. I am sure you originally left with an impression of informality in our office, but John is a serious man and is intent on making the best decision for the future of his firm. He is going through your references and work papers page by page, line by line. Oh, and you need to understand, that he expects to be called John. I know him well, I know he mentioned it at the outset, and you would do well to honor his request.

"Here, let me show you what I am presently working on."

I sat at Ira's side as he showed me briefs, decisions, letters, and more. We sat for what seemed like hours, but in actuality, it was only about thirty minutes before Ira's phone rang.

"John would like to see you now."

"Please be seated, Jim."

"Thank you."

I detected a hint of a smile, satisfaction almost. Suddenly, I felt more at ease.

"Your papers are orderly and complete. Your letters of recommendation are impressive. You should know two of these papers are submitted by friends and former classmates who are still colleagues. People whose opinions I value.

"You should know too, that I sent an inquiry to the former president of your firm. I know him by reputation. We are alumni of the same law school.

"So, your papers are in order, and impressive. Let's talk about you and why you are here.

"First, being one of the final candidates for Ira's position is not a small accomplishment. It seems this is a coveted opportunity.

"I have done research of my own. I know you were close to completing a law degree. I know you dropped out to help your father when your mother was ill. I admire your dedication to your family. I am disappointed you did not return to school once your mother recovered sufficiently. Two of your former professors told me they petitioned you to resume your studies. One even offered to help you financially. This speaks volumes about their respect for your abilities.

"It should come as no surprise to you, although I think it might, your employment is secure at your current firm. One of my former classmates is a junior partner there. He lauded your abilities and told me personally you are an important part of the firm. One who is thorough and prompt. This is praise that he does not give easily.

"Through Henry, I know of your help in his finding his daughter, Theresa, and about the loss of your dog, Walter. Your effort and diligence to retrieve what to others might seem excessive is heartwarming.

"These are thoughts and findings. Do you question the validity of any of them?"

"No, John. It is just I am surprised..."

"Don't be. This is the type of thoroughness I demand of myself, my colleagues, and my patrons. I would expect nothing less from you, should I offer you the position.

"Now, I know Henry wants to take you to lunch, so go enjoy your afternoon, and explore our town and the area around. Ira and I will discuss your application, and we will call you at three p.m. for a follow-up."

***

"Well, how did it go today?" Henry asked.

"I don't know. I think I presented well but John told me he and Ira will discuss and call me later."

"You didn't expect an offer today did you?"

"I didn't know what to expect. As I think about it, I'm not sure I can glean any clues."

"John told you there were six candidates, didn't he?"

"Well, yes, why?"

"John will not decide until he has conducted all the interviews. I believe you were only the second. Come on, get in the Mule, let's go to lunch - meatloaf and all the trimmings today."

"The Mule? I thought you couldn't drive the Mule to town."

"We have a new police chief. He's a little more relaxed," Henry grinned.

With no time pressure, Henry took me to different parts of town on the way to the restaurant. "I thought I should show you the older parts of town. I want you to have a more complete idea. You know, just in case," he grinned.

Does he know more than he is telling?

"Here, I took the liberty of picking up a brochure for you from a realtor. I think you should know how much more affordable life is here."

As we drove, I flipped the pages, searching houses in the one to two hundred thousand dollar range. *These places would be five times as much in my neighborhood, if there were any even available.*

"Here we are! Are you ready for another slice of the best meatloaf for miles around?

I smiled but didn't answer. I was reviewing houses, wondering what John and Ira were saying about me. It was all overwhelming. *This is happening so fast, should I step back? What if I have to decide today?*

"Good afternoon, Henry. Who's your friend?"

"Hi, Sandy, this is James Williams. He's the young man from New York I told you about."

"Hello Sandy, I'm glad to meet you."

"It was a nice thing you did for Henry, helping him find Theresa."

"Oh, you knew her?"

"Yes, she was a couple of years behind me in school. We used to take dance lessons together. I liked her a lot. Too bad she didn't like it here. I wish she'd stayed. I'm sorry I missed you when you were here before. I was on vacation then."

"That's nice, vacations are always refreshing, it's always nice to get away. Where did you go?"

"I stayed home. My sister drove over from Cherokee and we went to antique stores and garage sales.

"But I keep rambling on. Why don't you two take the table by the window, and I'll bring your drinks. Sweet tea as usual, Henry?"

"Yes, and my friend here will have a glass too. We need to get him drinking it right away," Henry answered.

Another hint?

"Our Saturday special is always meatloaf. I assume you both want it. Choices for sides are potato, baked or mashed, and your choice of either hominy, corn on the cob, or okra."

Henry eyed me to let me order first.

"I'd like a baked potato and hominy. I've never eaten okra before."

"Never eaten okra? Well, we'll have to change that. I'll have Myrt put a spoonful in a dish on the side.

"Henry?"

"Mashed as usual. I think I'll have the corn today, is it fresh?"

"You know it's fresh. I picked it up this morning on my way to work," She laughed. "I'll get your tea."

"She seems nice," I said to Henry as Sandy walked toward the kitchen.

"Yeah, but she's a kidder. She buys corn from a roadside stand on her way to work every morning. Potatoes too. Nothing beats a freshly baked potato next to a slice of meatloaf unless maybe a piece of made-from-scratch gooseberry pie," he grinned.

Sandy brought our food. Two heaping plates were balanced on her arm with a large bowl in her hand. She laughed as she set our plates, "Hope you boys are hungry. Mryt said she put a little extra in your okra bowl. She said, 'That boy's going to have to learn to like okra if he's going to eat in here.'"

We didn't say much while we ate. It's hard to talk with a mouthful, and the food was so good, conversation would have to wait.

"Well, what'd you think?" Sandy asked. "About the okra, I mean."

"I guess I will have to learn to like it," I answered.

"Okra and grits. If you are going to live down here, you are going to have to like okra and grits. It's a law," she laughed.

My cell phone rang as we were leaving. The number was not familiar, but it was a local area code. I showed it to Henry.

"Oh, that's Ira," he said.

"Hello."

"James?"

"Yes."

"We'd like you to come to the office at two instead of three. My hip is bothering me today, so John wants you to come in earlier so I can leave for the day. We apologize for the inconvenience."

"I'll be glad to. Henry and I just finished our lunch, I will be there shortly."

"Good news?" Henry asked as I put my phone away.

"Just news, I guess," I said. "They asked me to come earlier."

"Come in James," Ira said when we got back to the law firm. "John is waiting in his office."

"Good afternoon, John," I said.

"James, I want you to know you are our second interview. We intend to visit with the other four candidates before we make our decision, so don't expect this weekend's visit to be more or less than you expected. Please know your visit went well and your qualifications are more than acceptable. We have the other all candidates scheduled within the next three weeks. Ira and I will then make our selection. We expect our discussion will take approximately one week. Then we will notify all candidates of our choice. Should you be our pick, I will send you my benefits package. At that time, should you decide to accept my offer, I will expect you to inform your current employer and give them at least two weeks' notice.

"And understanding your current situation, should you be our pick, I would like you to consider completing your law degree.

"Now, if you have no questions, or even think of anything you wish to ask later, please contact Ira. You have his information."

I replied, "The law degree comes as a surprise to me, John."

"I know, but it is something to consider, should you be our selection."

⸎

"How did it go?" Henry asked.

"Fine, I guess. All he did was tell me he and Ira were going to interview every candidate before deciding. I didn't think about the process in its entirety, I guess I expected too much. I thought he might offer me the position before I went back to New York."

"No, John doesn't make decisions without first completing the process. I wouldn't expect him to do less. Don't be disappointed," Henry said. "Are you hungry?"

"Not really, but I can always eat."

After a piece of pie (I chose rhubarb tonight), Henry took me for a ride in the country. I didn't have much time though. My flight back to New York left at five in the morning and I needed to get some sleep.

"I wish there was time for you to go to Emma's Point," he mused.

Secretly, I was glad there wasn't time. The last trip up there, I thought I had solved all my problems and left with a sense of contentment I hadn't felt for a long time. But after I left, everything fell apart.

"It's okay," I told him. "I can't resolve anything until I hear from John."

"I know," he answered.

Chapter 20
The Wait

I was glad it was dark when I boarded the plane for the flight back. I had a restless night, wondering and worrying, so I still needed sleep. Nothing had changed except the interview was now behind me, and all I could do was wait.

An anxious Will and Rose waited as I carried my bag to the exit. I wished he was alone. I knew he would have a deluge of questions, none of which I could answer to his satisfaction. And I didn't want to talk about this in Rose's presence because, although she understood, she was still disappointed in me for letting Abby down.

The first words out of his mouth were, "Did you get the job?"

"I told you before I left, it was just an interview, and I wouldn't know anything right away."

"Yes, but I had to ask," he answered.

Rose interrupted, "You know, for selfish reasons, I don't want you to leave."

"I know, but it's an opportunity I should pursue. Sooner or later, you two will need to do the same."

"I know, but it's too much right now. I want you to move on, but not leave town. You know, get a job here with another firm if you think you have to leave this job."

"Besides, who am I going to beat at racquetball?" Will laughed.

"What do you mean? You can't beat me now."

We walked to the shuttle and rode to the parking lot without saying any more. All three of us were lost in thoughts about our futures.

Later, over sausage pizza (not Walter's favorite, but he would gladly eat it if he were here), we talked about my trip, John's firm, what Will should be doing, and what moving on would entail.

I was surprised such a seemingly small happening as a job interview could affect a relationship. Make that two relationships.

Racquetball games with Will now seemed emotionless. He no longer wanted to brag about beating me. He only went through the motions. Lacking now was the banter between us as we played. Sometimes when we were playing a game or match point, he didn't even try.

Pizza and beer after our games were now frequented with long moments of uncomfortable silence. Often we didn't discuss the game we just played. And neither one of us wanted to talk about work. Occasionally we might talk about the latest gossip, who was seeing who, who was cheating on their spouse, or a bulletin posted in the lounge.

I was willing to talk about North Carolina, my job interview, and the people I met down there, but the subject never seemed to come up.

I knew Will felt betrayed. He knew one of us would leave the company and move on, but the reality of it (even though my leaving was not certain) was distressing.

Rose, on the other hand, was willing to talk, but we lacked the opportunities. Will's reaction to what he saw as a betrayal made it nearly impossible for us to talk outside his presence.

Rose wanted to know about my interview and my thoughts. I was willing, almost anxious to discuss these things with her, but we could only find snippets of time to visit. In times like these, I wished I had a friend with a willing ear. Someone like Ingrid. I knew she would listen and understand. After all, she moved on and seemed at ease in her new life, what little I knew about it.

I decided to call her.

***

"Hello, James. It is nice to hear your voice. Do you have news about Walter?"

Before I even had a chance to talk about what I wanted to talk about, she changed the subject.

"Hi, no, I didn't call about him. I thought I would tell you I applied for a job in North Carolina."

"Really, what made you do that?" she asked.

"I think I told you, with the new CEO here, we don't know what direction our firm will take. The company has already sent some employees home and has announced they are going to re-evaluate again at the end of the next quarter. I don't want to work under such stressful conditions, so I have begun to search somewhere else. North Carolina seems like a good fit for me."

"Why North Carolina?"

"I met this nice man I told you about. He is the father of my ex-wife. He introduced me to his lawyer, and as if by fate, the lawyer's legal assistant was going to retire. They contacted me and asked me to interview. This might be a great opportunity for me; a chance to leave the city. You know, like you did."

"I haven't regretted moving; well, except for not getting to see you and Walter, of course," she answered.

"It's not like they offered me a job, but it's a start. I've promised myself to try to find something else. This opportunity came to me, so I thought it was a good place to begin. It would be farther from my friends, my folks, and my favorite veterinarian, but it's not like I would be moving to the West Coast or another country."

"I hope they offer it to you. How far away will you be?" she asked.

Her question caught me off guard. I took it as a sign of hope. *She must still think about me once in a while.*

"I don't know, I hadn't thought about it. Maybe two hundred miles," I stammered. I knew it was farther, but she seemed upbeat and I didn't want to spoil the moment.

"Have you thought about where you would live if you moved? Are there things to do there? You know, recreation, interesting places like museums. Would you live close to shopping?"

"I have an idea about lodging, but it is too soon to think about it. Shopping doesn't interest me, but there are some scenic places and nice roads. And the people I've met have all been friendly."

"I'm sorry, I have to go, our receptionist just told me my next patient is here. He's a black Lab by the way. Call me again with any news. I'm sure they will offer you the position. They couldn't find a better candidate. Just make sure you want it before you agree," Ingrid said.

I was relieved in a way. I told her what I wanted, and our conversation would now have turned to small talk, and I didn't want to hear about her boyfriend.

"Goodbye," I said. "It was nice to hear your voice. Call me sometime."

Call me sometime, really, how lame can you get?

The seriousness of what I was contemplating was beginning to sink in. A few years ago I quit law school to help Dad take care of Mom when she was sick. Once she was better, I decided to work for a while to build a nest egg since Dad was no longer in a position financially to help with school expenses. My favorite professor, Dr. Jay Fitzgerald Cummings, affectionately known as Dr. J, helped me find a job – the one I now hold. He contacted a former classmate, our now-retired partner and CEO, who conveniently had an opening in his company. So, in a sense, I merely fell into my current employment. Going out in the world to seek a job was a new undertaking for me.

The gravity of leaving friends with no intention of returning was also new. Before, I intended to return to school, but this was different, once I left Will, Rose, and my fellow workers, I would not be coming back. Most of whom I would never see again.

For the first time since I lost him, I began to think of the possibility, or maybe the probability Walter might be dead. The thought of him dying in some unfamiliar place, maybe lost in some woods somewhere, cold and alone, breathing his last breath with no one there to comfort him was painful. The pictures I painted in my mind were overwhelming.

And they wouldn't go away.

Several times, someone at work would startle me back into the present. I wondered how many times they tried to get my attention before I woke from my stupor.

Then there was Ingrid.

She now lived more than three hours away and now had a friend. She was quite possibly in a serious relationship. Was I being realistic in my hope for her in my future?

My mind raced. *If I get the position with John Gray, will it end any chance I have with her? Would she leave her job to follow me to North*

Carolina if I asked? Is she going to marry this guy? And what about Abby, was it foolish to break up with her? Could our relationship work if I hadn't cut it short?

There was a new posting at work this morning. The end of the quarter was quickly approaching, so everyone was watching it for word of any changes.

Employees were again huddling around the board. Most seemed relieved. I inched my way through the mob until I got close enough to read.

It announced our business was unexpectedly doing better. It went on to read "The Firm cannot at this time forecast the permanence of this turn. As a result, no changes will be made in the workforce at this time."

People were smiling in relief. I wasn't so enthusiastic about the news. To me, it read, "You will be expected to do more work without any change in compensation." I knew once this reality sunk in, corporate devotion would sink to a new low.

I hoped for a response from North Carolina.

Chapter 21
Change is good (and can be difficult)

My guess was correct.

The new grumbling was worse than before. Employees, myself included, were being asked to stay later at work. People who never took work home with them were now grudgingly leaving the office with bulging briefcases. I wondered if physical confrontations were in our near future.

I lugged an armload of folders up the steps, checked my mailbox, and found a manila envelope inside. It held the hoped-for return address. I put my work on the end table, put the envelope on top, and went to the bedroom to change. I sat on the edge of the bed for a few minutes to contemplate. I wanted to plan my reaction, no matter what the news. But I couldn't sit there, I needed to know.

Barefoot, I hurried back to my Barcalounger and fumbled through the end-table drawer in a vain search for my letter opener. I ripped the end of the envelope and yanked out the contents. Three long weeks I had waited for this moment.

My eyes rushed past the heading and greeting, before falling on the text. I scanned the greeting. The third paragraph held the information I craved.

"We wish to extend an offer of employment."

I read no more. I lay the letter on my lap, moved my recliner back, closed my eyes, and smiled.

All the "what ifs" I suffered in the last few weeks vanished now. A euphoria swept over me. It must have seemed silly to anyone who might see me now. But no one could, and I didn't care.

After enjoying the moment for probably twenty minutes, I sat up, lifted the papers from my lap, and turned the page, both literally and figuratively. An amalgam of words on a simple sheet of paper had just changed my life.

I turned my computer on and began to write my letter of acceptance. After writing and deleting, writing and deleting several times, I called John.

"Good afternoon, James. I assume you received my letter."

"Yes." Words struggled to escape my dry throat. "I am trying to write a letter of acceptance, and will, but I wanted to call to thank you first."

"I expected you to call. There is one thing I didn't include because I wanted to tell you personally, but over the phone will work. What I am about to tell you is not a condition of employment, but more than a request. I told you earlier that I talked to one of your professors during the application process. He hoped you would return to finish your degree. I share that hope," John said.

"Once you get here, and are comfortable with your position, I want you to consider returning to school. I would like you to finish your schooling, become a lawyer, and hopefully, stay with my firm. I understand this is unexpected, but it is my wish."

"I have been thinking about it for some time. There is so much to consider though," I said.

"I'm glad. Now is not the time to decide, but this is my hope. You should call Henry."

"I will, I assure you. I thought about calling him first, but it would have been inappropriate."

John laughed, "He is waiting for your call. He has even tried to figure out what time you get your mail each day. Ira and I are anxious for you to begin but remember, I expect you to give two weeks' notice. I know you will, and I know you will work diligently to the completion of your employment there."

"Hello, I've been expecting your call," Henry said a few minutes later. I sensed the joy in his voice.

"Hi, I called to tell you John has offered me the position."

"I know, he told me. He made me promise not to tell you. That promise has been driving me crazy. I didn't think the mail was ever going to deliver his packet. I am so happy for you. This is a prayer answered. Emma and I have talked about you."

I knew what he meant.

"I have a lot to think about. John made it clear he wants me to give two weeks' notice. But there is so much to plan and do. It will be hard to find the time for everything."

"Well, don't worry about where you will stay when you get here. Your room will be ready. Winnie and I can't wait. It will be so nice to have you as a house guest, and this time for a much longer time.

I take it you haven't heard any more about Walter. I know you would have told me if you did. Winnie will miss him, but she'll be happy you are here.

Walter! I guess I gave up hope, but Henry hadn't. Now what will I do about Walter?

"I'm sorry I brought him up. Once you get here, we can work on that," Henry apologized.

"It's okay. I just wanted to tell you first...well first after John. Do you think I should tell Ira?"

"He knows, but it is a courtesy I'm sure he would appreciate."

I called Ira next. He of course had been part of the discussion, but he thanked me graciously anyway. He told me he was looking forward to the opportunity to help me. He said his hip was bothering him more and he expected his doctor would recommend replacement at his next appointment.

I decided to wait until tomorrow at work to tell Will. I wanted to wait until then so he couldn't tell everyone I was leaving before I could turn in my resignation. This reminded me that I needed to compose a letter of resignation tonight too.

It was almost two a.m. before I got to bed. Composing my resignation took much longer than it should have. It was nearly impossible for me to focus.

I called my dad on the way to work in the morning. He was happy for me, sorry I would be moving farther from home, but we reconciled this a long time ago. His job was to take care of Mom until she passed, and mine was to make my way in life. Empathy didn't come easily to him, and he didn't expect any in return. He said simply, "Good luck, Son. I hope it works out for you."

I promised John I would keep up my work here until the end, but now it was hard to focus. I needed to be planning a move, keeping up with my work, and meeting my other obligations, which now included farewell parties.

⁓

Will took the news hard. He knew it was coming sooner or later but hoped it would be later. He tried to be positive, "I'm happy for you." But I could tell his heart wasn't in it, "I almost hoped they would offer the job to someone else."

I was surprised at his reaction but understood. He was being selfish in a way, but if the situation was reversed, I might have the same feelings.

In school, I had a mentor who liked to say, "Change is good." What he failed to add, was, "and it also can be hard."

I gave our secretary my letter, then went to my desk to work until I was asked to come to our senior partner's office.

"I am disappointed with this news," he said. "You are one of our key employees, the best researcher we have, our go-to guy. I believe you underestimated your value to our firm, but I won't ask you to reconsider. However, should this not work for you, and if you feel the need, we would be glad to accept you, should you choose to return."

We shook hands. When I opened his door to leave, everyone was standing, gaping, ready to attack me with questions. I didn't expect this either. It took some time to escape. I felt like a politician being bombarded by the press with questions I couldn't answer after an important legislative session.

At lunch I found a vacant office, locked the door, and called Ingrid.

"Hi, I called to tell you they offered me the position in North Carolina," I said.

"That's nice. Are you looking forward to it?" she asked.

"Absolutely!" I exclaimed.

"I'm happy for you. When do you start?"

"I'll be moving in two weeks," I answered.

"I'm sure you'll like it there," she said.

She ended our call with, "I need to go. I have a waiting room full of clients this morning."

Is she even happy for me? I thought I'd get a much better response. I wonder if it was because of her new friend.

Rose called. I wanted to call her first but thought it might be awkward. "Hi, Will told me the news. I'm so happy for you but wish it wasn't true. I hate to see you go. Are you sure?"

"Yes, I think I'm sure."

"You think you are sure?"

"No, I am sure, but it's all happening so fast. I feel overwhelmed."

"Abby will be so disappointed. She still was hoping."

"I'm sorry about Abby. I wish there was a way to… well, you know."

I was surprised at how much I accumulated since the divorce. I bought some containers at the hardware store and asked the liquor store around the corner to save boxes for me. Will came over to help but Rose was conspicuously absent.

Why do I feel guilty about leaving? I should be ecstatic and everyone should be supportive.

Ingrid called. "Do you have time to talk? I'm sorry I wasn't overjoyed with your news when you called yesterday morning. When I came to work, one of my patients worsened overnight and died just before you called."

"It's okay, I understand," I answered without emotion.

I found myself acting exactly the way she did the day before, yet now she was apologizing to me.

"I know you are going to love this move. I can't tell you how happy I am since I moved out of the city. It is so nice to see sunrises and sunsets. Will you be able to see them where you are going?" she went on.

"I don't know," I said. "The town is low, between some hills, but the scenery there is great. And the air is so fresh."

"I know what you mean. I don't know how I ever survived back there, what with the heavy air and nothing but tall buildings all around. I am so happy for you."

"I'm a little nervous about the whole thing. I hope I've made the right choice, moving so far, I mean."

"I don't think you'll ever regret it. Think of this as a fresh start. Not everyone gets one, you know. Keep in touch, okay?"

"Okay."

Our conversation ended on a friendly note, but nothing intimate. As

I thought about it, was this a signal? Did she just tell me this was the end? No, she said, "Please keep in touch!"

Chapter 22
The Move to North Carolina

Will came over evenings to help me pack. It was then I realized, I didn't have so much after all. My apartment seemed stuffed with furniture, a table, chairs, and a bed, but some of this came with the rental. The only furniture that was mine was the bed, the mattress and box spring set, the desk, the file cabinet, and the Barcalounger.

And Walter's bed. Walter's bed. Should I move it or donate it? Was there still hope? Did I want to move it? One thing was certain, I couldn't bring myself to throw it away. I couldn't face the finality of throwing it in a dumpster.

I should donate it.

But I didn't.

I opened a beer, sat on the couch and waited for Will, all the time staring at Walter's bed.

"Hey," Will shouted.

"Oh, hi," I answered.

"Don't you answer the doorbell anymore? I rang several times, then pounded on the door. Just because you are moving doesn't mean you should ignore people. What's up with the tears?"

"I don't know, just thinking about everything, I guess."

"You are moving, man. It's not the end of the world; it is the beginning of your new one. You are thinking about your dog again, aren't you?"

"Is it that obvious?"

"Yes, it is. Listen, moving isn't going to affect whether you ever find Walter. Besides, I don't want to sound unsympathetic, but it's time you face the fact that you may never find him. He may not even be alive anymore. You are moving away; maybe this is the time to move on.

"Last night Rose and I talked for a long time about you and your moving. We have come to grips with it. You and I have been friends since we first started working together, which Rose pointed out, was almost six years ago. The three of us have been good friends. We are going to stay good friends, even if we are far apart. We'll keep in touch, even visit each other from time to time. I admit, I want to see this wonderful North Carolina you talk about. Who knows what that might bring?

"As a friend, I feel compelled to tell you that you have a way of lingering. You can't let things go. You work your way into a funk when you shouldn't. I know you have mixed feelings about moving; you shouldn't. I know you still wonder if you did the right thing with Abby; it took me a while to realize, but I think you did. I know you still are clinging to hope about your relationship with your former vet, but she's gone. She's moved on and you need to face it. I know you still are clinging to hope about your dog; it's time to let that go too.

"Move on, man. You are getting a new start. Not everyone gets a chance. It's time to clean your slate, and let the past go. You are going to be just fine. I know I'll miss you, but I'll find a new racquetball player, someone I can beat a little easier. There's probably a racquetball court in your new digs; hopefully with someone who will trounce you regularly.

"And don't look at me like that. I told you Rose and I talked; we're good. Now you and I have talked, and we're good too. Wipe those tears off your cheeks, we've got work to do."

The moving van arrived shortly before eight. The men were there three times during the past week, finishing the packing, labeling boxes, and organizing them by the rooms they should go to.

Henry told me I could put everything I didn't need right away into his spare garage. "Just until we get you settled," he said.

I wasn't sure what he meant but appreciated his help.

The movers asked me if I wanted to ride in the truck.

"We can save room up front and tow your car, or if you want, you can follow us in your car."

The thought of spending a long day in their truck didn't appeal. "I'd rather drive," I said. Although listening to their chatter could have been a good distraction.

Will and Rose came over early to say goodbye. They brought Abby with them.

I dreaded this moment; saying goodbye for what might be the last time ever would be hard, but I hadn't expected to be saying goodbye to Abby too. I thought I would never see her again after our breakup and didn't want this last image to ponder.

"Don't be a stranger, write and call," Rose begged. "Come back to see us or we'll come to see you."

She hugged me for an uncomfortably long time.

"Come back anytime you need to be humbled on the court. I'm going to keep in shape," Will laughed. Then he shook my hand, pulled me close, and hugged me, "I'm going to miss you, buddy. It's hard to say goodbye to a best friend."

"I know, but it's not the end of the world. We'll talk. I won't promise to come back to see you, but I'll always have a place for you when you come to visit. You should start thinking seriously about a change too."

All this time, Abby stood to the side, uncomfortably watching our goodbyes. I could see she didn't know how to start, I didn't either. So I walked to her and extended my hand, "Thanks for coming to see me off. I didn't expect this."

"Oh, Jim, I so wanted it to work out between us. I came this morning, partly at Rose's insistence, but mostly because I want you to know if you ever change your mind..."

She broke into tears.

Suddenly, I felt like a heel for leaving.

She hugged me, kissed me on the cheek, and then turned away before either of us could say any more.

Thankfully, the van pulled up. The driver stuck his head out the window and yelled., "We need to get going; we gotta make this a three-day trip. You ready?"

"Ready as I'll ever be," I shrugged. I hugged Abby, Rose, and lastly, Will, one last time.

"I'll see you guys down the road," I said. Tears began to well up in my eyes as I turned away.

This was the biggest step I'd taken since I left for college. Fear of the unknown swept over me.

Chapter 23
My New Job

It was hard leading the moving van, driving into the unknown with the seat next to me empty. Before, everywhere I went in my car, Walter lay in the seat beside me. To the vet, to the park, even to the market, Walter was always my navigator.

This was my first trip alone.

A smiling Henry stood at the end of his driveway.

"Remember the widow's place I bought next to me? I thought you could store your stuff there. It won't be in our way over there. We can move it later when you get settled."

"Are you sure?" I asked.

"Yes, I haven't done anything with it, so the house is sitting empty."

"It's fine with me, I was worried about where I was going to put everything."

Henry got in my car and we drove toward the widow's place, the moving van following.

We directed the placing of boxes, then I shook hands with both the movers; gave each a tip, shook hands with them, and watched as the van drove away.

We stood in front of the widow's house, quietly soaking in the moment.

Henry spoke, "I've been thinking," he said, then paused before continuing. "Since the place is sitting empty, you may as well use it. I'd still like you to stay at my home for a couple of weeks. Between Bess and me, we can keep you fed, and in clean clothes. Besides, I would like your company, at least for a while."

I was happy to accept his offer. It didn't come as a surprise, an extension of this type of kindness is something I'd learned to expect from him. Not that I wasn't appreciative, I felt he more than repaid me for helping him find his daughter; he needn't do more. What I did then, leading him to his daughter, seemed more fate than effort. After all, I was married to her at the time and the particulars he told me of his search made their reunion predestined.

What little I did for him was nothing out of the ordinary; I would expect any other conscientious person to do the same thing.

"Don't you think we should wait until I see if working for John is going to be satisfactory?" I asked him.

"Have faith, young man. The difficult part is over; you have the job. You, John, Ira, and I all know you are well qualified, and you are here. All you have to do now is perform like we all know you can. We can wait to move you into the house until you think you are ready. Would that ease your mind?" he asked.

"Yes, I think it will."

"Then let's take your stuff to your room and get you full of meatloaf. You must be starved after your ride."

***

"Hi, Henry, I see your friend came back. He couldn't live without our good southern hospitality, I see."

"Hi, Sandy. No, he just came back for your meatloaf," Henry laughed.

***

It didn't take long to realize I was not prepared for my new job. In New York, I made very little contact with the company's clients. Research and writing was the largest part of my work. Here, with John and Ira, I learned I would be the first contact with clients, both longtime and new. The majority of my new firm's clients had been with John for years. They had access to John directly but often visited with Ira first. Any new or potential clients always were screened by Ira. In other words, if you called our firm, Ira answered.

This was new to me—a huge difference between being a researcher, and doing my work in a cubicle in the back of a huge office complex fronted by several secretaries.

On my first day, while sitting beside Ira, the phone rang for the first time. He smiled, handed me the handset, and said, "It's for you."

"Good morning, this is the law firm of John Gray, James Williams speaking. How may I help you?"

"Good morning, Mr. Williams, this is Henry Crane," a happy voice answered. "I wanted to be the first to congratulate you on your new position. Have a great day."

Now reassured and eager, I began.

I followed Ira as he took me through files, showed me where to find the various documents, and how his methods worked (and why). He showed me client lists, and where to find their earlier cases.

I thought of my dad and the sage advice he used to give me at the most proper times. He seemed to have one for each of my uncomfortable situations in my youth.

Two of his favorites came to mind. "Do the best you can all the time, every time," and "When someone pays you for a task, they are purchasing your loyalty, so don't let them down."

My mind was soon swimming with so much to do, learn, and so much responsibility.

"It's time for lunch," Ira said.

"Already?"

"Yes, we close at twelve-thirty unless we are with a client. John likes to stay in the office through the first part of the lunch hour, so I leave him alone.

"I go to Joy's every day, so if someone needs to visit but can't make it to the office during business hours, they can come there to see me. Liz keeps a table in the back of the room for me."

It was only a two-block walk to Joy's Café. Liz smiled from the cash register, "Table for two today, Ira?"

She led us to a table in the far corner of the room, "I remember you. You were in here a few months ago with Henry. Your name is James. I'm sorry I can't remember your last."

"Williams," I answered.

"Well, James Williams, you'll be Jimmie when you are in here. We don't do formality."

She turned to Ira, "Your usual?"

"Yes for the salad, but I think I'll have a fruit cup instead of cottage cheese today."

"And your friend here?"

"Do you have grilled cheese with tuna?" I asked.

"We do now," she grinned. Then she turned to Ira, "Eddy Miller is waiting to talk to you."

"Okay, give us a minute, then send him over," Ira answered.

A visually embarrassed young, heavy-set man dressed in dirty Carhartt bibs and a trucker's hat shuffled to our table. Everyone watched until he sat at Ira's behest, then turned back to their meals.

"Eddy, this is James Williams. He is going to take my place when I retire. You can talk in his presence. What's on your mind?"

"It's about Vicky," he said.

Later, as we walked back to the office, Ira spoke, "Everyone knows whatever they see at my lunch table is personal and confidential. No one, the regulars at least, will say anything to anyone about what they saw or heard today. Gossip does not originate from my table at lunchtime."

Throughout the afternoon, I was constantly struck by how organized Ira was. He was the epitome of 'There is a place for everything and everything in its place.'

"Oops, it's five-thirty already. Sorry, I kept you a little later than usual, I hope you don't mind."

"I don't mind, there is so much to learn."

"Don't worry," he smiled, "You'll be up to speed in no time."

"Where was John today?" I asked.

"Oh, he was here in his office. He wanted to stay out of our way today. He didn't want to be a distraction."

———

"How was your day?" Henry asked when I returned to his home.

"I think I'm going to like it here," I answered.

"I knew you would."

Chapter 24
Settling In

After a few weeks, I settled, almost too easily, into Henry's hospitality and Bess's cooking. I knew I needed to move into my own place, but this was so comfortable, and although I was making great progress (according to both Ira and John), I was still nervous, knowing someday soon, Ira was going to declare his freedom. I envied him but dreaded the day. It was too easy for me to fall back on his knowledge.

On a Saturday morning at breakfast, Henry asked, "Are you going to the office today?"

"No, for the first time since I started, I feel comfortable taking a weekend off."

"Good, then I can take a little of your time this morning. I have something to tell you."

"Oh?"

"Yes, once we finish breakfast, let's ride up to Emma's Point. I know it is later than usual; we won't see a sunrise, but I think it might do you good. You know, you haven't been up there since you came to work down here."

"Yes, I know, I've thought about it. Going up there has always helped, it might again."

"Good, we'll go up there and ponder a bit, then I have something to show you."

As I ate, I began to think. *The last time I went to Emma's Point, Walter was with me. I thought I had it all figured out, and had a plan, but then everything fell apart on the drive back. I haven't thought about Walter or Ingrid for some time. I'm not sure I can or want to do this.*

Henry seemed to sense my apprehension, "We'll leave Winnie behind. She won't know I'm going up there because it will be late, so she won't fuss."

We walked to the Mule in silence. Then neither of us spoke as we drove up the rocky path and climbed the slope to the summit. Silently, we sat on the bench, much as we did that first day in Fillmore Park.

The sun was already well up in the sky. Its warmth bordered on the uncomfortable, especially since it was an unusually strenuous climb because of the wind.

But it wasn't difficult to contemplate. My life had changed now. I was beginning to feel comfortable here, and confident in my new situation.

I left two important things behind. I gave up hope of both seeing Walter and Ingrid again. Did I really want that?

Henry interrupted my thoughts, "We should be getting back."

We descended the trail to the Mule and then started down the hill. As we approached the house, Henry smiled, "Let's go by the widow's place first."

Rather than open the gate between the two properties, Henry drove down his lane to the road, turned, and drove toward the lane to the widow's place. He stopped as we approached the entrance. "I fixed the fence and painted a bit; tell me what you think."

A fully repaired and newly painted wooden fence lined both sides of the freshly graveled and smoothed path to the house.

"Nice," I said, "Why did you do this?"

"There's more," he answered.

I first noticed some new shrubs around the foundation, then the freshly painted porch.

"Come on, I'll show you the inside."

In the living room all the old furniture was gone and in its place was my Barcalounger, couch, and end table set up, ready for a new occupant. Missing though was new paint on the walls.

"I'll show you the kitchen," he said and led me in.

A new stove, refrigerator, and dishwasher greeted me. The old cabinets were freshly cleaned.

"Go ahead, open one," he said.

Inside the cabinets, I found new dishes, pots, and pans. The silverware drawer was freshly filled.

By now, I was beginning to understand.

"Only the bedroom is left," he grinned.

A completely new bedroom suite welcomed me.

"I didn't have the walls painted. I wanted you to choose the colors. Ed, down at Reese's Hardware is expecting you. He will send the paint and a painter. The place is yours to live in as long as you wish," he said.

"But..." I began to protest.

"Don't worry, the rent is reasonable," he laughed.

"This is too much; you shouldn't have."

"Why? You need a place of your own. Besides, we are working poor Bess too hard. Just keep the barnyard gate open. Winnie will want to come visit."

Chapter 25
My New Home

"Ed, I don't know anything about colors. Can you decide for me?"

"No, Henry wants you to feel at home at the place. I will make a suggestion though. Why don't you ask Bess? I think she would love to pick colors for you; besides, women are better at this type of thing. But don't tell her you want white," Ed answered.

～

After only two weeks of clutter, each room had a new coat on the walls. I found a desk and chair at the furniture store and had it delivered. They also had a rocking chair I liked. I bought two for the front porch.

Poor Bess, though. Her transition back to her more sedate life didn't come as soon as it might have. I asked her for help. I wanted to learn some of her easier recipes. The local pizza shop didn't deliver outside the city limits, I didn't know where to shop in town, and most importantly, I needed to learn how to make sweet tea.

～

My desk was soon inundated by an onslaught of clutter. I began making copies of old briefs, wills, and other documents. I brought books and documents home, not just to work on, but also to study. I needed to glean all the information I could from Ira before he left. He told me I could call him anytime, but I didn't want to impose on his much-deserved retirement any more than necessary. I hinted that I would be willing to buy his home library but he was reluctant.

I began to build my library. I went back to the furniture store to buy an expandable bookcase.

Still, unpacking took a surprisingly long time. The stack of boxes stored in the garage seemed endless. As I worked toward the last of them, I found a box marked only 'desk.' I didn't remember packing it; the movers must have. I carried it in, set it on the coffee table, and opened it. Inside, I found two forgotten photos–the photo of Walter and me that Will took as we walked one day, and a photo of Ingrid, the studio picture she gave me and one I believed she posed for just for me.

I held them for a while, wondering, remembering, wishing.

Misty-eyed, I placed them on the back corner of my desk, then moved them under my desk lamp, so they would be the first things I stared at each time I sat to work.

Later, when realizing how distracting they were, I moved them to the coffee table.

This new location also proved to be disconcerting. They were the last images I saw when I reclined in the Barca. Images I pondered when I closed my eyes.

Becoming acclimated to my new life was hard, unexpectedly hard. It was not so much that I missed city life; it was more the isolation I felt here. The euphoria I felt on my first visit and then my move here began to wear off.

I was beginning to make new acquaintances through work. I got to know people at the café, the grocery store, even at the filling station – I now drove my car more than ever before. The people I met were friendly, but they weren't my friends, they were Henry's. The quiet bothered me. Evenings spent on the porch alone, watching the day wither from the approaching night, next to an empty rocking chair, brought an unwelcome isolation.

Am I cut out for this life?

I drove up Henry's lane Friday evening after work. Winnie ran to meet me. "I just sat down with a glass of tea. I'll get you one if you have time to sit for a spell. Bess left me some chocolate chip cookies, the ones with pecan chunks in them. Would you like to sit?"

"Yes, I'd like to."

"What's on your mind, Son?"

Henry had an uncanny knack. He could read my mood better than either my mother or father ever could.

We sat quietly, sipping and snacking, Henry waiting for my thoughts.

"Are you busy tomorrow morning?"

"My mornings are always free; I always have time for you," he answered. "What do you have in mind?"

"I'd like to go to Emma's Point again, and I want you to go with me."

The words sounded odd. I didn't plan to ask him to go with me. Why had I?

"I'll put the top on the Mule and have it warmed up," he said.

I saw the half-smiling anticipatory grin. He sensed my unease.

Winnie was already in the Mule, resting on her blanket when I arrived. Henry came out of the door with two thermoses. "I brought each of us one. It's a might chilly this morning."

The Mule seemed to know the way and easily managed the path this morning with some expediency. My flashlight anticipated the boulders as we climbed. Winnie led us to the bench. The wind obligingly switched to our backs, making our sit more comfortable. The sun and the cumulous clouds honored us with a spectacular show.

Henry finally spoke, "What's on your mind, son?"

"I am having a hard time believing."

"Believing what?"

How does he do this? How does he know when to speak and what to say?

"Believing I belong here," I answered.

"You know you weren't happy before. You know this is a better life. You know you are accepted here."

"I know, but…"

"Do you think it's the honesty?"

"The honesty?"

"Yes. You have met many people since you moved here. They have all accepted you. Do you question the honesty in all that has happened here?"

"I haven't thought of it that way," I answered.

"Well, maybe honesty isn't the best word. Let me put it another way. do you think the people here are superficial?"

"No, I guess not."

"Then don't you think you honestly belong here?"

"I don't know yet."

"Try to understand the circumstances which caused your move. You weren't happy with your job and you met me through an almost unimaginable coincidence. The coincidence led you to a new job, a new life if you will. Do you think all this may have been fate?"

"I've never believed in fate, but when you put it that way…"

"Then what is keeping you from relishing and embracing your new life here?"

"But I still have questions."

"Don't you believe those questions can be answered better here than where you were before?"

"Yes, I suppose so."

"It's time for breakfast, let's go back down the hill," Henry smiled.

My bookcase began to fill. Ira told me of a lawyer who was closing his practice in a small town about sixty miles away.

"I took the liberty of calling him. He and John have been friendly adversaries for years. I think he would consider selling his library to you if you meet him and make a favorable impression," Ira said.

"I'll call and introduce myself," I answered.

We drove there the next Saturday.

The highway was as scenic as any I'd seen. I wondered why the population was so sparse.

"Why is there so much pristine area here?" I asked on the way.

"Most of the land around here is National Forest. The rest has soil so poor it is hard to make a living from it. If you drive on the back roads in this area, you will see many run-down shacks; the only sign left by the folks who tried to make it farming. Some of them turned to moonshine, but when the government came in, most gave up and moved on."

In a residential area off the main street, we found a sign in front of a stately old house. It read "J. P. Henderson, Attorney at Law."

"I'll wait in the car," Ira said.

The wooden steps creaked under my weight as I climbed. A porch board sank under my feet. *This is nothing like John's office.* A hand-painted *Welcome, Step Inside* sign hung by a single hook next to a heavy wooden door. I ignored the sign and knocked.

The old oak door swung open, and an overweight, squat, balding man with wire glasses hanging precariously from his nose smiled up at me.

"James Williams?"

"Yes."

"Come in son, I've been expecting you," he said.

"Thank you, Mr. Henderson."

"Just J. P. if you like. May I call you James?"

"Yes, thank you," I answered. "Ira Jacobs sent me. I am beginning employment with John Gray and would like to build a home law library. Ira says you are retiring and might be willing to sell at least a part of yours."

"Come in and sit a spell, James," he said.

His eyes sparkled as we began. "My dad started this practice over fifty years ago. He took me in when I was just a pup, like John is doing with you. Dad died about thirty-five years ago. Been here alone ever since. It's time for me to give it up. We have some good lawyers in the area now and I have a little place on the edge of town with flowers and a garden that needs tending.

"Ira tells me you are new to the Carolinas, down here from New York. Made friends with old Henry Crane through his daughter. Tell me, how do you see your future?"

I told J. P. about the firm in New York and why I left. I said I liked North Carolina the instant I crossed the state line for the first time. I wanted to grow roots here.

We fell into casual conversation. It felt like a visit with an old friend. It was J. P. who turned the conversation back to the books. "I could take them home after I close my office, but I fear I might be tempted if they're still around. I'd like to be rid of the entire lot. I could sell them by auction or maybe online, but don't need the bother."

"I'd like to buy them all, sir, but not sure I can afford them now," I said.

"Son, I feel they would be in the best place possible if you had them." Then with a sly grin said, "I'm sure you can afford them."

Only now I remembered poor Ira was still waiting in the car and went out to ask him a favor.

"Can you drive my car back? I need to rent a small truck."

"You made a deal, huh?"

"Yes, he made me an offer I couldn't refuse," I laughed. "I bought everything but his personal papers."

"I thought you might. I know the guy who runs a rental place," he said.

He knows everything and everybody. I'll never learn all this.

"How do you know all these people?" I asked.

"I was green like you once. It just takes time, Jim."

With renewed vigor, I began to study. I went through John's old cases and studied his references to better understand the what and why in his work.

Evenings, I would study all I could find on the subject. Many times I became so engrossed that I'd be surprised how late it was when I glanced at my watch.

Late one afternoon, John asked me to come to his office.

"It seems you've settled in nicely. I am happy with your progress, your attitude, and your instincts. Ira and I have been talking. I believe it is time. Yesterday, I accepted his written two-week notice. Beginning next Monday, the position is yours."

Even with the understanding when John brought me into the firm, the thought that one day Ira would leave and I would be on my own seemed remote. Today was the day I both hoped for and dreaded.

"I'll do my best," was the only response I could muster.

"I know you will," John answered.

"I guess he told you," Ira said when I returned to my desk.

"Yes. I'll sure miss you," I said.

"I know, but it's not like I'm leaving the country, or dying yet," he laughed. "If you need anything, call me, I'll be happy to help, but the job is yours now. All I ask is, do it the way it should be done."

"I will."

~

On Monday, my first day without Ira, I opened the office door, turned on the lights, and started the coffee maker. It wasn't so much, I had done this many times already, but today, the office was mine–well, John's, but the front was mine. I sat at my desk, arranged some papers, then leaned back, closed my eyes, and took a long deep breath.

The phone rang.

"Good morning, is this the law firm of John Gray and James Williams?" a familiar voice asked.

"Good morning, Henry," I laughed.

"I wanted to be the first. Have a great day," he said.

The phone went dead. I grinned.

I am home!

Chapter 26
Everyday Life

I settled in. Each morning as I turned on the lights in the office, I felt more at ease. I worked diligently on each brief John wanted. Our phone rang occasionally, but each call was either congratulatory or a referral to John. I don't know why I expected catastrophe or mayhem, but I did. No crying housewife bursting through the door, swearing about her cheating husband. No embittered farmer amid a dispute with a neighbor. Nothing.

Not to say it was boring, but it was quiet.

Most days at lunch at the café, I ate alone. My only interruptions came from Liz,

"Ira tells me you're single."

"Yes." I didn't feel the need to elaborate or tell her or anyone else that I was once married to Henry's daughter.

"Are you looking for that special friend?"

"No. I'm still getting acclimated. I don't have the time and I've been so busy, I haven't thought much about my social life."

"Don't you think you should? There seems to be an interest in 'that new guy down at the lawyer's office.'"

"Maybe someday, but not now."

"I could set you up. I could start a lottery. You know, draw names, bring them to you one at a time. How about a new one to share lunch with every day for a week? Maybe you could start a spreadsheet to keep track. List their pros and cons. That sort of thing," she laughed.

"No, you know lunches are reserved for business. It's what John wants and Ira did. I am going to do the same."

"Just let me know when you are ready, but don't wait too long. You won't be a hot commodity forever, you know. Someone else might move into your territory," she laughed.

I knew she was joking at my expense. I knew that she knew she was making me uncomfortable. I also knew there was an element of sincerity in her voice.

Maybe someday, but not now.

Friday of my second week alone in the office, I went to lunch as usual, almost hoping a potential client might join me. As I entered, I saw a person with a hoodie sitting with their back to the door. I approached the table with a mixture of apprehension and glee.

I could see it was a man but I couldn't see his face.

As I reached to pull my chair back, a face appeared from the sweatshirt. Under the brim of a baseball cap a scruffy beard appeared, then a smile.

"I thought I'd join you today. How do you like my beard? It's only two weeks old, but it will fill out more. I always wondered how I'd look with one. What do you think?" Ira asked.

"You look like a vagrant," I laughed.

"I know, but I like it. I've wanted to grow one for over thirty years, but John would always say, 'It won't look professional.'

"I wondered how it's going, so I thought I'd drop in, check on you; you know, answer any questions. This is the end of your second week, and you haven't called. I'm a little disappointed but can't say I'm surprised."

"I didn't want to bother you," I answered. "I thought a person who worked all his life deserved to be left alone for as long as he wants."

"I've tried to sleep in, but just can't break the habit. I get up at the same time as always.

"Uh oh, Liz is giving me the eye. She has someone who wants to talk to you, I better go so you can get on with your business lunch," Ira said.

I watched as he walked toward the counter, said something to Liz as he passed, and then sat on a stool, alone.

Does he miss working that much? Will I be like Ira someday?

Sometimes my mind wanders to places it doesn't need to go.

"Good morning, sir, have a seat. Would you like some coffee? How can I help you?" I said to the man.

My life began to assume some order. I fell into routines, both at work and at home. I convinced Liz to abandon the hunt. "I am not interested at the present. Someday, if I feel the urge, you will be the first to know," I reassured her.

Visits from Henry became less and less frequent. He was comfortable alone. He spent his time making the rounds, so to speak; pie for lunch, meatloaf for dinner, coffee with his fellow farmers, helping at the Salvation Army Store, and talking up the local widow ladies. He lived alone, but he certainly wasn't lonely.

The local YMCA had a racquetball court, but it was almost abandoned. I talked the local manager into approaching the few locals who played at one time, and we started an informal league. Most of my opponents were older men. Even with diminished skills, they felt rejuvenated when they scored a good point or made an excellent shot. And relaxing after the games was great. These guys had some stories to tell, and they loved having someone fresh to lie to. I especially enjoyed it when, after doubles, or when a couple of guys who hadn't played with us today dropped in. After sitting back and enjoying the banter, each trying to tell a more colorful tale, I began to feel accepted.

Life was good here. Most of the folks have lived here all their lives. Those who didn't, like me, had moved here for one reason or another, and stayed, just as I expected I would. I learned the few locals who moved away did so because of family issues, like divorce, or a sick relative somewhere that needed help. A few who left did so because they didn't think there were enough amenities here.

Chapter 27
The Phone Call

Today was an unusually busy one. Three clients, two of them new, came to us with issues. John was due in court next week. Between interruptions, I was trying to compose an opening for him. I assumed the next few days would be hectic, so I brought his speech home to work on.

His trial was going to be sensitive; a divorce between two people who had been married a long time. John was good friends with both and hadn't been able to excuse himself. The soon-to-be ex-wife insisted he represent her. This was made worse because there was a third party, a man who also was a friend of both parties.

I worked all day on the opening paragraph without much success. I made three different drafts and wanted to ask John to choose but thought I should work it out myself. He was under enough strain already, caught between three friends.

My phone rang.

It wasn't the familiar ringtone of John, Henry, or even Ira. I let it go to messages.

I purposely left it on the kitchen table so it wouldn't bother me while I worked. *I wish I had set it to vibrate.*

About two minutes later, it rang again. Grudgingly, I got up from my desk and walked toward the kitchen. It quit ringing before I got to it. *I'll turn it off, then get a soda from the refrigerator, and go back to work.*

I was startled when it rang a third time as I held it. *I may as well answer. Whoever it is may keep interrupting until I do.*

"Hello."

"Hello, James."

It was Ingrid's voice. *But why is she calling me James? I thought we were past this. When last we spoke, she called me Jim, and I was sure she was getting close to using Jimmie. Why James again? Was this about Dylan? Did she have good news to share? Good for her, bad for me?*

"Hi, Ingrid."

"James, we've found Walter!"

My world collapsed. My legs went limp. My brain ceased to function. I reached for a chair to stabilize but needed to sit. I clenched the phone to keep it from falling. Tears gushed, instantly dripping from my chin. My heart raced. Then came the thoughts–first elation, then guilt. It was weeks since I last thought about my dog. *How could I have abandoned the best friend I ever had? Why didn't I continue searching for him? I thought of Fillmore Park, Mike the squirrel., the biker punks, the stolen money, the day he cut his leg, the old man on the bench. This was the phone call I hoped for, waited for, wished for, and had given up hope for.*

"James, are you still there?" she asked.

"Yes, sorry. Is he okay? Where is he? I'll go get him. I can leave right away."

"It's not that simple."

"What do you mean, it's not that simple?'

"He's not well. He can't travel."

"What?"

Suddenly, I felt sick. I thought I was going to vomit. I scrambled from the chair and rushed toward the bathroom, still clutching my phone.

"Why?"

"He's not well," she repeated.

"You already said that."

"Please, James, let me explain."

I stopped short of the bathroom and sat on the edge of my bed.

"What?" I yelled.

"Please, try to stay calm and listen. They found Walter…"

"Who found him?"

"Please, James, just listen."

"Okay."

"They found Walter in a little town in south-central Pennsylvania. He was tied to a light post in front of a humane shelter there. Employees found him unresponsive lying in the grass. They carried him inside, wrapped him in blankets, and called the local veterinarian clinic to put him down…"

"Put him down! What the hell?"

"Please, just listen. At the clinic, they discovered he was chipped, so they decided to do what they could for him while they tried to find his owner. He was registered at the Fillmore Clinic so they called and talked to Dr. Schmidt. He remembered Walter. Apparently, you two made a good impression; anyway, Dr. Schmidt called me."

"And?"

"I called the clinic in Pennsylvania. I told them I knew Walter, and I knew his owner. I begged them to do what they could for him because he is loved and wanted.

"Walter was emaciated; he was nothing but skin and bones. They don't know who brought him in or even why, considering his condition. And their security cameras don't show that part of the property."

"I don't care about the details about the shelter, tell me more about Walter."

"He can't walk, or even stand. He can't even lift his head. His eyes are open, but they don't focus. They are trying to keep him alive, but right now… well, right now, it is too soon to know. I talked to the vet. He seems caring and very competent. I asked him to do all he could."

"Tell me where he is, I want to go see him."

"I understand. I knew you would say that. I've thought about it and don't think you should. At least not yet. I don't think Walter would know you were there, and if he did, the excitement might be too much for him."

"But I want to go. I can leave right now."

"Jimmie, please trust me. I think this is best. Let's wait, at least until the weekend. Maybe we will know more then."

"Okay, I guess."

"Jimmie, promise me you'll leave them alone while they try to save him."

"I'm not sure I can."

"I know, but you need to think of what is best for Walter. When he gets better, you two will have all the time you want to be together. It will

be like it was before, only better. Please wait, I think it's best.
  "Jimmie, I'm sorry."
  My phone went silent, then flashed "call ended."

Chapter 28
Finding Walter

The phone fell from my hand and landed on my desk, face up. The words "call ended" flashed for a few seconds, then the screen turned black. It lay there, a vacant, dark screen staring at me. I could only stare back.

Several minutes passed before I finally began forming thoughts. Was I sleeping? Was this all a dream? Did I just talk to Ingrid? Was Walter coming home?

Sleep came hard that night, and morning came long before I was ready. I woke to more questions. What was I going to do about John's presentation? How was I going to bring Walter home without compromising the firm? Had Ingrid told me the whole truth about Walter's health? Why did she finally call me Jimmie?

I scrambled to assemble my papers, stuffed them in my bag, showered, shaved, grabbed a cup of coffee on my way out the door, and stopped at the filling station for a bagel on the way to the office.

Hurriedly, I turned on the lights, started a fresh pot, and then sat to finish John's paper.

"Good morning. You are a mess this morning. Do you not feel well?" he asked.

"I'm sorry, it was a short night," I answered.

"I hope you weren't up working on our opening."

"No, although I am checking it now, readying it for print."

"Are you sure you aren't ill? It is okay to stay home when you are sick, you know."

"No, it isn't that. I received a phone call last night. They found my dog."

"Your dog? I wasn't aware you owned a dog."

"I lost him several months ago. On my return from my first trip down here, Henry originally asked me to come for a visit. Walter got away at a rest stop in Virginia and has been missing ever since."

"Walter?"

"Yes, Walter, he's my dog."

"Is your dog alright? Where did they find him? Do you need time to retrieve him?"

"It's not that simple. Walter is not well. It seems he was abandoned. He was found in south-central Pennsylvania; someone left him at a humane shelter. He's being cared for at a veterinarian clinic there."

"I can finish my opening remarks if you need to go."

"No, it won't help. There is nothing for me to do but wait and pray. I'll keep working until there are new developments."

—❧—

I called Ingrid.

With a calm voice she answered, "Hello, James,"

"Hi, I called to check on Walter. Do you have any new information?"

"I called this morning. He hasn't changed. He is neither better nor worse. It's too soon to know. It is going to take time. I know it is hard, but we'll have to be patient. I told the clinic we'd like to move him as soon as possible. They said they would keep me apprised of his condition."

"Will you give me the name and number of the place?"

"Yes, but remember, you promised. Don't show up at their door unannounced. We need to do what is best for Walter."

"Okay, I'll wait, and I'll keep my promise, but I can't be patient."

"I know."

—❧—

I couldn't stand it anymore, being patient. I called after lunch while John was in court.

"Hello, my name is James Williams. I am the owner of the black Lab you have. The one you just got from your humane shelter. The sick one."

"Yes, we have your dog. He is not doing very well, but his health hasn't deteriorated."

"Is he going to be okay?" I asked the receptionist.

The phone was silent for a moment, then, "There is a chance he will get better, but it is not a good chance. It would be easier if he were younger. He must have been in good health once because he seems to have the inner strength, and a will to fight. We are a small clinic, but we are doing the best we can. Our vet is top-notch; your dog is getting excellent care. I wish I could tell you more. It will take some time for him to regain his health if he does. And he probably will never be the dog he was before," she said.

"Can you tell me how long?"

"I'm sorry, it's impossible to predict at this time."

After the call ended, I suffered the inevitable selfish thought; who is paying for this? Then felt small and callous for thinking about money.

I suffered through an agonizing next few days. The importance of John's court case was the only thing that kept me remotely focused. I was thankful for my job. If it weren't for the responsibility and pride I felt, I wouldn't have been able to concentrate on anything but Walter. Still, it was an excruciatingly long week. Every morning I called the clinic to ask about Walter. Then I called Ingrid to have her interpret what I was told.

I tried to mask my urgency and worry; I didn't want to be a nuisance, but I needed to know, so I didn't feel apologetic.

Thursday's call gave me some encouragement. The clinic told me Walter raised his head and was trying to stand.

Knowing he was trying gave me a sliver of hope.

Maybe, just maybe.

I asked Henry to join me for dinner. I felt a whisp of hope now and wanted to share it.

"Walter is getting better," I said. "He is going to be okay, I know it."

"That's great," he smiled. "But you have to remember, this could take a long time."

"I know."

My phone rang. It was Ingrid (I'd put her number back in my contacts list).

"James, it's Ingrid."

"Hi, I'm glad you called. I am having dinner with my friend Henry."

"Please say 'Hi' to him for me. James, I talked at length to my colleague who is caring for Walter this afternoon. He feels Walter is well enough to move, but still needs more care and rehabilitation. We decided to move him here…"

"Here?"

"Yes, here, to my clinic. We have better facilities and I have three fellow doctors. We feel we can give Walter the around-the-clock attention he will need as he heals."

"But…"

"Hear me out, please. I have some vacation time to use. With your permission, of course, I am going to bring him here. We have a van we use as a portable clinic. I am going to drive the van there and bring Walter back. Molly, my assistant, will go with me. We are going to leave early in the morning. We will drive over, stay one night on the way, then arrive late Saturday morning. We should be able to transfer Walter to the van and return. We will have to stop somewhere on the way back and have agreed to sleep in shifts at a motel, so one of us can be in the van all night."

"Can I meet you there?"

"I've thought about it, but don't think it can work. If you drove up, you would have to drive your car back, or the three of us would take turns driving two vehicles. When we return, you will still have to drive back to North Carolina. I know it will be hard for you, but why don't you wait until we get Walter here, and let him recuperate a little before you visit? The trip will be hard on Walter, so you may be disappointed when you see him."

"I can't stand all this waiting."

"I know, but think of Walter. This is going to be a long, hard struggle for him."

"Okay, I suppose, but are you sure?"

"I think this is best."

"Did you hear all that Henry?"

"Yes. I think she is doing the right thing, Jim. Let's trust her judgment; she is a professional. We need to be thinking of Walter's health first. All the rest can be managed."

My weekend was miserable. The thought of Ingrid driving to see Walter, and then taking him back to her clinic was unbearable. It was over a week ago since he'd been found at the humane shelter and I still hadn't been able to see him. No one even sent me a picture of confirmation, which, when I thought about it, was probably good. *They must not want me to see him like he is.*

The following week was better only in the sense that the trial ended abruptly, and we had an unanticipated lull. John managed to avoid the resentment of both protagonists, and the verdict was agreeable. Also, and more importantly to me, Ira returned from visiting his brother and sister-in-law in Arizona.

When I told Ira and John my lost dog story, they happily agreed to let Ira fill in for me for a few days. "I should be back Wednesday morning," I told them.

I called Ingrid.

"I'll send you driving instructions and reserve a motel room close to our clinic," she told me. "It will be great to see you again. I am eager for us to spend time together. Brace yourself though. Walter is not the same dog you remember. It has been a long time. I hope he will recognize you."

Walter and I had been together for years. I couldn't imagine we wouldn't recognize each other.

This drive was not like the others. Without the frequent Walter stops, I made the trip in one long traveling day.

Still, it was almost nine o'clock when I drove into the motel parking lot. I rushed into the lobby, checked in, and left without taking anything to my room.

The clinic was dark, except for one light in the lobby. I knocked on the locked door.

Ingrid appeared and rushed toward me. My eyes were already tearing. My promised attempt to keep my composure vanished. She opened the door and hugged me. Her arms held me so tightly, I couldn't catch my breath.

"Oh, Jimmie, I'm so glad to see you. It has been so long."

I didn't expect this. I didn't know what I expected, but not this, definitely not this. From the time I first heard her utter Dylan's name, I thought I'd lost her. But this? I didn't know how to react, so I didn't. She must think she is hugging a statue.

She finally let go, stepped back, and smiled. Tears were flowing from two sets of eyes. "Now remember, he's been through a lot. Try not to be disappointed."

"How can I possibly be disappointed? I've been without him for months."

"He's not the same. Be quiet, we don't want to startle him. He is probably asleep."

We crept down the hallway, carefully opened the door to the back, and approached his cage.

I saw a mottled mound of black hair with gray strands scattered through it. I saw ribs poking from under the tight skin like they were trying to escape their bodily restraints. I saw his side raise only slightly with each labored breath. This must be a mistake. This isn't Walter. He's a lot bigger than this, and his coat is sleek and black.

Like she was speaking to a newborn baby, Ingrid said, "Walter, there is someone here to see you."

An ear twitched on the far end of the scraggly mound. Then a head slowly moved. I could see one dull eye. The mischievous sparkle was gone.

"Hi, boy," I blurted then lost my composure. I started crying. Unable to stand, I fell to my knees. My fingers clung to the cage door. Holding on was all that kept me from collapsing completely. Walter lifted his head, his sunken eyes glimmered; he smiled.

No one can tell me dogs can't smile.

I was sobbing uncontrollably. A flood of tears covered my cheeks. "Can you open the cage?" I begged.

A weeping Ingrid fumbled with the latch.

My trembling hand touched Walter's side. I could feel his heart racing.

"I'll get you a stool," Ingrid said.

Motionless, we sat, each of us on a stool, my hand on Walter's side; Ingrid's hand on mine.

"Can we take him out?" I finally asked.

"Yes, but understand, his legs are weak. He can stand but can only walk a few steps. We also need to remember he is tired and should be sleeping. We dare not do too much."

"I just want to hold him."

We pulled him from his cage as gently as possible. He stood on shaky legs unwilling or unable to move. I embraced him with my arms and held his frail body to keep him from falling. Neither of us could move.

"Can I stay with him tonight?"

"It is against our policy, but yes. I'll get you a pillow and some blankets."

"Can you let Walter lay with me?"

"We don't allow that either, but yes, you can do that too."

⸺

Daylight beginning to stream through a window woke me. Walter was lying motionless beside me. I placed my hand on his side to search for a heartbeat.

It was faint, but it was there. I tried to remain still but couldn't resist. I began to stroke Walter's scrawny body.

When I heard his faint whimper, I began to cry again. Walter had been lost for almost a year – a year!

"I heard some noise, I knew you guys were up," Ingrid smiled. She stood, gazing down at Walter and me. Her hair was mussed and she was wearing the same clothes as last night.

"Our receptionist, Linda, will be in shortly. I need to get home and clean up. I'm on duty today."

"Have you been here all night?"

She smiled sheepishly, "Yes, we have two pillows, several blankets, and a slightly uncomfortable couch in the lobby. Don't worry about Linda; she's nice, you'll like her. I'll talk to her before I leave. She'll understand. You should probably clean up too. Tom will be here to check on Walter."

"Can I wait until he gets here?"

"Yes, he won't mind. I've told him about you. You'll like him too."

⸺

The motel clerk gave me an odd gaze when I walked through the lobby with frazzled hair, in wrinkled clothes. He probably thinks I'm just another drunken salesman on the road. Damn! That made me think of Dylan.

Chapter 29
The Healing

I showered, put on a fresh shirt, and returned. Ingrid was with clients, so Molly took me back, helped Walter out of his cage, spread a blanket, and left us.

"I need to go back tomorrow, can I take Walter with me?" I begged Ingrid.

"I won't forbid it, but I don't think you should. Why don't you leave him for another week? Then we'll decide," she answered.

It was the wrong answer. I wanted to take him back. If we left first thing in the morning, we could avoid the interstate, take some of the older highways, cruise along slowly, and stop a few times.

I wanted to take my dog home!

Finally, Ingrid finished work for the day and came back to sit with us.

"We should get something to eat," she said.

If this is my last day, I want to spend all the time I can here with her and Walter. "Can we order something and have it delivered?" I asked.

"I was thinking something nicer, but I understand. We have a good Chinese restaurant close by. They deliver."

"What is Walter's diet? Can he eat solid food?" I asked.

"Yes, he's been on solid food for several days, why do you ask?"

"Can he eat pizza?"

"Pizza?"

"Yes, could we order pizza and give Walter a slice?"

"I suppose. Although I must say, this surprises me. Why would you want to share a pizza?"

"When Walter and I were alone in the apartment, we often ordered pizza. I would manage a couple of slices, then he'd eat the rest."

"Okay, there's a pizza place not too far. What kind do you want?"

"Pepperoni is his favorite."

"Your dog has a favorite pizza?"

"Yes. Pepperoni, please."

The smell of fresh pepperoni pizza several minutes later made his nose twitch.

Ingrid found a card table and unfolded it, moved our stools up to it, laid out our table, and then gave Walter the box with the two remaining slices.

"He usually gets half," I said.

She smiled and said, "There are three of us tonight. He'll have to share."

We sat in silence, Ingrid and I enjoying our pizza. Walter finished his and begged for more.

"How was your drive to get Walter the other day?" I asked.

She broke into tears.

"Did I say something wrong?"

"No, it's just… I wasn't going to tell you, but I guess…"

I knew I shouldn't pry, but I did. "You weren't going to tell me what?"

Ingrid left the room and came back shortly dabbing her eyes with a tissue. Then she began.

"Molly and I started driving shortly after work to get Walter. I wanted to leave sooner, but things got hectic here that afternoon. Anyway, it was late before we left. I knew we couldn't get to Walter that night, so I thought we'd stop along the way and stay for the night."

"That makes sense," I said.

"Please, Jim, this is hard for me."

"Sorry, I won't interrupt again."

"As I was saying, we knew we would need to stop for the night. I thought the town where Dylan lives wasn't too far out of the way, so I suggested we take a detour so we could surprise him. I thought we could get a nice dinner somewhere, the three of us."

Oh, God, Dylan again? Here we go, just what I didn't want to hear.

"Molly thought it was a good idea, so we put a new destination in the GPS. His house wasn't hard to find and the computer led us right to it."

Jeez, why did I have to ask?

Ingrid continued, "Molly and I went to the door together since she knows him too. I was a little nervous, thinking we should have called first, but I rang the doorbell. We didn't hear a response, so I pushed the button again.

"A female voice from inside yelled, 'Just a minute, I'm busy.' Shortly, a woman came to the door. A nice-looking woman with a baby in her arms.

"I said, 'I'm sorry to bother you. We're hunting for the home of Dylan Callahan. We must have the wrong address.'

"She said, 'You have the correct address, this is Dylan's place.'"

"Is he here?" I asked.

"She said, 'No, but he should be, he left me home with the kids. He's probably out somewhere, chasing skirts again.'

"I was so embarrassed, I couldn't think of anything to say. Molly and I rushed to the van, drove to the next town, and found a motel.

"Oh, Jimmie, I thought he was the one. I never dreamed…"

I couldn't react. I knew I should but didn't know how. How does a person react when someone they care about has a broken heart and it makes you feel great?

Finally, I muttered, without conviction, "I'm sorry."

We finished our dinner without another word.

I wanted to do or say something but didn't know what, and I didn't have a clue what Ingrid expected from me.

Finally, she said, "I'll get you the pillow and blanket. I need to run an errand in the morning before I come to work, so please don't leave before I get here."

"Can I take Walter with me?"

"Not yet, please. We can talk about it tomorrow."

I snuggled up to Walter, and with bellies full of pepperoni pizza, we soon fell asleep.

"Mr. Williams, it's time to get up, we open soon," Molly said.

Walter stood over me and gently licked my face. This was the first time he'd stood on his own.

"Hi, did you have a good night?" Ingrid asked.

"Yes, can you get Walter ready? I am ready to take him home."

"He isn't going, Jim. He can hardly stand on his own. He needs at least another week. I don't think you realize how far he has come in this last week, and how far he needs to go. You can't take him home, and then leave him alone during the day. He still needs professional care."

"But Henry will be there, and his dog, Winnie, too."

"I'm sorry, Jim, it's not good enough. Walter isn't well; he can easily relapse. I told you earlier that you needed to be patient. You still do."

"I think you are being too strict, but I'm going to oblige you. I'll go home because I promised you, but you need to promise me that as soon as he is able, I can come get him."

"I promise as soon as he is able, but I think I should bring him. I want to monitor Walter's ride back, and if I take the van, I will have everything he might need along the way. Once I get there, I will want to see the facilities at your clinic. I still have three vacation days left, and remember, we are equipped for this sort of thing."

"Okay, but I am not going back in there to say goodbye. I don't think I could stand it, and Walter would know."

The drive back was almost as hard as the day I drove back to New York after I lost him. Now knowing Walter was alive and would probably get well, and having to leave without him a second time was too much.

I called Henry on the way.

"Are you bringing Walter? Winnie wants to know," he asked.

"No, they made me leave him. They told me he wasn't well enough to travel yet."

"Did you tell them I was here to help take care of him?"

"Yes, but I wasn't convincing. Ingrid said she wanted to bring him herself and see our clinic's facilities."

"I'm sorry, I hoped…"

"I did too."

I called Ingrid every night the following week.

During each phone call, she was optimistic, but wouldn't promise. She said he could get up on his own easily, and each day he was more stable and walked a little more.

On the sixth evening, I asked, "How's he doing today?"

"We are outside. It is such a beautiful day here, I thought he'd like to lay in the sun for a while. Besides, Dylan's monthly visit was today, and I didn't want to see him, let alone talk. Molly is out here too."

I didn't answer, but today I didn't feel any guilt about being happy to hear the news. I shouldn't even think this, but I wasn't sure which made me happier–Walter lying in the sun, or more news about Dylan. Now, in the most selfish sort of way, I was glad she'd met him. It was tough for me while they were together but after her relationship with such a sleazy character…

Ira was glad I was back. "It didn't take long to get used to retirement," he told me. "It is nice to sleep in whenever the spirit moves me. Your job is safe from me," he laughed.

For a second week, I called Ingrid every day. In the beginning, I called her first thing in the morning, but she protested. "It's too early, I have rounds to make early every day, and it includes checking on Walter. You're asking me questions before I have an opportunity to know the answers."

This was frustrating, but I agreed to call during our lunch hours. That didn't work either, because I might be sitting with a client at the café. So we agreed that she would call me as she drove home from work. I didn't like it, but I reconciled it as the best bad compromise.

At the end of almost two weeks of anguish, she called me as she drove home and said, "I think it is time."

Thankfully, I was home alone, but still wondered if Henry could hear my exhilaration at his place almost a mile away. "Woo Hoo!" I screamed. "Shall I come get him?"

"No, we talked about that, remember? The ride there is going to be stressful for him. I am going to use my three days of vacation and bring him. I want to go to your clinic and talk to them about what Walter's been through and the care he still needs. He's still not the same dog he was." She paused, then said, "And never will be."

The last part, 'never will be' sucked my breath out of me. She'd said it before, but I ignored the thought. Now, it was about to become reality.

It caught me off guard and I lost my train of thought, "Well, yeah, that will work," I stammered.

"Can you recommend a motel?"

This caught me off guard too. "I can do better. You can stay here, I have an extra bedroom."

The words fell out, without any real thought. "I mean…"

"A motel room will do just fine," she answered.

An awkward silence followed. This was a situation I caused by not thinking before speaking.

"It's alright. Molly will be with me and we can share a motel room. It will be less awkward that way."

"I could take vacation too." I knew I shouldn't; we were busy at the office.

"No, you needn't do that. I want Walter to stay at your clinic for a few days, and I'd like to see your community and the surroundings."

"Henry will be glad to be your guide," I said, again without knowing if it could work.

"I'll drive down Sunday, then take Walter to the clinic on Monday morning."

"Okay, see you then. I can't wait."

I was so happy I was bursting and felt compelled to share my news. I called Henry, "Walter is coming home."

Chapter 30
The Reunion

Mine was a weekend filled with anxiety and anticipation. I spent both days burning off energy by cleaning. I cleaned the house. I organized my desk and filed papers. I raked the front yard, twice. I walked the lane with a trash bag. I dug Walter's bed out of the closet, then spent the longest time trying to decide whether to wash it. I did. I thought about putting up a welcome home banner but decided not to. He couldn't read it anyway and Ingrid might think it inappropriate.

On the day they were to arrive, I carried a folding chair to the end of my drive. Winnie and Henry waited on the porch.

I knew they were close because Ingrid texted me from town, but still the next few minutes dragged on.

Finally, a white van with printing on the side appeared in the distance. I could make out the word "Veterinary." I couldn't (and didn't make much of an effort to) control myself. I ran to meet it.

Walter is home!

Ingrid stopped, I climbed in on the passenger side, and like I was riding on a float in a homecoming parade, we drove up to the house, me waving like some silly teenage boy.

Winnie and Henry sprang from the porch and stood at the end of the drive, eager to meet us as we stopped.

Introductions didn't take long, "Ingrid, I'd like you to meet my friend, Henry. Henry, this is Ingrid. I've told you about her. She's the one who's nursed Walter back to health. And this is Winnie, she's Henry's dog and Walter's best friend, in the dog world, that is."

"And this is Molly. She works at our clinic. She has been invaluable in helping Walter. Our clinic couldn't function without her," Ingrid said.

"Hi Winnie," Molly said, as she leaned to pat her head. "Would you like to see Walter?"

She slid the van door open and she and Ingrid climbed in, opened the cage door, and helped Walter to his feet. The step down to the ground was too high for him, so they helped him down. Instantly it became a Winnie–Walter reunion. With a ton of joy and an ounce of jealousy, I watched. Winnie frolicked around the unsteady Walter. She galloped up and down the lane and ran circles around our little group. Walter broke from my grasp and vainly tried to follow. When Winnie realized Walter couldn't keep up, she came back and lovingly walked by his side, at his speed, gently brushing him as they moved.

Winnie returned when Henry called, and then the six of us made our way to the porch where Winnie and Walter collapsed - side by side.

"This has to be the best dog reunion of all time," Henry said.

I escaped to the kitchen and brought out sweet tea and chocolate cookies for four (Bess made them for me just this morning) and fresh water and dog chewies for two.

I imagined the image we made–four adults sitting and watching two dogs lying side by side on a blanket, all this on the porch of a distinctive older cottage. This time the picture would be a Norman Rockwell painting, with the picket fence in the foreground leading to my home.

We sat quietly for a while, watching and smiling, sipping our tea, and eating cookies until the plate was empty.

"Henry, will you stay for dinner? It won't be fancy, just pizza from town," I asked.

"No, I think I should be getting along. Winnie can stay though, the gate is open; she knows the way home. If she wants to come, that is."

We watched as Henry shuffled out to his Mule, climbed in, and drove off.

"He seems like a nice man," Ingrid said.

"He's my best friend here. He's honest, intelligent, and has been so good to me. I'd still be alone and miserable in the apartment back in New York if it weren't for him."

I scooched my chair closer and touched the back of her hand. "Thanks so much for all you've done too. I'd still be alone and miserable without Walter if it weren't for you. I am very happy right now."

She smiled, but not at me. I could sense she was lost in thought; I hoped they were good ones. And about me.

We sat for what seemed forever but was probably only a few minutes. "Jimmie, we need to be going. We haven't checked into the motel yet, and this has been a long, and in a good way, exhausting day. We'll be back in the morning to take Walter to the clinic. We need to meet their staff and discuss Walter's care," She said.

"Can't you both stay here, tomorrow I mean?"

"No Jimmie, Walter needs to be examined. We'll be back by the time you get home from work. But Walter is going to need to stay at the clinic during the day for quite some time. They will want to watch his progress. Understand, if he gets worse–and he might, he still isn't strong–they may want to keep him nights too. We have to do what's best for him. You should know that by now."

"But…"

"You promised, remember?"

"Whatever you say, you're the doc," I answered.

Boy, you sounded dumb. It just came out. I can't believe I said that.

Walter slept on the bed with me. I knew this could easily turn into a bad habit, but tonight was not a night for discipline.

His whining woke me. He was hungry. This is one habit he hadn't changed. Before I lost him, I never worried about oversleeping, even on weekends. Walter always woke up before me, and he always woke up hungry.

I trudged to the kitchen, retrieved some of Ingrid's special dog food, poured him a bowl, and started the coffee. I peered through the window and saw the clinic's van coming. Still in my pajamas, I wasn't ready to entertain guests, especially guests of this importance. I ran for the bedroom, threw on yesterday's clothes, did a quick brush job on my hair, and ran back to the kitchen to pretend I was awake for some time.

With my cup in hand, I answered the door, "Come in."

How does she do it? Here I am wearing yesterday's wrinkled shirt and a pair of jeans, barefoot, greeting a woman who this early in the morning is already ravishing.

"Hi, I thought I should get an early start today. I want to get Walter to the clinic and meet the people there. I want to spend time helping him get acclimated. Hopefully, it will be an easy adjustment, since he's been penned up so much in the last two weeks. But now that he has been home and seen you, well, we'll see. How did you two do last night?"

"We're okay. Happy, really. It was great, feeling his warmth all night."

"Better be careful with that," she laughed. "You could be starting a habit you can't break."

We took our coffee to the table. I wanted to go to the porch, but it was too cold. Walter lay between us getting a two-fer (as in both of us petting him at the same time.)

I heard scratching at the door and got up to let Winnie in.

I sipped my coffee and enjoyed the perfection of my morning. Me, Ingrid, Molly, Walter, and Winnie, all together in my kitchen.

The euphoria ended with the morning sun burning through the window, a sign telling me it was time to begin. With regret I said, "I need to get ready for work."

"I know, I need to get going. I told them I'd be in early with Walter."

From my porch, I watched the woman I wanted walk the dog she'd found toward her van.

Life is good!

About eleven o'clock, Ingrid appeared at our office.

Still as stunning as the first time I saw her in the Fillmore Street Clinic, she strolled to my office, sat in the seat I offered, smiled, and said, "I think Walter is going to do nicely. I planned to stay longer today but didn't see the need. The people there are nice and seem very competent, and the facility is very clean."

"Would you like to join me for lunch? Nothing fancy. I go to the café every day and sit at a reserved table in the back of the room so people who need to talk but can't get here during the day have a place to bring their issues. Most days, no one joins me."

"I'd like to, but Henry is taking me to Joy's for lunch, then this afternoon he is going to be my tour guide. You don't mind, do you?"

Of course I minded. She was here. I wanted to spend every minute possible with her. And here was Henry, keeping her away. But if she liked what she saw… I am getting ahead of myself.

"Of course not. Henry loves to show off his town. Who knows, you might like it here" I said.

Why did I add the last sentence?

❧

She was sitting alone on the porch with a glass of tea when I came home after work.

"Where is Walter?" I asked.

"He's with Winnie. He didn't want to come home, so I left him."

"Where is Molly?"

"She stayed at the clinic. Tom is taking her for dinner later, then back to the motel."

"Tom?"

"He's the vet there. They seemed to hit it off."

"Would you like to get something to eat, maybe meatloaf at the Family Café?"

"Okay, but can we come back here? I'd like to sit on your porch some more, it's so peaceful here."

As we drove to town Ingrid started telling me more than I knew about my newly adopted village, "Peter and Jennie live there. They moved from Ohio. Ron lives there. People say he flew a fighter plane in the war. He's never been married. Andy and Edna live in that house; Edna's parents built it by themselves. Did you know Henry's family lived in the same house for four generations? There used to be a still down by the creek. Did you know there was a Civil War battle here?"

"Henry told you all this in one afternoon?"

"Yes, he's such a nice man. I like him."

❧

We ate our early dinner; I ordered meatloaf and Ingrid ordered the chicken fried steak. "I've eaten meatloaf before, Mom used to make it all the time, but never chicken fried steak."

We drove around a little more, then drove home. "Walter is probably getting anxious," I said.

"I doubt it. He was content to be with Winnie."

I poured two glasses of sweet tea and we retired to the rockers on the porch.

Ingrid grew quiet. When I turned to her, she was leaning back, rocking gently, and smiling with closed eyes. I moved my chair closer.

A breeze came up, bringing with it a slight chill.

"I should be getting you back to your motel," I said.

"Could you bring me a blanket? I want to sit here until the stars come out."

I brought a blanket large enough to cover both chairs and we sat. I moved my hand. It found hers and held it.

"I like it here," she said.

"I'm glad. I like it too."

"Jimmie."

"Yes."

"Are the sunrises pretty?"

"Yes."

"Can we watch a sunrise too?"

Chapter 31
Sunrises

I awoke to the smell of coffee brewing.

"Get up sleepyhead, you'll miss the sunrise if you don't start moving. Here's a cup of coffee. Come on, we need to hurry to the porch."

Clouds muted some of the colors. Today's sunrise threatened not to be the most beautiful ever, but it was already the most perfect. I picked last night's crumpled blanket from the couch and carried it to the rockers. We sat next to each other, just as we had last night.

This morning, when I found her hand and squeezed it, she squeezed back.

The thought of work entered my mind. Why can't this be the weekend?

The words came painfully, "I have to go to work."

"I know. Can you take me to the motel on your way? I need to get the van and go get Walter. He spent the night with Winnie," she smiled.

Then, "What's so funny?" she asked.

"I just thought of you hurrying through a motel lobby wearing the same clothes you left in yesterday, just like I did the first night when I stayed with Walter. The people in the lobby were all smiling, knowingly, as I passed wearing wrinkled clothes."

"They won't notice mine; they aren't wrinkled, I didn't sleep in them," she smiled.

I knew I was blushing but I didn't care.

On the way to the motel she said, "Jimmie, I need to leave tomorrow morning. There is a horse show this weekend. We need to be there with the van. I have to get back."

"Damn it!" I blurted.

"I know, me too."

I don't even know if she curses. I've never seen her drop a coffee cup or pinch a finger. There is so much about this woman I don't know, but I want to.

From euphoria to despair in a split second. From no care to the biggest, worst sorrow imaginable. I wanted to say, "Do you have to?" but there wasn't any use. I knew this was going to happen. But I didn't imagine this circumstance. How can I live without her after last night?

"This breaks my heart," I moaned.

"I know how you feel. It breaks mine too, but we have lives and responsibilities. It hurts, but I have to go. I'll bring Walter this afternoon, then we can have one more evening."

At work, I listened to messages, sent notes to John, answered some emails, and called Henry. "I would like to take Ingrid to Emma's Point in the morning before she leaves tomorrow. I need to see a sunrise, and I think it will help Ingrid too. May I borrow the Mule?"

"I was hoping you would ask. I'll get it and have it ready for you this afternoon," he said. Then he added, "She's very nice. I like her and you two make a fine couple."

"I checked out of the motel a day early and left Molly at the clinic. I'll just leave from your place in the morning if it's okay with you?" she said.

"I'm glad you want to," I smiled. "We will need to get up early in the morning. At least an hour before sunrise. Do you have any warm clothes?"

"Just a light jacket and a raincoat."

"It won't be enough. I'll get an extra from the store room. We'll need the blanket too."

"Sounds exciting. Where is this place?"

"It's on the far end of Henry's land. We'll take his Mule up a rock road, then have to hike about a quarter mile. I'll leave Walter here. I think he'd have a fit when he sees us leave with Winnie."

"Winnie will want to go?"

"Yes, Henry says he never goes without her. He has made a place for her in the back. As soon as she hears the Mule start, she'll hop in."

I loaded the coats, blankets, stocking caps, and gloves in the trunk of my car before we went to bed. I didn't want Walter to suspect anything when we left in the morning.

We sat on the porch to watch the sunset. Then I said, "We better go in, it will be a short night."

I didn't bother to fill thermos bottles or pack any snacks. I knew Henry would be up, the goodies would be packed and the Mule warmed up when we got there.

Walter threw a fit when we left. I could hear him whining as we drove down the lane.

"The Mule's packed and ready with plenty of gas. You better get started, Winnie's already in the back waiting."

I helped Ingrid into the passenger seat, then got in and began the ascent to the top.

Once there, I parked the Mule, helped her out, handed her a flashlight and we slowly began making our way to the top. As we climbed, I sensed it was a time for silence. We both had thoughts we didn't need to share.

"Let's spread one of the blankets on the bench, it gets cold sitting on the bare wood."

"Oh, Jimmie, this is so romantic."

I was hoping for a spectacular sunrise but knew any sunrise would work its magic. "Just watch, it gets better."

She quietly laid her head on my shoulder.

The sky began to brighten. In moments, birds started their morning songs. As the deep gray began to show the first shades of blue, I put my arm around her waist. I felt her arm move and then hold me as the reds, oranges, yellows, and purples stole the sky from the dark blue hues. The first hint of the sun as it broke from behind the distant mountains made the tears on her cheeks glow. We didn't speak.

We sat until the sun warmed us before removing our jackets. Still, we huddled under our shared blanket.

As the bright colors succumbed to the bright sky, I knew it was time to leave.

Without a word, we followed Winnie's lead to the Mule.

Henry was gone when we got to his house. We left Winnie and drove to mine.

"No, Walter, you don't have to go this time," she said. "I hate to leave," she said. "I don't want this to end."

"It isn't ending. It's beginning. We just have to figure this out," I answered.

I rubbed Walter's head as we watched her van disappear. There was nothing to do now but return to the house and get ready for work.

Chapter 32
The Miles Between Us

I returned to the house, cleaned up the kitchen, dressed for work, and called for Walter. He didn't answer. I called again, and still, he didn't come. I went to the porch, thinking he may not have followed me in. I called again. He didn't respond.

For an instant, I panicked. I thought about that day at the rest stop. Did he try to follow Ingrid?

I ran to the end of the lane. Exasperated and scared, I stood at the edge of the road looking and hoping.

I hurried back to the house, trying to decide what to do next. I looked at my car. The windows were closed, so no way for him to crawl inside. I thought about chasing after Ingrid in the car.

I rushed into the house to get my jacket, still not having formed a plan. There lay Walter, in his bed, unwilling to get up.

I couldn't scold him; I understood what he was thinking and why. I might have the same reaction if I were in his situation. I am in his situation!

I carried my unwilling partner to my car, laid him in the back seat, and drove my Toyota toward my new normal.

I introduced myself to the nice lady at the reception desk of the clinic. Of course she knew Walter, but this was my first time here. I purposely avoided the place as long as possible as I knew it would be depressing for me bringing Walter and leaving him every day.

But when she said, "Good morning, my name is Elaine. You must be Jim, I've heard a lot about you," I thought of Mary at the Fillmore Clinic, and my trepidation vanished.

Then she turned toward the back hallway and called, "Ben, Walter is here to see us."

A sophisticated-looking young man with jet-black hair (the same as a younger Walter's) appeared, polished and professional with his perfectly groomed hair and beard. He was wearing a fresh white smock and smiled at me.

At once, I felt at ease. This is the best place for Walter to spend his days – at least until he is well.

"Has your visitor left?" a knowing Liz asked when I came for lunch.

"Yes, this morning. She needed to get back for the weekend. Her clinic is supporting a horse show of some kind. She has to be there."

"I'll tell the girls you are back on the market. I have to say though, they've got some pretty stiff competition in that young lady. She's pretty and seems nice. I think she's real smart too."

I didn't want to say anything that might continue the conversation. "Is anyone waiting to see me?" I asked.

"One girl is waiting. She's been here for a while. I don't know her; she might be some of the competition," Liz said with her sly, accustomed grin.

"I told you, Liz, strictly business."

She laughed. "You want a salad today, or are you up for some real food? You're probably worn out. You know, from lack of sleep."

"Enough," I growled. "Any rhubarb pie today?"

"Okay, just pie and just business it is. But remember, I can help with matters of the heart."

"Liz," I growled.

"I'm going. I'm going," she grinned.

No 'girl' was waiting to see me.

Sometimes I fail to understand Liz's humor, but she doesn't mean any harm. I should learn to let it roll off my back. Maybe I will work on it. But not today.

No one came to my table today. I finished my pie and began to drink tea refills.

These last few days were the best of my life, getting Walter home and being alone with Ingrid. I wish she could have stayed longer. I wonder how far she is by now. Probably only about one hundred and fifty miles. It may as well be one hundred and fifty thousand miles. I guess it's not possible to be that far away, but she's not here and she won't be here when I get home tonight. And I don't know when she will be here again.

"Jim, it's after one o'clock, shouldn't you be getting back?" Liz said.

"Uh, yeah, I was daydreaming, I guess."

"I wonder what about?" she grinned.

Nothing at the office was pressing this afternoon, which was good since I couldn't concentrate. Words on paper seemed to run together, then lose focus.

"I have an errand to run," John told me later. "I won't be back to the office this afternoon. Have a good weekend. I'll see you Monday," he said, then left me alone with my thoughts.

Walter and I sat on the porch until the morning sun became uncomfortable. He didn't follow me into the house, so I filled my drink cup and took his leash down from its hanger. In those days before he was lost, he would hear the faint sound I made when taking it down and would be at my feet begging to go.

Today, he only raised his head. "Come on boy, let's see if Hannah's brought the mail yet."

Grudgingly, he let me fasten the clasp.

We only made it about halfway down the drive when I realized this was too much for him. I walked him back, then went for the mail alone.

Walter spent his afternoon in his spot on the porch, basking in the sun. Winnie soon joined him. I got out a book to read but couldn't concentrate.

I wasted my afternoon in my Barca with the television on, my eyes closed, daydreaming.

I knew Ingrid would be tired from her drive, so I waited as long as I could before calling her. I thought it would be nice if I sat on the porch in her rocker when I did.

She didn't answer. Her phone went to messages, but I didn't leave one. I returned to the kitchen, refilled my glass, and started toward the porch. My phone rang, just as I stepped out. Before answering, I checked the caller ID. Ingrid.

I sat before answering. "Hi, I tried to call you. I am sitting on the porch, in your rocker, watching the sun sink. It will set soon. I'll be thinking of you as it does."

"That's so nice. I wish I could be there with you. I called to tell you I had the best time with three of the best men I know."

"Three?"

"Yes, three: Henry, Walter, and some guy named Jimmie. I like them all, but one is more special than the others. I'd like to talk; we could talk for hours, but I am tired and this is going to be a long weekend. I don't know if I'll get a chance to call you, and you probably shouldn't call me. It will be hectic here. Just know I will be thinking about you and our wonderful few days together, and I'm looking forward to many more."

"Me too."

"I need to get off here now and get to bed. I love you, Jimmie."

"Me too," I answered and watched my screen go blank.

Me too? Me too! God, Me Too was all you could come up with? The woman you love, have loved for a long time, just said, 'I love you' and all you could say was, 'Me too.'

My nervous fingers touched redial.

"I love you, Ingrid. I wish I'd said it first."

It was a long, difficult weekend; I wanted to call her but said I wouldn't. I wondered if she was thinking the same.

Where do we go from here? How can we make this work? Is it even possible?

I was relieved when Monday finally arrived. I could go to work and focus on something other than my problems. Walter woke me. We hadn't done anything all weekend, so he was rested and ready. He stood at my bed and for the first time since he'd been home, begged for breakfast. I filled his bowl, poured a fresh cup, and sat on the floor beside him as he ate.

"How are you doing, boy?"

He peeked at me between bites. For the first time, his eyes were clear, and I could see the beginnings of the old Walter coming back. I rubbed his head and then wished it wasn't Monday so I could stay home with him. We could go for a ride, find a park bench. Maybe we would see a squirrel…

~

"I hope you had a good weekend. I met with a new client on Friday afternoon. We have work to do," John said.

Ingrid called.

"Hi, I miss you. How was your weekend?" she asked.

I told her how much I missed her, how lonely I was, how empty the house was without her. Then, "Walter is feeling better. He ran to the car when I came to pick him up after work. The vet told me it won't be long now. Winnie was there waiting when we got home. We all walked to the mailbox and back when we heard Hannah bring the mail."

"What are we going to do?" she asked.

"About what?"

"About the miles between us."

"I don't know. I thought about it a lot. I don't see a good solution."

"Me neither, but we have to do something."

"I know, but we're both settled. I wish this had happened when we both lived in the city."

"It might have if a certain someone would have acted on the hints."

I pictured the smirk on her face.

"Yes, I know. But I didn't, and believe me, I've kicked myself hard and often. Sorry."

"I shouldn't have said that. It isn't the issue now. But back to our problem, do you have any ideas?"

"No, other than we could meet on weekends."

"I've thought of that, but we are so far apart. And you have to consider that I share weekend duty here, so I am on call every third one. We may not have anything to do but watch our boarders, but someone needs to be here in case of a sick or wounded animal," she said.

"Sorry, but weekends are the best I can think of. At least there are three of you at your clinic. I occasionally work on Saturday and sometimes Sunday too. The issue with me though, is I often don't know ahead of time, so I can't schedule. And saying I can't is not an option because when John needs assistance, I'm the only one available," I answered.

"So what do you suggest?" she asked.

"Let's try to schedule one weekend a month. Meet halfway, stay in a motel, and go to a movie or visit a museum or local attraction. We can pick the first one after your on-call weekend, that way, if I have to work, we can move it to the next one," I said.

"We won't have very much time together."

"I know, but I can't think of another possibility. It will have to do for now."

"Okay, I suppose. It can't be this coming weekend though. I'm on duty."

"You just worked all weekend. Why two in a row?" I whined.

"We all worked this last weekend, so it didn't count in our rotation. And it wouldn't be right to ask one of the others to trade. It would mean three in a row for one, then two for the other, and they both have families…"

"But…"

"I'm sorry Jimmie, but it can't be this weekend."

"Okay, I'll figure it out and rent two rooms somewhere the following weekend."

"Two rooms?"

I took Walter to the clinic Friday after work. I wanted to get an early start; for this first weekend anyway, I didn't want to take him. All those "necessary stops" along the way would take up too much time. And if he could understand he would be an inconvenience, he would probably agree to stay.

I messaged Ingrid early in the morning, "It's five forty-five; I'm driving." I wanted to be waiting for her when she arrived.

I selected a nice little out-of-the-way place on the edge of a small town. I was hoping for nice weather and pictured a walk along a creek in a park. This was one–if not the main– reason for my choice. I picked adjacent rooms with connecting balconies and connecting doors.

"Hi, where's Walter?" she asked.

"Did you drive all this way to see me or my dog?"

"Both of you, really, but you will have to do," she grinned.

I was beginning to see a new side to her–mischievous. I liked it.

"No, I couldn't wait to see you, so I didn't want to make all the stops he requires."

We walked the steps to our rooms. When I made the reservations, I asked for rooms on the back side of the building. There was a wooded lot behind and I thought it was better than a view of the parking lot and the car dealership across the street.

"Which room is mine?" she asked.

"Take your pick," I answered.

"I'll take the one on the right," she said and led me in. "Put my bag on the stand, if you will, kind sir. Oh, I see there's a door between. I'll be sure to keep mine locked. I don't want any prowlers in the middle of the night."

I watched as she flopped on the bed, fluffed the pillow, and said, "Ooh, nice, it's comfy, and it's king-sized. This will be just fine. Call me when you are ready. To go eat, I mean."

Somewhat dejected, I carried my bag to the other room, sat my suitcase on the stand, and began to unpack.

I heard the door between us unlock.

Chapter 33
Change is Good – Again

It seemed like a good idea at the time; a best/bad compromise, but Ingrid and I only managed three visits in four months. We learned our lives were not easily governed. We had to expect the unexpected and we didn't like it.

Also, after our first visit, and at her insistence, I always brought Walter. Yes, I loved my dog. We've gone through a lot together, and he was my best friend. But the extra time it took to drive to and from our weekend trysts was making me bitter. But, as I reasoned, Walter wants to see her too.

Ingrid and I had long discussions about our situations but neither of us could come up with a real, workable solution.

This is all my fault. If I'd just done something when we were meeting at the Fillmore Clinic…but I didn't.

I was beginning to worry about where we were headed. I suspected she was too.

"Hi, Jim," she said on one of our evening phone calls. "I need to tell you, I talked to Dylan today."

Dylan again? I thought you were over him. What now? Is this a 'Dear James' call?

"What did he want?"

I knew my answer was curt and gruff, but I was in no mood to talk about Dylan ever again.

"He dropped in unannounced today."

"And?"

"He demanded to see me. Our receptionist, Jenny, paged me. I told her we weren't expecting Dylan, and I didn't want to talk to him. Then Dylan got abusive, so Jenny paged Dan, my colleague, who happens to be a very big man.

"A big argument started. Dylan yelled he wouldn't leave without seeing me. Dan yelled back, telling Dylan he needed to leave or he would call the police.

"And unfortunately for the clinic, the lobby was full of customers and their dogs. The dogs started barking and a couple of the male customers got up and tried to ease the situation. It all ended with Dan and two of the men dragging Dylan outside.

"Dan told him we would no longer use any of his products, and if he ever came back, we would call the police.

"After it was over, Dan told me he smelled alcohol on Dylan's breath. I confess I watched from the hallway. It was so embarrassing."

I wondered why she was telling me this, but I confess, I enjoyed her story.

At least I don't have to worry about Dylan again.

Later that week, John called me into his office. "James, as you remember, we talked early on about you finishing your education and getting your law license."

"Yes," I answered.

Where is this conversation going?

"I think it is time. The business is thriving. We have acquired several new clients, and there are prospects for more. Our little town is growing and we need to expand with it. There is a need, and if we don't fill it, I fear others will. What do you think?"

"Well, first, this comes as a surprise. And second, how will I manage both my work and school?"

"I've thought about it. There are two good schools within two hundred miles. Either will accept you. Both will offer some of your work online, but you will have to attend some classes in person. In addition, I have decided to hire another person, an office manager to assist you with your everyday tasks. It will mean longer hours for you, driving to and from, teaching a new employee, and continuing with the bulk of your current duties. Short term, it will be burdensome on both of us, but in the end, we will have a more fluid, accommodating practice."

"Thank you. I appreciate your faith in me. This comes at an unexpected time. Can you give me a little time to digest this, to organize my thoughts?"

"Yes, but we must begin. We need to adapt to these changing times. Also, I would like you to be involved in the interview process."

Again, my life was taking an unexpected turn.

John had talked about this in the past, but still, I didn't expect it now. My head was swimming with these new complications.

I called Ingrid.

"Hi, I have news. It is both good and bad," I said.

"What is it?" she asked, with concern in her voice.

"I just came from John's office. He wants me to go back to law school. I don't remember telling you, but one of the things he asked of me when I started was I go back and finish my schooling and take the bar exam."

"Why is it both good and bad?"

"It is good because I will eventually be a lawyer. It is bad because it means I am going to be inundated for the next year, maybe more. I'll have to continue to work in the office, take what courses I can online, and drive to and from college for the classroom work. And it is going to be terrible because I don't know how I will ever find time to see you."

Ingrid's phone was silent. I waited. "Are you still there?"

"Yes."

"What are you thinking?"

"I wasn't going to say anything about this until it was firmed up."

"Firmed up? What are you talking about?"

"I've been thinking about our relationship."

Oh, God, what now?

"It's not working. We can't continue this way. It's just a matter of time. About two weeks ago I contacted Benjamin Raymond at your clinic. We visited quite a bit when I brought Walter, and he hinted at being overworked. So I asked him if he would consider selling a partnership in his business.

"As I said, I wasn't going to say anything to you until I was reasonably certain he was willing, but I know he is considering it, and seemed open to my suggestion."

"That would be great. It would solve all of our problems."

"I don't think it would be fair to say anything to Benjamin. I should work this out on my own, but it would be great if we could live in the same town. No more five-hour drives for just a short weekend. I wish you wouldn't say anything to either John or Henry, at least until I know."

It was impossible to hide my joy, but why should I, and certainly not from Ingrid?

With a muted response I had practiced, I told John I was willing and eager to go back to school. I enrolled in the next term and eagerly established a rapport with our new office manager, Kathryn.

Walter was now well enough to be on his own. I left food and water for him every morning and when I got home in the evening, his food bowl was empty and most of the water was gone. According to Henry, Winnie came to visit Walter every day. He laughed when he told me he had to keep her well-fed so she wouldn't want any of Walter's food.

Now, every day, he waited at the end of the drive, most times with Winnie, and would trot alongside my car as I drove to the house. It made me feel so good, knowing he felt better. Still, the gray hairs didn't vanish from his coat and his eyes no longer had the deep, dark sparkle they once did. When I could squeeze in the time, we went for walks for as long as possible. The timber on Henry's farm was his favorite. I felt guilty taking papers from work or school with me, but Walter didn't seem to mind. I watched as he explored while I studied, each of us learning new things.

Ingrid was mostly memory now. In the past two months, I'd only seen her once. She still beamed with optimism about the possibility of her move, but I wasn't seeing any progress.

Why do these things have to take so long?

We discovered FaceTime. It was better than no contact at all, but not much. Contact was the key word.

Late, on a Friday evening, she called and said, "I turned in my resignation today. I gave them a month's notice; it seemed only fair. I know a month seems like forever right now, but in a month, our time apart will only be a memory. Can you find me an apartment?"

Euphoric, I answered, "You can stay with me."

"No, it wouldn't be proper, at least not yet."

Yet another delay. One more month I had to wait before we could be together. Will there ever be a last time? Why the seemingly endless setbacks?

I started calling her every night, hoping she would leave before the month ended.

"You are not helping," she said. "I have many things to do before I leave and I have to pack my personal belongings. I know this is hard, it's hard for me too, but please be patient. I plan to leave on Friday the thirteenth. I will have a moving van packed and the drivers ready. They are having a farewell party for me that afternoon, so I will leave directly from the clinic. I'll call you when we are on the way."

I tried to ignore the Friday the thirteenth part. I'm not a superstitious person but please!

"I'm sorry it is so late. I never expected so many people at my party. They kept talking, offering their regards and wishing me well. One after another asked me to change my mind. I'm sorry but we are on the road now and should be there in about nine hours," Ingrid said.

"I have rooms for you and the drivers at the Travelodge, I'll meet you in the parking lot," I said.

"It will be late. Why don't you wait? We can meet for breakfast," she answered.

"No, I'll be waiting."

"Suit yourself."

—⁓—

"I hope you have a great weekend," John smiled knowingly as we left for the day.

I stopped to pick up a pepperoni pizza on the way, Walter and I had something to celebrate. Once we finished our meal, I cleaned the house as best I could, swept the front porch, moved the rockers closer to each other, then sat on the steps with Walter until the last of the day's color disappeared.

I knew Ingrid couldn't get here before ten but by nine o'clock, I couldn't stand the wait any longer. I woke my snoozing dog, we drove to town, I circled the motel parking lot before finding a spot where I could best see the street and parked.

I'm sure this late-night adventure confused him, but soon Walter was contentedly sleeping in the back seat. After intently watching the street for more than two hours my eyelids grew heavy and I too fell asleep.

Headlights flashed across my windshield alerting me to a moving van, followed by a car sporting a Pennsylvania license plate, pulling into the lot. I followed as it slowly drove to the back of the motel. I glanced at my watch; 2:15 a.m.

Walter and I hurried across the pavement, "I am so happy to see you. We thought you would get here sooner."

"The van had mechanical trouble on the way, so we had to stop at a service area," Ingrid answered.

I offered to let her spend the night at my house but she said, "No, I don't want to begin this way, and I am really tired and need to get some sleep. Tomorrow will be a hard day. Is the apartment ready? The moving guys will want to get started as soon as possible."

I tried to coax her, "Can't you stay, at least for the first night?" I begged.

"No, it wouldn't be right, at least not yet" she said, again.

"I could stay at Henry's and you would have the house to yourself."

"No, I don't want to be an imposition, and I don't want to begin my life here with a scandal–of any size."

I was too happy to object, but 'keeping up appearances' wasn't going to fool anyone. I made it clear to everyone I spoke to, 'My girlfriend is moving to town.'

<hr>

Ingrid leased a townhouse on the far side of town. I didn't like it, but fourteen minutes was so much better than the four hours before. And now, most importantly, I can see her evenings, weekends, almost any time. Of course, the problem was that I didn't have evenings, weekends, or almost any time because of school and my workload.

She now walked Walter more than I did. And he loved it!

He was doing so much better now. His hair had a sheen back, but the gray ones didn't go away. He only showed a slight limp when he trotted, but only those of us who knew the limp was there saw it. I attributed some of his limp to the day he cut his leg in Fillmore Park.

Fillmore Park...it was so long ago.

Still, the memory of him being lost didn't go away, and I didn't want it to. I never left him or tied him up when we walked. Ingrid didn't either. Our local soft-serve ice cream parlor had a drive-up window (walk up for us), so his walks with Ingrid always included a cone. The little traitor let her order a large cone and he ate the entire thing.

Chapter 34
The Three of Us, Together

After all we'd gone through to get to this point in our lives, being all together seemed odd. Looking back, the many *if-onlys* and *I-wishes* I would do over if I had the chance couldn't cloud the way I felt now. My life was hectic, almost beyond belief. I needed to keep up with my work, help train our new employee, study, and (most importantly) my girlfriend was living right here in town.

Walter was back home too. He was doing so much better now. We went on walks whenever I could find the time. Ingrid went with us when she could. Sometimes Ingrid and Walter went alone. Those times when I stood on the porch and watched as Ingrid and Walter walked away, him trotting around her, brushing up to her, demanding she pet him, were exhilarating.

Henry told me about a meadow on the south edge of town. "The city annexed it a few years ago. They thought they had a developer secured, but it didn't work out. The meadow lies fallow now. The fence was good, and a stream ran through it. It reminds me of the park where we met. It might be a good place for you to walk Walter."

We settled into our new life, Ingrid and me and Walter. However, it wasn't what I pictured. I knew I would be busy for the next several months. I expected to go days without seeing her, but the long-term benefits made it seem like the right thing to do. Living it, however, wasn't so easy. Days went by, sometimes several, without seeing her. Here we were, living within minutes of each other, yet we still couldn't find time to be together. On days when I needed to attend school, I left before dawn and returned late in the evening, tired and not good company. My work weeks at the office now stretched into seven-day weeks, when school allowed. There was so much to be done and I needed to keep up, so I asked John if I could limit my business lunches at Joy's to three days a week. At least I could share the hour with Ingrid. But lunch together was not enough for either of us.

Most of Walter's walks now were with her. I didn't have the time. I wished I could explain the reasons to him.

We did enjoy those times in this new meadow whenever I could manage. I named it "Walter's Acres" in his honor. It was an oblong meadow with a smattering of oak trees, some overgrown bushes, and tall grasses. The stream carried much more water than the one in Fillmore Park, and it was much, much cleaner. If Walter hurt his leg here, I wouldn't have worried about infection.

I hoped our law firm might have some connection when it was finally developed. It would be nice to save these old trees.

The fence was good and even had a nice gate. An old lean-to shed sat in the middle, needing repair.

I went to the lumber yard and bought material. Then with instructions from the yard man, I shored up the lean-to and built a bench designed to imitate Henry's on Emma's Point. I dragged it to the lean-to and left it for Walter and me to enjoy and anyone else who might need to rest and refresh in "Walter's Acres."

This was my first wood project ever. It may not be impressive to others who might see it, but I was proud of the result. It bothered me that Ingrid and Walter spent more time resting on it than I did.

It wore me down, this new normal. I was living alone with my dog. Ingrid was living across town. Our only contact was occasional, at best. As I thought about it, it seemed selfish, but it was the best we could manage.

I bought a ring and kept the next Sunday open.

"I'd like to borrow the Mule Sunday morning," I told Henry.

"Are Winnie and Walter invited?" he smiled.

"Definitely."

I made a small breakfast and had it ready when Ingrid arrived. We filled our thermos bottles, loaded Walter, and drove to Henry's. Then, with Winnie and Walter in the back, we started the Mule up the hill.

"I am looking forward to this," she said. We haven't been up here for quite a while."

"I hope the sky is pretty," I said.

"It will be, I know it."

The dogs leaped from the Mule and hurried up the hill, leaving us alone for the climb. Silently, we climbed. I was nervous, wondering. She didn't have any idea as to my thoughts or motives.

We wrapped ourselves in the blanket and sat silently, watching the sky begin to turn. She was lost in thought, and I was at a loss for words. It took a while, quite a while, but I managed to finally slip from the blanket and drop to my knee.

"Yes," she blurted before I could find my words.

I told John I couldn't work next Saturday.

I asked a local magistrate to perform the service. Ingrid asked Molly to be her maid of honor. Henry was the best man. Guests were limited to a few friends in town and employees of the clinic: John, Ira, and Kathryn, the employees at Joy's Café and The Family Café. My mother was too sick to make the trip, and Ingrid's parents lived in Sweden, so we recorded the service for them.

I promised her a honeymoon once I passed the bar.

"We could spend our first night in the motel where we used to meet. We could sign in as Mr. and Mrs. and just take one room," Ingrid laughed.

"Or we could sit on OUR porch and watch OUR sunset, then ride the Mule to Emma's Point in the morning," I said.

"That will have to wait for another day," she grinned.

I took my (our) mailbox to a local graphic designer and asked her to reinstall it when she finished. When it was ready, I asked Ingrid to walk with Walter and me to get the mail.

"I'm writing thank you notes, can't you go alone?"

"I have something to show you; it'll just take a few minutes."

I asked her to cover her eyes and led her for the last few yards.

Our mailbox now read,

Dr. Ingrid & Mr. James Williams
And Walter

"Oh, Jimmie, I love it."

I was so happy with how warm and inviting it appeared. I stopped to admire it almost every time I came or went. It was a dream come true and I couldn't be happier.

Our lives were so much better now. I was happy to hear her footsteps on the hardwood floor, see her sitting on the porch waiting for me to join her, smell her perfume early in the morning, watch her move, and enjoy the odors emitting from her kitchen.

I attacked my studies with new ferocity. Long days at the office flew by, and the drives to and from school were easier now, all because she would be there when I got home.

"Home," held a new meaning for me. In the past, I listened to others speak of home. Sometimes they simply meant the place where they live now. Other times, they meant where they grew up or the country they came from, but I never thought much about home. Before, I called Mom and Dad's house home; the apartment where I paid rent was home; even the widow's place was home. But in reality, all these places were not home but were only places I lived; nothing more.

Now for the first time, I understood the meaning. This place where I lived with my wife and dog was home. I belonged here, this was my place. And it was not only the house that was this home. Henry's farm, the town I lived close to, the people here– all this was my home!

I passed the bar exam on my first attempt.

We spent a long weekend in an oceanside hotel in Playa del Carmen, Mexico for our promised honeymoon and to celebrate this achievement. We lay in the sun on afternoons, walked in the surf, ate some wonderful meals and watched every sunrise from our deck.

"The sunrises are great here, but I like the ones on our porch better," she said.

Our porch, she said, 'Our porch!'

Tuesday morning we rode a shuttle to the airport for our flight back to Ashville. That first night together in our own bed as husband and wife ended with the sound of our alarm. *Our alarm!* Even something trivial and mundane as an alarm clock sounding was special. Everything was different; better.

My new wife and I walked to our cars together and each of us would return to spend our evenings together. I arrived at the office renewed, ambitious, and happy.

John knocked on my office door. "I have three items," he said. "First, I am having a new sign made for the front of the building. It will read, "John Crane and James Williams, Attorneys at Law," Second, I have a new sign for your door. It reads "James Williams, Attorney at Law." And third is an item I withheld until you passed your bar because I didn't want to cause you an extra burden, but I am sure you are aware that a new, ultramodern lumber mill and distribution center will break ground near here. We will be their legal representative in all their transactions. This will be a significant workload but I have no doubt we can manage it."

"John, I want to thank you for all you've done. Not just your support, but also your faith and belief in me. I couldn't have succeeded without you."

"Thanks, Jim. But you are wrong. You would have found a way without any help. I saw that in you, it's why I brought you in."

I relished the new opportunities, the challenges, and the rewards. The general population thinks of lawyers as staid, stuffy, standoffish, aloof, and maybe a necessary evil. But this was fun. I felt important now. John, Kathryn, and I were a team; professional and courteous when necessary, friendly and sympathetic when needed. I worked at a dream job in a great community with a wonderful life. As one of our clients says, "It don't get no better." He uses it as sarcasm, I think of it as the utmost compliment.

Chapter 35
Our New Life

"Honey," Ingrid said.

"Yes?"

"Have you ever thought about the future?"

"I don't need to think about the future, I have the here and now, with you."

"No, I mean have you ever thought about our future?"

This isn't like her. Where is this conversation headed?

"What do you mean?" I asked.

"Have you thought about our lives five, ten, even fifteen years from now?"

"No. Why? What are you getting at?"

"Have you ever thought about a family?"

"We are a family–you, me, and Walter."

I don't get it. What is she saying?

"Have you ever thought about a bigger family?"

"Oh, my God! Really?"

"Yes, really. You are going to be a father!"

Suddenly, pictures of waving goodbye as my child started the first day in preschool, bringing home report cards, (all A's of course), teaching him to drive, going to a high school prom, going to college. Would I need to buy cardigan sweaters and start smoking a pipe?

"I haven't mentioned it, but I haven't been feeling well lately, especially in the morning. Last week, I took the morning off to go to my doctor. I didn't say anything to you about going because you were busy.

"My doctor told me I was pregnant."

With my mouth agape, I stared at her. I couldn't form any words. As she smiled at me, I saw the glow on her face, one I'd never seen before.

"Well?"

"You surprised me, this isn't something I've ever thought about."

"It is happening, so you need to think about it now. We are going to be parents. Isn't it awesome?"

"I'm thrilled, I guess. This is a lot…"

"A lot of great," she grinned.

—⁓—

I soon became the proud Papa of a little girl. I never dreamed of being a father, and certainly not the father to a little girl. We named her Sophia in honor of her grandma back in Sweden. She was the prettiest thing. Fair skin and blond hair, just like her momma.

Now, sitting on the porch watching the sunset with my beautiful wife holding our beautiful daughter in the rocker next to me, was more beautiful than ever.

Walter liked Sophia too. From the day we brought her home he was next to her. When Sophia was in her mother's arms in a rocker, either in the bedroom or on the porch, Walter lay beside them. When Sophia was put down for her nap, Walter lay beside the crib. When Ingrid carried Sophia from one room to another or outdoors, Walter followed.

I might have felt bad for Winnie, but she was with the baby all the time when she came from Henry's, which seemed more often now.

Henry came more often too. He wanted to be with Sophia as much as he could; hold her at every opportunity. Sophia was the granddaughter he probably would never have.

Soon, when Sophia began to crawl, Walter followed her everywhere. In the evenings, I would sit at my desk working; Ingrid would sit in her rocker reading, and together, we both watched the parade with joy and amusement; Sophia crawling, Walter following all through the rooms. As Sophia's abilities began to improve, we needed to close doors to corral them. To Walter's dismay, he was no longer able to enter such now forbidden places as our bedroom, the kitchen, and most importantly, the front porch.

"It took some time, but I think I am the luckiest man on earth," I told Ingrid.

In her impish way, she replied, "I agree. I think you are too."

As Sophia began to stand and attempt her first steps, Walter happily assumed new duties. When Sophia pulled herself up to the coffee table, Walter stood next to her so she could hold on to his collar if she lost her balance. If she fell, Walter was there to comfort her. His nuzzling and licking turned crying to laughter in an instant. When Ingrid put Sophia in her crib, Walter lay in front of it, guarding her.

My walks to the mailbox were now solitary. Walter only rolled his eyes at me when I implored him. He wouldn't leave Sophia. The meadow where we used to walk was now abandoned. A contractor could be building houses there, but I didn't know; we hadn't been there for months.

I heard a scratching and whimpering at the front door. Ingrid was feeding Sophia in the highchair. Walter was standing guard and I was having a cup of coffee, grinning as I watched their show.

The whimpering and scratching didn't stop.

"See about the commotion will you, Honey?" Ingrid asked.

I went to the door to find Winnie. "Come in," I offered, as I opened the door.

Normally, Winnie would bound into the house in search of Sophia and Walter. Today she refused.

"Come on, Winnie," I begged.

But she refused and ran toward the fence.

"Come here, Winnie," I ordered.

But she stood at the fence and began to bark.

"What is it?" Ingrid called from the kitchen.

"It's Winnie. She's acting strangely."

With Sophia in her arms, Ingrid came to the door. "There must be something wrong," she said. "It might be Henry. We should check."

Winnie was now pacing back and forth in front of the fence. "I'll run over there," I said. "Why don't you drive around with the baby and Walter?"

I ran to the gate and jumped over it as Winnie went through her doggie door, and then I raced toward the house.

I heard Ingrid's car wheels on the lane as I entered the house.

"Henry! Henry? Are you in here, Henry?" I yelled.

I could hear Henry's teapot boiling over. I ran to the kitchen. His contorted body lay between the stove and the table.

"Henry, are you okay?"

I rolled my unconscious friend onto his back. His eyes were open with a vacant stare.

"Honey, call 911! It's Henry! He's fallen!"

Chapter 36
Complications and Recovery

Ingrid sat holding Henry's hand while I leaned against the hospital room's wall gazing hopefully at my unconscious friend. Haltingly, he began to stir, then his eyes opened to unfamiliar surroundings, "Where am I? What is happening?" he asked.

"You are in the hospital, Henry," I said.

"How did I get here?"

"Winnie came to the house and made such a fuss we knew something must be wrong. When I came to the door, she ran to the edge of the yard then turned toward me and barked. I knew she wanted me to follow. Ingrid and I found you on the floor in your kitchen."

"Where's Winnie? Is she okay?" Henry asked.

"She's okay, Walter is taking care of her," I said.

"And the baby? How is she?" Henry asked.

"She is okay Henry. Everyone is okay. You gave us quite a scare," Ingrid said. "We are more worried about you. What happened?"

"I was going to make a pitcher of tea. I started the water boiling, then got a terrible headache. I tried to sit down, but I guess I kind of missed the chair. I tried to think about what to do, but my brain went all fuzzy. I wanted to call for help, but my phone was in the living room. I knew I needed to turn off the stove first. When I tried to move, I couldn't sit up. I remember hearing Winnie bark, and then she quit. It was quiet and I couldn't move. It's the most scared I've ever been."

"Well, you're safe now. Thank God Winnie knew what to do. The reason she quit barking was because she left to fetch us. We heard her scratching and whimpering on our porch. She wouldn't stop until I followed her. When we found you, we knew what she did and why she did it," I said.

"What are the doctors saying? They won't tell me anything."

"They won't tell us either. I'm not sure they know yet. We think they may keep you for a while," Ingrid said.

"What about the house?" he asked.

"Don't worry about anything. We've called Theresa. We had to leave a message because her ship was at sea. Her company called us back and she is going to get off at their next port. She'll be here by the end of the week. Bess is taking care of things in the meantime. Ira is going to drive to the airport to get her when she arrives. We have everything under control. Your job now is to focus on getting better," I said.

"We need to be going, Henry. You need to be quiet and rest," Ingrid said. "We will be back this evening. Is there anything we can bring you?"

"Do you have a photo of my beautiful little Sophia? I would love to have her picture on the bedside table. She cheers me up every time I see her."

"I'll be happy to bring you one. She cheers us up too. She is walking now and getting into everything. Poor Walter, she keeps him busy following her all over the house. It's fun to watch.

"Once the staff here lets you get up and move around, we will bring her with us. You take care now, we all miss you – especially Winnie."

It took several attempts with me trying to take a picture while Ingrid tried to get both dogs and Sophia to cooperate.

"I'll stop on the way home from work and have it printed at the pharmacy. I'll buy a frame too. Henry will appreciate it," she said.

Henry's recovery was slow. He was tired and worn now. Every time we went to see him, I tried to keep a positive outlook, but he wasn't making much progress. For the first time, I thought about his age. When I looked at my friend lying in a hospital bed with tubes stuck in his arms, I now saw an old man.

He was a popular patient though. Many times we would wait until someone left before we were allowed to see him. Bess, John, Ira, Hannah, Sandy, Joy, Myrt, all the regulars at The Family Café and Joy's all came frequently. One person who didn't seem to be there often was Theresa. I tried not to think critically of her, but she was conspicuous in her absence. Even Ingrid noticed.

Of all his visitors though, I think his favorite was Sophia. She was beginning to talk now and talk she did. When I listened to her ramble on and on, I said, "She didn't get it from her father."

Ingrid laughed. "Don't I know it."

Sophia couldn't pronounce his name correctly, so she called him Hany.

At home, when one of us appeared to be leaving the house, she'd ask, "Go see Hany?"

Ingrid always had Thursday afternoons free. She used this time to shop, clean the house, take Walter for walks, sit on the porch, and read.

With nothing pressing today, I told John I was going to spend an afternoon with Henry. "Maybe they will let me push him around the grounds or let me take him for a drive."

I assumed the hospital staff would nix the ride idea, but I was determined to ask. His doctor thought it was a good idea.

Ingrid and I wheeled him outside. I knew he would love to see his place and thought about taking him there. It was tempting to defy the 'no automobile rides' edict, but I didn't.

What if something went wrong? What would we do? I couldn't fathom the thought, so we found a bench at the edge of a small pond in the back of the facility.

After a period of quiet, Henry said, "I don't know if they are ever going to let me out of here. And if they do, I wonder if they will let me go home."

I interrupted, "Henry, you shouldn't even think those things."

"Maybe, but I need to be realistic. I am getting on in years. I have some things to tell you."

"Let's just enjoy the sunshine," I said.

"I have some things I need to tell you and this is the perfect time, so please listen. These are decisions I've made; they affect you and Ingrid. You need to hear me out."

"Okay," I answered, wondering and fearing what he was about to tell us.

"You don't know, but I have worked this out with John. He made me do this with a law firm in Asheville, to avoid any conflicts of interest. It is all finished now. This is the way I want it.

"First, the widow's place is yours. The deed is in your name."

"But we've only begun to pay you." I protested.

"Jim," he went on. "This is what I want, so please don't argue. The place is yours, no more payments will be accepted. You two can live there as long as you want. Now about my farm. Theresa is my daughter, and as you know, the place has been in our family for four generations. It is hers if she chooses to live there. I made a provision saying she cannot deny you access to Emma's Point and have created an access in the deed. I don't know if she will stay; I doubt she will. So, in that case, I made another provision. If she does stay, it probably won't be for long. If or when she decides to leave, she must offer my farm to you first. She must sell it to you for fifty percent of the fair market value. The place will pay for itself by renting it out, just as it does now for me. John told me this is very unusual but assured me it is legal and binding."

"Henry, this is too much."

"It is not too much. It is what I want. You are a son to me, and your wife," he smiled at Ingrid and with a quivering voice said, "She is something special. I love her like she is my own."

They both began to tear. "Oh, Henry," Ingrid cried.

"Please call me Hany," he grinned.

<hr>

It was almost a week from the time she was notified until Theresa arrived. I am sure there were logistical problems but I wondered if she understood the severity of Henry's health issues. In the five days since her arrival, to my knowledge, she only visited Henry three times and never when either Ingrid, Sophia, or I were at the hospital.

After her second visit, with him, Henry no longer spoke to me about her. I didn't know what transpired between them and didn't feel I should ask.

We fell into what for Ingrid and me was an uncomfortable avoidance routine.

So it came as a surprise to me when I was washing Ingrid's car in the back yard when Ingrid yelled to me, "Theresa called; she wants to come over. Is it going to be a problem?"

"Not for me," I answered.

"Do you think she knows about the will?"

"I don't think so. Henry didn't want to tell her yet. He wanted to wait until he knew whether the doctors would let him go home first. I guess we are about to find out though."

Ingrid answered the door, "Hello, Theresa. I assume you want to see Jimmie."

"Yes," she answered bluntly.

"He's out back, I'll fetch him. Can I get you something to drink?"

"No thank you."

"Have a seat, I'll be right back with him."

⸎

"Hey, Jimmie, Theresa's here. She wants to see you. She's waiting in the living room."

"Is she upset?"

"She doesn't seem to be, but I don't know her well enough to tell."

Fearing the worst, but knowing that talking to Theresa was inevitable, we walked to the house.

Just as we entered, I heard Walter growl, and then Theresa screamed.

The noise was coming from Sophia's bedroom. I hurried to the door only to see Sophia calmly lying on Walter's side. Walter's teeth were bared, and he was snarling.

Theresa stood cowering against the far wall. When I entered, she shrieked, "Your damned dog just growled and tried to bite me!"

"He doesn't bite; he was only being protective of Sophia," I answered.

But apologizing for Walter's actions was too little too late. Theresa stormed past me, through the living room, out the front door, down the steps, slammed her car door, and roared down the lane.

Ingrid and I stood in the doorway, half grinning, as we watched her speed away.

"I wonder what that was about?" she asked.

"We may never know, but I doubt she will be coming back," I answered.

I stood in front of the house for a few moments wondering what, if anything, I should do. When I walked back into the house, Ingrid was standing at the entrance to Sophia's bedroom smiling.

"What are you smiling about?" I asked.

She shushed me, then motioned for me to come. over. I peeked through the doorway to see why she was smiling. Walter lay on the floor, eyes open and fully contented. Sophia was lying against his side with her little arm around his front leg.

Ingrid put her arm around my waist, looked at me, grinned, and said, "It looks to me like Walter is no longer your dog."

About the Author

Roger K. Droz was born and raised in Fairfield, Iowa. He graduated from Parsons College with a BA in History and Political Science.

Roger became involved in writing later in life through his interest in memoirs. He felt the need to tell his children and grandchildren about his world, growing up in a small Midwestern town in the middle of the twentieth century.

His memoir essay, *Bikes and Basketball* was published in the June/July 2021 issue of *Our Iowa* magazine. Another memoir, *First Beer* was the winner in the Creative Nonfiction category of the 2016 Kansas Voices contest. His story, *The Curse of the Catalpa Tree, Learning About Bees* was awarded first place in the 2023 Kansas Authors Club, 2023 Literary Contest, memoir division. A memoir, *Uncle Cal's Knife,* is included in the 2024 edition of Meadowlark Press's 105 Meadowlark Reader. Also his first novel, *Rusty's Repair* is available on Amazon.

Roger and his wife Margo grew up in Southeast Iowa and are now twenty-year Kansas transplants happily residing in Topeka, Kansas.